# RIVER BRAIDS

## A NOVEL

*To Carol — Enjoy!! [signature]*

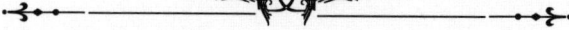

## Marcy Luikart

# River Braids

## A NOVEL

Sea Hill Press, Santa Barbara

Sea Hill Press Inc.

www.seahillpress.com

Santa Barbara, California

The characters and events in this book are fictitious. Names, characters, places, and incidents are either the product of the author's imagination or are used fictitiously, and any similarity to actual events, locals, or persons, living or dead, is coincidental and not intended by the author.

ISBN: 978-1-937720-16-2

Printed in the United States of America

# Acknowledgments

I would like to thank my husband, Ralph, for realizing his childhood dream of rafting down the Mississippi, which created the spark for this book. I want to acknowledge Shelly Lowenkopf for his generous edits as well as the little voice in my head that is always asking, "where is the story?" I would also like to thank my writing buddies, Melody, Christine, Jennifer, Shirley, Mike, and Greg, for their encouragement. Thanks to the University of California at Santa Barbara Women's Rowing team. And most especially thanks to Dale DeLaPorte of Hannibal, Missouri, without whose assistance we never would have been able to build the raft and begin the adventure.

# Prologue

# JOE

If you walk into the East Side Boat Club, the first thing you'll see is an antique mahogany bar, darkened from a hundred years of drinks and tears. You'll see an old jukebox that still plays five songs for a quarter and a pool table with a level attached to the edge. Around the room, lining the walls, you'll see glass cases filled with all kinds of taxidermied critters: owls, foxes, birds, and even bugs. There's a mountain lion nursing its cub, a badger that looks as if it's about to reach out and swat you, and a couple of squirrels chewing on acorns.

And you'll see photos. Lots of photos. Mostly black-and-white, but some in color, the reds already faded to pink. Then there are the medals, team medals from the good old days when the river ran free, before the locks and dams restricted, before the factories closed, before the young people left.

If you take a bit more time and look at one particular picture—the one of the dream team, the rowing gods of the 1904 Olympics—if you look at that one up close, you'll see I'm not there. No, I'm not in that photo, even though everyone thinks I am. But I'm not. I'm standing behind the photographer, looking over his shoulder. I hold the box of light, the chemical flash that temporarily blinds everyone.

We're long gone now, dust and ashes, compost one and all. But look at the faces in that picture. We were so very young back then, Greer, Johnson, Smith, Tucker, and me: Joe.

# Chapter One

# SONNY

## 2004

Sonny left the rental car in the hospital parking lot, so he could make the walk to the East Side Boat Club. A dented blue '64 Corvair was the only car in the side parking lot. Sonny ran his hand over the hood and smiled. He paused for a moment but didn't take the gravel walkway toward the Mississippi. Instead, he made a right turn up the path to the clubhouse. A rusted grill lay on the ground next to the barbecue, and the tire swing was still attached to the old oak tree. The branch looked rotten now, like it could barely hold a chipmunk.

At the bottom of the stairs a sign read EAST SIDE BOAT CLUB TEMPORARY ENTRANCE. Sonny had put the sign there the last time he'd been in town, after the big flood of 1993 destroyed most of the original main building. That's when the club was moved to what had been the bowling alley. Just for a while, it's only temporary, everyone had said. It looked to Sonny like temporary had become permanent. The old clubhouse had been a grand old structure, with wood beams and sweeping windows and an impressive hand-carved entry door. His Grandpa Joe always said there were stories in that door, "Some could be told, but most of them had to be discovered." Sonny guessed he'd never get to discover them.

It was only four o'clock, but someone was playing old '60s music on the jukebox, *Light my fire, light my fire come on baby* . . . Sonny took a deep breath and pushed open the door. He was glad he'd taken that breath. He'd forgotten how much everyone here liked their smoke, and they liked it thick. He coughed. The room wasn't crowded yet. He knew it would be later on.

Frank walked toward Sonny with his arms out, ready for a hug or a handshake. He wore a Chicago Cub's baseball cap with the brim turned backward.

"Well, guys, look who finally made it." The guys consisted of Roy. "Sorry about your dad being sick and all, but damn it's good to see you, buddy. You been gone a hell of a long time. What is it, nine, ten years? Way too long." Frank held Sonny at arm's length and then pulled him in for a bear hug.

Sonny hugged back. "Frank Johnson, you river rat. I saw that old Corvair of yours. Can't believe you're still driving it." Frank was the one person Sonny had been sorry to leave behind. The one person who probably really cared that he'd left. "Shit, I hope I don't look as old as you do." Frank's beer belly was new. When they were kids, he and Frank used to make fun of the old guys whose stomachs hung over their belt buckles. Now Frank was one of them.

"Hell, Sonny, no one looks as old as I do. But you, you've hardly aged a week. You still got all your hair, even though I do see a bit of gray." Leave it to Frank to mention the gray. "What took you so long getting over here?"

"I've been stuck sitting in that damn hospital for the past two days. Sure could use a beer."

A perky brunette behind the bar smiled at him as she dried off glasses. Sonny always liked brunettes. He couldn't tell how old she was, maybe thirty-five or forty. They all looked the same to him these days, young. "Hi, I'm Grace. You must be Sonny Barton. I've heard a lot about you. What can I get you?"

Frank put his arm around Sonny's shoulder. "Get him a real beer, Grace. I bet they serve sissy beer out there in California."

Nothing had changed.

"Hey, Roy." Sonny sat at the bar. "I see you still got your same seat. How's the family?"

Roy pointed to his glass of beer. "Me and the family are doing just fine, thank you, aging well."

"Always a joker, Roy, always a joker."

"Yeah," said Frank. "He's funny as long as you don't sit on his goddamn stool."

"Have you guys seen my brother?" Sonny asked.

"We thought he was with you."

"He was, but he disappeared."

"Oh hell, you know Charlie. He'll show up when he's ready." Frank slapped a twenty-dollar bill on bar. "Beers all around."

Sonny smiled. Frank managed to comp the room before it got too crowded. Three beers wouldn't set him back too much.

Grace reached for the spigot, and Sonny noticed the tattoo. A turquoise-and-black feathered wing ran from her shoulder to her wrist. The drawing was so intricately detailed that it was hard for him to believe it was a tattoo. He couldn't take his eyes off it. Did it hurt while she lay there and the tattoo artist dipped ink into her pores as if she were a stretched piece of blank canvas?

Sonny looked away from her arm to the large picture window that framed their slice of the river, the murky silver water a liquid road. Empty barges lined up on the far bank. He almost expected to see parking meters. The rusty red barges were splashed with white and blue paint and gang graffiti. He hadn't realized they had gangs here, or maybe the graffiti came from someplace else and landed here.

The grain elevator was upriver from the clubhouse, and the waiting barges were stretched out a quarter-mile long, lined up like animals at the feeding trough. A constant flow of yellow gold filled one barge and then the next. He could hear the low rumble from the idling towboat that pushed the barges up and down the river. The elevator was the beating heart, pumping the grain from train to barge, sucking from barge to train. Off to the right he could see the end of a bridge as it stretched across to the Missouri side. It always seemed quieter in Missouri.

"Here's your beer." Grace brushed his hand with hers.

Frank walked over to the pool table and slapped down a quarter. "We'll see if you still got the edge, Sonny." Sonny knew he could trust Frank with his life. There weren't many people he could say that about. Not many people he could trust with a nickel for that matter. But he and Frank went way back.

It was so easy to fall into the old routine, like a time warp or time travel. The same old people doing the same old things. Sonny's California life seemed like a dream. He reached in his pocket and checked his cell phone. There were no messages.

Grace stood in front of the pictures that hung on the wall. There were pictures of men with boats, men holding trophies, and groups of men smiling into the camera. "I've heard a lot about your Grandpa Joe, Sonny. Seems he was quite a character."

Sonny glanced at the photo gallery. The water line left by the big flood of '93 ran just below them. There didn't seem to be any new pictures, not since long before he'd left.

"Two ball, side pocket." Sonny felt the tip of the cue skid as he tapped the ball, white against blue against black. "Shit."

Frank let out a hoot. "Scratch. That was fast. You're off your game, buddy boy. Rack 'em up again, but remember, you buy this time." He picked up the chalk and rubbed it on the end of his cue. Then he leaned forward for the break. "Rumor is you might be moving back."

"I wouldn't place any bets on that one, Frank." Sonny put down the cue stick and walked over to Grace. She stared at the pictures that hung in the glass cases with all the trophies. In the old days the East Side Boat Club ruled the Mississippi. The names of the legends were etched in his memory like the ABC song or *Itsy Bitsy Spider*—Greer, Johnson, Smith, Tucker, Barton. They were lanky men in black-and-white. The wall covered with their class pictures, only they were of a different class back then.

Sonny stood behind her; his chin grazed the top of her head. Somehow, she looked bigger behind the bar.

"Which one's your grandpa?" she asked.

"The one on the end. Grandpa Joe always stood on the end. Always ready to make an exit."

"That's odd," she said.

"What's odd?"

A stuffed badger stared at him from behind its glass case, its paw frozen mid-swipe. When Sonny was a kid he had nightmares about that badger, about it busting out of the case and tracking him down, stuffing him and leaving him in the case, his arms frozen for eternity. Grandpa Joe said badgers were rare in these parts. They came from out West. Badgers and prairie dogs. The characters were real to him, like Ratty and Moley. When Sonny read *The Wind in the Willows,* he'd thought of all the animals stuffed and sitting in the glass case at the boat club, and he'd swore that one day he'd set all of them free. But they were still here, just like his friends. It seemed like he was the only one who'd gotten out after all. Charlie, Frank, Roy, and somehow Grace had ended up here. A fly caught in the spider's web. He wondered where she came from.

"Look at this. It looks like your grandpa's picture was pasted on."

"Pasted?"

"Pasted, glued, it's added on. Look, here."

"I don't see anything."

"Well, look closer."

He reached up and lifted the picture off the wall. The yellow-flowered pattern of the wallpaper looked new underneath the spot where the picture had hung. Yellow roses seemed odd for a bar. He took the picture over to a table and laid it down.

"See?" Grace leaned next to him. "Right there, you can see the edges of his picture. I swear it's pasted on." Her hair smelled like grape bubble gum. Frank and Roy stood in front of the jukebox arguing the merits of country versus zydeco.

The door opened. His brother, Charlie, posed in the doorway. Sonny nodded at him then looked back down at the men in the picture. They all looked pasted on, their positions stiff and unnatural. It was hard to imagine them as real people, hard to image them sweating. And now they were dead and buried, nothing more than crosses and dandelions.

He slid out the cardboard backing and removed the photo. The paper was thicker back then. Sonny ran a finger over the surface. When his finger brushed his grandfather's face, Sonny felt the barest hint of an edge, and then his grandfather fell away.

# Chapter Two

# ANNIE

## 1904

July 11

Dear Diary,

I got two letters today, one from Joe and one from John. I've never gotten a real letter before, one that was just for me, from a faraway place. I don't think they're good letters, at least they don't feel good when I read them. Something is wrong. I know that much. Here, you'll see what I mean.

*Dear Annie,*

*I hope this finds you well. The fair is very nice.*

*Lots of interesting people and things to see. It is amazing what is happening these days. It is a wonderful time we live in. There are so many inventions and cultural exhibits. I think you would like them. I am well.*

*Yours Truly,*

*Joe Barton*

There's nothing of Joe in this letter. Not his smell, not his voice, not his smile. That's what bothers me so much. I wish I could hear his smile.

And I don't understand the letter from John, but I know it can't be good.

*Dear Annie,*

*I assume you've heard about Joe and the Olympic committee. All us guys are convinced that there's been some horrible mistake. Joe's as white as the rest of us. I'm sure it'll work out, but frankly, I'm worried about him. He doesn't talk much when we see him, and he keeps to himself, not even coming around to the practices. Got himself hired on in the Wild West Show as one of the Indians. It's just not right.*

*We're all getting excited here. It's pretty incredible being surrounded by so many athletes from so far away. The lake is always crowded with teams practicing. Sometimes things get a little rough. I'm not convinced that all the dunkings are entirely accidental, but it's to be expected.*

*You would love the Exposition.*

*Gotta go. They're calling me and I want to be sure this letter gets out in today's post.*

*Best wishes.*

*Your brother,*

*John*

What is this committee, and what's happened to Joe? I couldn't even brush my hair properly—I only got to fifty strokes tonight. I pushed the stiff bristles so hard onto my scalp that they hurt, but somehow the hurting felt good, as if it would help me understand.

Me and Joe have a lot in common, us both being raised by our fathers. Sometimes I think I can remember my mother. I remember that she had soft skin, and she would sit on my bed next to me and brush my hair while we both counted to a hundred. I'd fall asleep with her sitting there looking at me, and then she'd lean over and kiss me on the forehead before she left, saying, "Sweet Dreams, Annie." I'd always have sweet dreams just to make her happy. If she were still alive, I know she'd have hands as soft as a baby kitten's fur, not dried and cracked like most women's hands seem to get from washing and cleaning and cooking, like mine are getting already. Forever soft her hands would be. That's how I imagine her. And maybe she'd understand what these letters mean. Mothers are supposed to know everything.

There's a bird in my room. It's driving me crazy. Daddy must have left the door open again. Since he retired he seems to forget things like doors and dinner. The bird should be outside. That's where it belongs. It's watching me. I think it wants something. But I don't have anything to give it. I'm trying to ignore it, but it cocks its head from side to side as if it's trying to tell me something. Maybe I should sneak downstairs and get it a piece of bread.

Now the silly bird has gone and flown into the window. When I tried to let him out he just sat on the windowsill and stared at me. Maybe he wants me to fly away with him. Maybe I could. Maybe I could climb out that window and fly far away, find Joe and tell him I love him, and then he'd come back home and everything would be fine.

# Chapter Three

# JOE

# 1904

I was late for my first day of work at the Cummins Indian Congress and Wild West Show. I had the letter in my pocket written on the official Louisiana Purchase Exposition letterhead.

> *Dear Mr. Barton,*
>
> *We regret to inform you that due to the current regulations you will not be able to participate in the rowing competition at the 1904 Olympic Games. Given your American Indian heritage we are pleased to offer you a place in the Anthropology Games. These games represent a unique opportunity for the world to become better acquainted with the types of activities indigenous to your people. We are sure that you will be proud to represent your race in this unique event. We have also recommended you to Colonel Frederick T. Cummins. Please present this letter as verification.*
>
> *Thank you for your interest in, and contribution to, the Louisiana Purchase Exposition of 1904.*
>
> *Sincerely Yours,*

The letter had three signatures, and I couldn't read any of them. I doubted there was much sincerity anywhere in the letter. We don't want you, but we want you. We can't use you, but you'll be useful. It was all double talk. They didn't even know me.

The entrance to the Wild West Indian Congress and Rough Riders of the World was a town built to augment the ego of Colonel Frederick T. Cummins. He was a celebrity, not quite the same caliber as Wild Bill, but the fair couldn't get Wild Bill. He was off on a tour of Europe. Colonel Cummins wasn't going to let the opportunity for self-promotion slide. He'd built an almost genuine Wild West town; the only thing missing was the whiskey. The sign at the entrance read *Next Show High Noon*. It was long past high noon, but I saw there was still some activity going on inside. A guard dozed in a chair by the box office, and leaning against the ticket window was a board that read CLOSED.

"Excuse me," I said. The guard snored. A leather canteen dangled from a string around his neck. "Excuse me." I leaned forward and tapped him on the shoulder. He stirred but didn't open his eyes.

"Closed, can't you see the sign," he muttered without lifting his head.

"I was told to come here and report in. I'm the new Injun."

The guard opened one eye. "You ain't no Injun."

"I have a letter," I held the piece of paper for him. He gave it a glance and spit on the ground. "They're rehearsing. Go on in. Ask for Colonel Mulhall. But I still say you ain't no Injun."

The scene inside the fake fort looked like pictures of the old days out on the prairie, when the West was still wild. Here we were at the beginning of the twentieth century in the most exciting place on earth, where all the testaments to technology and civilization were on display. We had long ago tamed the West. My own father had been part of it. In this make-believe world the cavalry and the Indians relaxed while waiting for their cues. Instead of blood and mayhem, they were all laughing and joking together. A pack of horses grazed nearby. The large quarter horses were obviously for the cavalry. I figured the Indians would get the smaller black-and-white pintos. The Indians were in full battle regalia, most of them dressed in buckskins and feathers, while the soldiers were decked out in gray dress uniforms with swords dangling from their sides.

I called out to a boy pulling a water cart, "Hey, you! Can you tell me where I can find Colonel Mulhall?"

"I take it yur new. You ain't got no costume. Yur gonna need a costume."

"I'm supposed to find Colonel Mulhall."

"I heard you, but yur gonna need a costume. Mulhall's in charge of you guys, and he's not gonna like it that yur not in yur costume. Can you ride?"

"A horse?"

He rolled his eyes at me. "Of course, a horse. What else you gonna ride?"

"I can ride a little."

"Well, a little ain't good enough. They'll probably put you in with the guys on the ground. You got to be a pretty fancy rider to handle this action. They'll probably make you a body."

That sounded easy. I could be a body.

He must have decided that I was okay. "That's Mulhall over there. Big guy with the loud voice." He picked up the handle of the cart. The last thing I heard as he made his way over to a group of riders was, "If they make you a body, try not to let a horse step on you."

A group of soldiers in gray uniforms stood at attention in front of Mulhall.

"You are a bunch of pansy-assed soldiers. I want to feel your rage and anger. I want you to hate and massacre. I don't want any of this namby-pamby horseback riding. I want a charge, a big hell-bent charge. People are paying good money to see a show, and if we aren't careful they'll get Wild Bill in here faster than you can say 'Little Big Horn.'" Mulhall had a thick Irish accent that made the curses sound like a song.

I stood off to one side. He saw me out of the corner of his eye. "What the hell do you want?"

"I was told to see you. I guess I'm the replacement."

"I told them I needed a' Injun, a real Injun. I pride myself on giving them the real thing here."

"I am the real thing."

"No, you ain't. You got red hair."

"My mother was Indian."

Mulhall put his face up close to mine. The odor of tobacco and whiskey on his breath was so strong I could almost taste it.

"No way. I can smell it, and you don't smell like a' Injun. You smell like something else. I don't know what it is, but you sure don't smell like a' Injun. These clowns . . . ," he waved his hand around the field, "now they smell like Injuns."

So that was how it was going to be. I couldn't row with the guys because I wasn't American enough, and I couldn't ride with the Indians because I didn't smell enough.

"Hey, Zach," someone called from somewhere, "we gotta do this. The troops are getting restless."

"Okay, you, what the hell's your name?" He didn't wait for me to answer, "Pinky," he laughed when he said it, "Pinky, get suited up. Go over there with the Apache, and when you see someone shoot, you drop. That's your cue. Clutch your chest and fall to the ground. And I don't want to see you move so much as a toenail again until you hear me tell you." He walked over to the side of the field and picked up a megaphone like the one Greer used when he was calling our strokes.

I ran off to the changing room, behind an old Indian blanket attached to a clothesline. I put on stiff buckskins, leather chaps, and moccasins. "Places!" Mulhall called through a megaphone. As I ran out from behind the blanket, someone stuck a black wig with a long braid onto my head. "Here put this on. We can't have no redheads runnin' with the 'paches, boy." I headed out to the field, pulling the wig down tight as I ran. I took my place next to one of the Apache. His costume was tattered and dirty. Probably another body, I thought. I was glad I didn't have to fall off a horse.

"Where do we go?"

The tattered man stared at my clean outfit. "You'll figure it out."

"And GO!"

And then there was chaos. We Apache were yelling, trilling, and whooping while waving decorated spears and small axes.

I hadn't expected all the sounds, the explosions of rifles going off and pistols shooting. I heard names called out, Big Feather, Little Foot, and with each name someone dropped right where they were, in the middle of the mayhem. I didn't want to drop; I didn't want to fall; I didn't want to be trampled by the horses that came up from behind, so I ran faster and farther. My side ached. "Yell. Wave your arms. Pretend you're attacking," someone shouted beside me. "I am yelling," I shouted back. My whole head was yelling.

I nearly ran into a horse coming straight at me. There was a rifle pointed at my chest, and a puff of smoke came out of the opening.

I felt a pain in my chest, a piercing pain. I clutched my chest. I was sure I'd been shot, that the rifle pointing right at me had just shot me. I was dead. I was going to die right here on this stupid dusty field, in this ridiculous costume, and I couldn't even smell the river. I clutched my chest where I thought I'd been hit, my heart pounding so hard I felt it in my ears, heard it in my throat. I fell to my knees first, then my head dropped back. I was panting, I could hardly breathe anymore, and then I fell forward, my face in the dirt. The mayhem passed me by. It got quiet. I wasn't dead.

A muffled voice next to me whispered, "Nice drop, Pinky. Are you a real actor?"

I couldn't answer. I lay there, the dust thick on my tongue. All I could think was that from now on I needed to drop with my head sideways and keep my mouth shut.

# Chapter Four

# SONNY

## 2004

"Looks like the old man was a crackpot fake after all." Charlie slapped Sonny on the back. "I knew it. I always knew it."

"What exactly did you always know?" Sonny wished Charlie would shut up and go away.

"I knew he was too good to be true."

"Charlie, you don't know squat." Sonny picked up the small picture from where it landed on the floor and held it in the palm of his hand.

Charlie lifted a beer. "To fools and their heroes." He poured the liquid down his throat, then wiped his mouth with the back of his hand. "I know he had you hoodwinked, bro. Not me, though, I ain't nobody's patsy."

Sonny felt Grace's breath as she looked over his shoulder. "What do you think it means?"

Greer, Tucker, Johnson, Smith were all still there in their crisp linens, smiling into the camera, but where Grandpa Joe's picture had been was nothing.

"I don't have a clue."

The door opened. Two men dressed in leather paused in the doorway with the light behind them, posed like the bad guys in a Western movie. The smell of gasoline wafted in with them. One of them saw Charlie, waved at him, and they both sat down in a booth.

"Excuse me, I got business." Charlie walked over to the booth and sat down. He's swaggering, thought Sonny. He wants me to see how important he is. He's got business, and business means you are somebody.

Frank nudged Sonny. "O boy, there's a couple a losers. Haven't seen them around in a while."

"Who are they?" Sonny asked.

"The Evans twins."

"You've got to be kidding. Those are the Evans twins? What happened?" Sonny stared at the two barrel-chested men with gray beards. He remembered the Evans twins as undersized mama's boys.

"You been gone way too long, Sonny boy. Those are the Evans twins."

"I never could tell those two apart."

Frank lowered his voice, "It's easy. Billy went and got himself an earring a few years back. They didn't speak for almost two months, Bobby was so mad. Then one night Bobby comes in, and he'd got his left ear pierced just so no one could tell 'em apart again, but he went and pierced the wrong ear. So just look at the ears. That's how you'll know."

Sonny laughed and watched his brother with the twins. Charlie held up three fingers and then made a thumbs-down sign. They had two choices for the cheap stuff at the East Side Boat Club. Thumbs up was house beer, thumbs down, house whiskey.

Sonny took out his wallet and placed the picture of Grandpa Joe in with his credit cards and driver's license, and then he walked over to the pool table. He'd think about the picture and Grandpa Joe later. Frank was waiting for him. The Evans twins stood up at the same time as if joined by a cord. Bobby walked over to the table. "Hey, Sonny. It's been a long time. I hear you're a hot shot out West."

Sonny stared at the hoop hanging from Bobby's left ear. "Not so hot."

"Ha, yeah, I hear you. Not so hot. Well, it's hotter 'n hell here, so maybe you should have stayed. Ain't that right, bro?" Billy laughed and nodded.

As soon as the twins left, Sonny went over to his brother. "Hey, Charlie. What's going on?"

"What business is it of yours? You're not my babysitter."

Charlie downed his whiskey in one gulp, then he followed the twins. The screen door banged behind him.

Frank stood by the pool table watching. Sonny walked toward him.

"What's he up to Frank?"

"Nothing too serious, just the usual: pissing you off."

"Things never change." Sonny threw a five-dollar bill on the bar and walked outside, passing a couple guys he didn't recognize on their way in. The air was heavy. He took a deep breath and walked down to the dock. The old dock was gone, washed out by the flood. The new one was gray plastic, temporary. He squatted down, leaned over, and put his hand in the water. It had been a long time since he'd been on the river. Not since Grandpa Joe's big party.

❧

"Come on, Sonny, wake up." Grandpa Joe's voice mixed with his dream about Jenny the head cheerleader. Grandpa Joe wasn't supposed to be in that dream.

Sonny opened one eye. It was still dark. Grandpa Joe's face looked down at him.

"What's wrong?"

"Nothing's wrong. I need you to get up."

"What time is it?"

"It's four thirty. Get up, and keep your voice down."

"I'm sleeping." Sonny pulled the cover over his head.

Grandpa Joe shook him. " Sonny, wake up. We gotta go."

"Go where? It's not even light out."

Grandpa Joe pulled the pillow out from under his head and threw it across the room. "It's my birthday, Sleeping Beauty, and I need you to take me out on the river."

"I can't take you out on the river." Sonny pushed himself up on one elbow.

"Why not?"

"Because Dad will have a fit."

Grandpa Joe laughed. "Now that would be worth seeing. But who's going to tell him?"

"Believe me, what with half the town coming to your party, he'll notice if we're not here."

"We can tell 'em we went to check out the birthday cake. That we had to make sure they didn't spell 'Joe' wrong. I'm not letting you get back to sleep, so you might as well just take me."

Sonny threw back the covers and sat on the edge of the bed. In the distance a rooster crowed. Sonny never got up with the roosters.

They kept a rowboat tied up at the boat club. "No one's gonna steal this old boat," Grandpa Joe always said. And he was right. No one wanted a rusty old boat that didn't even have a motor.

Sonny looked at the steep incline from the parking lot down to the dock.

He wished he had a wheel chair, but Grandpa Joe wouldn't let them get one. "Are you sure you can walk down there?"

Grandpa Joe held on to Sonny's arm. "I may not make it into heaven, boy, but I can certainly get these sorry old bones down to the dock."

There weren't any other boats on the river yet. "This is the best time of day, you know, Sonny."

"Aren't you cold, Grandpa?"

"Don't mind the cold. Makes me feel young."

Sonny pulled a blanket from behind the seat of the old pickup and wrapped it around the old man's shoulders. "Well, Dad'll kill me if you get a chill, so here, I want you to wear this."

Grandpa Joe climbed into the boat with an ease that surprised Sonny. His whole body seemed to relax once he was seated. He pointed at the milky white mist that covered the river. "I bet you don't know what that is, Sonny."

"That's water vapor, Gramps."

"No, it ain't. That's the ghosts of all the old oarsman."

"There ain't no such thing as ghosts. That's water vapor." Sonny leaned forward and pulled back on the oars.

"Well, maybe to them that can't see, they call it water vapor, but if you look real close you'll see 'em. Each and every one of 'em: Tucker, Johnson, Greer, Smith." He looked at me. His lips were blue from the cold. "It don't matter if you can't see them, boy," he patted Sonny on the knee, "just don't forget them."

The door of the club opened and Grace walked outside. Sonny watched her light a cigarette. He could see her silhouette and the slow movement of her arm as she lifted a cigarette that glowed like a firefly. A low mist hung over the surface of the water. He could hear the sounds from the club, the clack of the ivory billiard balls, the bass line of the rock and roll, and the laughter. He didn't want her to see him, but she must have sensed his presence.

"Hello?" she called out. "Who's there?"

"It's just me, Sonny." He walked up the ramp to where she stood under the burned-out lightbulb.

"I thought you took off."

"I needed to put my hand in the river."

She threw her cigarette on the ground and rolled her toe on the end. "I've never been down close to the water. I hear the river's a dangerous place, that there's strong currents that can grab you before you even know it." She leaned closer to Sonny and whispered, "and I hear there's ghosts in the river."

"Grandpa Joe said the river mist is the spirits of all the river people. I don't know about that. I've never seen any spirits in the river, but I've seen broken spirits. I've seen people who get as stuck here as if they were mired in the mud, as beached as that barge over there that no one has ever bothered to move."

"I believe there's spirits here," she said. I think that's what brought me here. And a man." She had a small dimple that appeared when she smiled.

"And the man?" Sonny asked.

"Long gone."

She wrapped her arms around her body. The detail of the tattooed wings faded in the night, and it looked like she had a dark smudge on her arm. Sonny wanted to wipe it clean.

"Are you cold?" he asked.

She shook her head and shrugged. "Guess I felt a spirit."

"You know, Grace, I'd like to take you out on the river sometime, show you its magic."

"Grace!" he heard Roy yell from inside, "I need another beer."

She turned to Sonny. "I'd like that. I'd like that very much." She turned and skipped up the path to the club. When she opened the door, the inside light made a gold carpet on the gray deck. "Take it easy, boys. I'm coming. I'm coming. Can't a girl get a break around here? " The screen door slammed behind her—a tinny slam. And she was gone.

Sonny took a deep breath. Thunder rumbled in the distance. They could use a good rain.

His cell phone rang. The vibration in his pocket startled him. He hadn't had a call for days.

"Hello?"

"Mr. Barton. This is the hospital. I think you'd better come right over. There's been a change."

# Chapter Five

# ANNIE

## 1904

July 19

Dear Diary,

This morning Papa knocked on my door early, which isn't like him at all, "Pack your bags, Annie," he said. "We're going right now."

So here we are on an honest-to-goodness riverboat paddling our way down the Mississippi River. It's much bigger inside than I thought it would be. You can't tell from the outside how much room there really is. And there are so many fine people on board. Everyone looks like they're going to a party or to church on Easter Sunday with their bonnets and all. It's such a happy, excited place. My Daddy is an important person on the boat. He's an important person wherever he goes, being a doctor and all. So I guess that makes me an important person, too, even though my bonnet is a bit shabby. Daddy knows the captain quite well, and surprise of all surprises, the captain is a very large woman who's as tall as most of the men. Her chest is so large that it seems to push everyone out of the way. I wish I had a large chest. Mine is nearly as flat as a boy's is. I can't tell what my mother's was like. The picture of her is from the neck up, so I can't see all of her. I don't know if she was tall or short. When I ask Daddy, he says that she was just the right size. I don't know what that means.

Captain Irene laughs a lot, a big hoot of a laugh at the end of every sentence. It's hard for me to imagine a woman boat captain. Father told me not to get too excited, that she didn't start out to be a boat captain. It just happened. It turns out that she was the former captain's widow, who kept on with the boat after her husband died. But she had to get permission and know about being a captain and all. It makes me think, is what it does, because if a woman could captain a boat, why, what else could a woman do?

The boat itself is like a layer cake, a frosted cake with frills and candy. I have my own room, and I can walk outside straight onto a balcony and feel the wind. It's a wonderful boat. I think I might like to be a boat captain and have my own boat and ride up and down the river and laugh at everything.

I spent the morning with Captain Irene. Father was at a poker game, and I think she felt sorry for me. It's strange, this river life. On the way down to Hannibal I watched the shoreline pass by. Each bend in the river was a new surprise. Every now and then I saw the chimney of a farmhouse and some smoke that meant someone was cooking.

The houses right next to the river are built up high on poles. I think about the people who live in them and what they're doing. Are they watching me as I float by? Captain Irene says I'm her guest. I realize I've never been a guest before. I'm not sure what one is supposed to do.

When I asked her about it, she stared at me for what seemed to be a very long time, and then she told me to just enjoy myself and look pretty.

I never thought of myself as pretty before, but I'll try.

We are now docked in Hannibal for some repairs.

<hr />

July 19, Later

Dear Diary,

The repairs took longer than expected, and we haven't left yet. Irene says we'll be ready to leave by early morning.

I told Captain Irene about Joe. She asked me lots of questions about him. Like if he drank too much or swore or if he went to church. I told her no and no and no. I even told her that I was planning on marrying him.

"Ain't nothing like marrying a good man," she told me. "My Robert was one of the best."

Just about then, one of the crew came up to Irene and whispered something in her ear. "He's here now?" I heard her say, and then she started off without saying a word and was out the door already when she came back in and motioned to me to follow her. We went up to the pilothouse. That's what they called the very top of the boat, the top layer of the cake. I was higher above the ground than I'd ever been before, and I could see as far as the next bend in the river. Charts and maps covered the table. An old man with white hair wearing a white morning coat sat in an armchair. Irene burst into the room with a big grin on her face, "Well, I'll be damned, Samuel Clemens. When did you get here? I thought you were back East in Connecticut." Then she paused for a moment and said, "Sorry about Olivia."

He shrugged his shoulder like Daddy did when I asked him about Mama, and then he said, "I saw your boat and thought I'd scare the hell out of you."

Captain Irene turned to me. "Annie, I'd like you to meet an old friend of mine, Samuel Clemens."

Sitting right in front of me in the same room was the great Mark Twain himself. I was tongue-tied. I'd never met a real famous person before. And here I was face-to-face with the man who wrote *Huckleberry Finn*. I never really liked the book much, but Joe always says it's his most favorite book in the whole world, and so I said that right out loud.

Mr. Twain smiled and looked at Captain Irene and said that I reminded him of Livy. I supposed that was a compliment, then Mr. Clemens asked me about Joe. There was something about him that made me want to tell him everything, so I told him about the Olympic Games and how much Joe loved to be on the river, and that my Daddy said they wouldn't let him row because he was part Indian.

Mr. Clemens nodded, and when I said that about Joe being part Indian, he said, "Oh, he's a bit like my Injun Joe." His Injun Joe wasn't a nice person, as far as I could remember. But Captain Irene thought that was funny, and she laughed right out loud. I noticed that her teeth were tobacco-stained brown. I never knew a woman who smoked tobacco before. Maybe she'll let me try some. Then Mr. Clemens told me that he was born right here in Hannibal, and that he had a secret that not many people knew. He pointed at an island on the other side of the river, and his voice got low, almost a whisper, and he told me that I was looking at the real Shucks Island where Tom and Huck had their hideout. He said that most folks around here think it's on Glasscox Island, a bit further down, but they were wrong. I couldn't tell if he was fooling with me or not, but I thanked him for the information.

Then he picked up a copy of *Huckleberry Finn* that lay on the table, and he opened it. He took out a pen and wrote on the inside cover, and then gave me the book. I opened it. He'd written, "To Joe. From one river rat to another, Sam Clemens."

"This is for your Injun Joe." Then he pushed himself up to standing and said he needed to be going before they wondered where he went. I thought it funny that even a grown famous man couldn't slip away without people worrying.

I stood there with the book in my hand. Captain Irene came over to me and cupped my cheek in her hand. It was a rough hand. Her hair was pulled back into a tight bun, so tight that I could see the skin of her scalp beneath the gray. I wonder if my mother's hair would be gray if she'd been alive.

"This will help your Joe find his way." While she talked she rubbed at the whiskers on her chin.

I wonder what her whiskers feel like. Are they sharp like my Daddy's when he hasn't had a shave, or are they soft like the hair on the top of my head? I guess you have to have whiskers to be a captain, even if you're a woman.

## Chapter Six

# JOE

# 1904

"Creve Couer is right. That lake'll break anyone's heart." Greer shook his head. "I mean it, Joe. It's horrible, really bad. No one's got a straight shot. There's a bloody bend in it, and a layer of green algae so thick that it slows you down. You're not missing anything. If you ask me, the whole race is a farce."

I wanted to say, "Why don't we just go home? Let's all leave. Let's pack it in, all of us, together, tonight, now. Forget the farce." That's what I wanted to say, but I didn't.

"Yeah, and not only that, it's all the way out in the middle of nowhere. Takes a bloody train to get there. Who's going to go that far to watch us anyway?"

Greer, Johnson, Smith, and Tucker stood close to the edge of the small lake, skipping stones. I sat behind them on a tree stump. We were more than eight miles from my Mississippi, and I couldn't smell it anymore.

"Tucker leads, six skips. How about upping the ante?" Greer reached into his pocket and held up a coin.

"I'll take that bet." Seven skips. I'd never done a seven.

We were in our secret spot, the place me and the guys came to get away from the crowds and the noise at the fair. I'd found it before I got the letter, just after we'd all arrived, a bunch of fresh-faced boy-men, excited and ready to win one for our country, one for our town, one for us. The letter was in my pocket. I should have burned it.

"So who'd you get to take my place?" Those words, "take my place," left a nasty taste in my mouth. I hadn't said them out loud before, hadn't really believed that some arbitrary rule was actually going to keep me out of the games. I was glad it was dark, glad that they couldn't see me, couldn't see how hard it was to be with them, but not with them. It was as if I were a ghost. That was it. I was a ghost, and not really here. I wished it were true, because it would be easier not being alive. If I could be dead, then it would make more sense. Poor Joe, everyone would say, too bad he couldn't be in the games because he was dead. That was something you could say with pride.

Greer reached over and put his hand on Johnson's shoulder. "We've got Johnson here for now, but we keep hoping that something will change, that they'll let you back in. My dad's writing letters, and there's a petition going around the town."

I picked up a stone. It was flat and smooth, perfect for skipping. I pulled my hand back and let the motion of my wrist propel it forward. One, two, three, four . . .

"I'll owe you." I knelt next to the edge and dipped my hand in the water. It was cold for that time of year. "Congratulations, Tucker. You'll do good."

Tucker looked me straight in the eye and said, "I'd rather it was you, Joe." At least he could still look me in the eye.

Greer stood up. "We gotta go. They want us all tucked into our beds by ten thirty."

I wasn't supposed to be out either. Mulhall kept a tight rein on the hired help, but I'd learned a long time ago, way back in the Indian school, how to make my bed so someone thought I was sleeping in it.

"I'm gonna stay here a bit longer. I'll see you guys later."

Just before they were about to disappear into the woods, Greer looked back at me. He had that grin on his face, that one that meant we were about to get ourselves in a whole boatload of trouble.

"Oh, Joe, I almost forgot, I got a letter from Annie." Greer reached into his pocket and held out a pink envelope. "It says, Joe Barton. Now, why do you think my sister would be sending a letter to Joe Barton? Must be a different Joe Barton. I guess I'll just have to send it back."

He had four inches on me, and he held it up out of reach so that I had to jump like a trick dog. Just like the good old days, me and Greer playing keep away.

"I didn't say you could read it. I just said I got a letter," he laughed.

"Come on, guys, help me."

Smith stood behind Greer. Smith was always the strategic thinker. Block the bugger. Johnson, who was as tall as Greer, reached up and pulled the letter out of his hand and handed it off to me. Just like the good old days.

The envelope was already opened. "This is addressed to me. You had no right to open it."

"Relax, Joe, it wasn't me. Coach opened it. It's part of the training. It's like we're in jail."

The pink paper smelled like vanilla. Annie always dabbed a bit of vanilla behind her ears, said it kept the bugs away.

"Well, aren't you going to read it?" Greer asked. Then they all started in singing, *Joe and Annie sitting in a tree, k-i-s-s-i-n-g.*

"I'll read it later." I put the envelope in my pocket. I could feel the edges of it through my shirt.

Greer put his hand on my shoulder and squeezed. "You do that, Joe. But just remember, she's my sister."

"Don't worry, I'll remember." He slapped me on the back, and I watched them go.

Their voices faded. It was just me, the water, and a sliver of a moon, too dark to read. Maybe if I sat still long enough the beavers would think I was a tree. Maybe they'd try to carry me off and make a dam out of me. Maybe I'd let them.

I'd just about dozed off when I heard something thrash behind me. It didn't sound like a beaver or any other animal that I knew of. Nothing makes that much noise except a man.

Whoever it was seemed to be cussing up a storm. Not in any language I could understand, but cussing is cussing. "Hello!" I called out. I figured the sound of my voice would help.

The thrashing stopped.

"Hello!" I called again. "Are you okay?"

"No."

"Follow my voice."

I kept my eye on the trees. I felt him before I saw him. He was as black as the shadows, and I wasn't expecting a black man to be wandering around in the woods at night. Not around here.

He was so small I could see over the top of his head. He wore loose pants and was barefoot.

He came up close and pinched me on the arm.

"Ow, what do you think you're doing?"

"Good. You are real. I thought you might be a ghost." He squatted with his rear end resting on his heels, as if he sat in a chair.

He didn't sound like any of the black men that lived around these parts.

He sounded educated, British, probably had gone to a missionary school. He took a corncob pipe out of his pocket. His hand shook. "I got lost. Confusion spirits lured me into the woods. Someone must want to be rid of me to send such powerful spirits." He handed me the pipe.

Whatever he was smoking smelled like dried skunk. I passed it back to him.

"Why would someone want to get rid of you?"

"Because I am Aday, the fastest man in the world." He pointed a finger at his chest and tapped. "That is who I am."

"And I am Joe, the fastest oarsman in the world. That is who I am."

"Because of me, the Boers lost the war. That is who I am."

The Boer War, the name always reminded me of wild pigs. "Well, at least I'm not lost."

"Aaaaaah. Then I am not lost either." He smiled at me. His mouth opened so wide I could see the empty spaces in the back where teeth had been. A yellow smile, a jack-o-lantern smile.

He was lost, I thought. He was crazy lost. "You know, it's not a good idea to be wandering around these woods at night. You could get yourself shot. Or worse, you could fall in the lake."

Aday leaned forward and stared at the still water. The high-pitched whine of a mosquito rang in my ear. I slapped at the air.

"Some men may run faster for short little distances, but that is not the mark of a true runner. A true runner can run for days. A true runner can sleep while he runs. A true runner can drink the sweat from his brow and live on the insects that fly into his mouth. I am a true runner."

And I am a river rat, I thought, but didn't say.

"I am going to win the marathon medal, and then the British will let me go home. That is what they said. Win them a medal, and then I am done."

He was going to win a medal? How could he win a medal? The only medals were the ones they were giving out for the official Olympic Games. Us primitives got ribbons and flags for our games.

"You're running in the real marathon?"

"That's what I said. I am the greatest runner in the world."

Here I was a homegrown boy, born to the river, local through and through, and the blasted committee was going to let him in the games—a black man from a place that sounded like a pig—they were going to let him run the marathon. Him? And they wouldn't let me paddle around on a slimy lake?

A white scar ran down the black man's back like a zipper. I could push him in, I thought, I could push him in and no one would ever know.

I turned away. "I need to get back."

Aday didn't move.

"You better follow me," I said. "You don't want to fall into this water. There's horrible creatures that live in this lake." I was feeling mean and wanted to rile someone, and this odd little man was as good as any. "Who knows, there might be currents and undercurrents and mud that'll suck you in so deep you'll end up on other side of the world."

Aday squatted on the edge of the bank and tossed a handful of dirt into the water. The ripples caught the edges of moonlight. "The other side of the world is not such a bad place to be."

# Chapter Seven

# SONNY

## 2004

"Wait here, Mr. Barton," the nurse said. "The doctor will be with you in a moment."

Sonny looked at his watch. Not that it made any difference. Time wasn't the same in the hospital as it was outside. Sick time, dying time. It dragged out and speeded up all at once. Sonny picked up a magazine. He'd already read this one. "The Best Summer Camps" was the lead story. When he and Charlie were kids they'd never gone to an official summer camp. The river was their summer camp. Quite a threesome they'd made: Charlie, Frank, and Sonny. They were always in and out of the house, and Sonny's mom never yelled, never got angry, and she always had a batch of homemade chocolate chip cookies ready for them. His mom—she'd been gone a long time. He could picture the tray of cookies, and he could picture her hands, but he couldn't picture her face or remember the color of her hair. Had she been pretty back then? He didn't know. He'd only been twelve when she died, and they were left with their dad and Grandpa Joe and a succession of housekeepers who tried to make it all okay.

He tossed the magazine on the table and walked over to the window. He could make out the silver reflection of the river between the buildings at the other end of town. Just catching a glimpse of it was enough to let him know that somehow everything would be okay.

A smell of stale smoke and beer mixed with the hospital Lysol. Charlie stood next to him. "What's so fascinating out there?"

"The river. I can see it from here."

"You and that damn river. You're as nuts as Grandpa Joe used to be. The crazy old fake. Look, if you want me, I'm gonna go sit over there and watch TV." The television in the corner was tuned to *Wheel of Fortune*. Someone with an odd sense of humor must have decided on that channel.

Sonny wondered if the shack by the river was still there, the one that Grandpa Joe had taken him to visit.

---

"Don't tell your folks about this," he'd said. "They wouldn't approve." Sonny crossed his heart.

"I won't tell."

"Atta boy. Your dad gets funny about some things. But I want you to meet someone who lives here, one of my oldest friends." Grandpa Joe knocked on the door. There didn't seem to be a doorbell.

"Who is it?" a voice from inside called out. It was a raspy voice with a funny lilt to it, not like any voice Sonny had ever heard before.

Grandpa Joe turned the handle and opened the door. It wasn't locked. "Who else would be visiting you, you old coot? It's me, and I brought my grandson, Sonny."

Sonny's eyes had a hard time getting used to the dark. The window curtains were made of blue plastic tarps tied back with yellow cord. Plastic buckets were scattered around the room. There didn't seem to be a ceiling, just wood nailed onto beams and bits of light coming in through the cracks. An old black man sat in an easy chair, his feet up on the coffee table. A cane rested against the chair. Sonny had never been in a black man's house before.

"So what do you think, Addy?" Grandpa Joe asked the man in the chair.

Addy, it sounded like a woman's name.

The old man looked in their direction, but not at them. Sonny turned around, thinking maybe something was behind them, but there wasn't anything there except for the closed door.

"Don't know yet." He smiled. "Can he read?"

Grandpa Joe took a book out of his pocket. He never went anywhere without it. "Sit down, Sonny." Then Grandpa Joe sat on the couch and put his feet up on the table next to the black man's. Addy wasn't wearing any shoes. His feet were as cracked as the river mud in August.

Sonny's eyes finally got used to the light. On the wall hung a framed picture of a black man waving an American flag. That was the only decoration on the pale green mold and chipped paint that peeled away from the wall.

Grandpa Joe handed the book to Sonny. "Let's hear what you got."

Sonny looked down at the book, placed his finger under the first word, just like Grandpa Joe had taught him. He took a deep breath and began, "You don't know about me . . ."

❧❦❧

"Mr. Barton."

"Yes?" Sonny and Charlie both answered at the same time.

The doctor stood at the entrance to the waiting room. "Your father is stable now, but there really isn't anything more I can do. Just keep him comfortable."

They walked down the hall and into the room. Neither of them spoke.

Their father lay in the hospital bed. He had tubes coming out of his nose and his left arm. A white blanket was pulled up under his armpits. He was neat and tidy in the bed—perfectly arranged, a model sick person. The television was on, but his eyes were closed.

"He doesn't look real," Charlie said.

Sonny leaned over and put his head next to his father's, but he didn't open his eyes. "Hey, Dad, how're you doing? It's us—me and Charlie."

Sonny didn't know why he expected his father to care. Maybe it was because it was near the end. Then, without warning, his father's eyes opened, and Sonny felt the faintest touch against his hand. His father's hand. Which of them had moved closer?

The nurse walked in. "Well, isn't this nice, Mr. Barton, you're awake. Boys, your father woke up just for you. Isn't that nice? Let me just fluff this pillow a bit and set you up higher so you can see them."

She spoke constantly, narrating every action as if she knew the thoughts that passed through his head. Sonny looked at his father. His eyes were open, but it didn't seem as if he were really awake, at least not in this world. It was as if he were in between worlds. Seeing what? Maybe their mother, maybe Grandpa Joe, maybe nothing.

"It's a beautiful day, Mr. Barton," the nurse rambled as she put the blood pressure cuff around his arm and stuck a thermometer in his mouth. "It's a perfect late-summer day. I even thought I saw a maple tree starting to change. Why I bet the apple picking is perfect now. I just love a good caramel apple, don't you? I'm going to straighten your bed sheets now. Can't have you looking disheveled for your sons. Sonny has come a long way to see you. And what would he think if . . . ?"

Sonny tuned out the banter. The sheets looked fine to him, not a wrinkle. His father barely moved. Fine white hairs covered his chin. Apparently the beard still grew, even though everything else was shutting down. He glanced over at Charlie, who sat in a chair tucked back in the corner and tugged at his mustache.

With his free hand Sonny rubbed his father's brow. In the past few years he'd gotten old, as old as Grandpa Joe had been. With each exhale a faint whistle came from deep inside his father's chest. The sound of it was no more than a whisper, a trail of bread crumbs to the gingerbread house, and then there was no more whistling, no more movement, no more breath.

Now he'd never get to take his father to California or the Grand Canyon, and he'd never get to ask him what was his favorite cake or why Grandpa Joe wasn't in the picture.

Charlie jumped up and ran to the door and shouted into the hall. "Nurse, nurse, we need help, nurse."

"She's not going to be able to do anything, Charlie."

"Don't say that. Don't ever say that. He's just sleeping. You don't know. You don't know anything. You're not a doctor. You don't know. He's fine, he's fine . . ."

The nurse rushed in. "What's going on here?" She turned to Charlie. "You can't carry on like that. This is a hospital. Now what's hap— . . ." She walked over to the bed and looked down at their father. "Ohhhhh." She looked up at them. "What a blessing. It's because you were here, you know, because you were here he went so easy."

Charlie grabbed on to Sonny's arm. Sonny felt the heaviness of him. He was shaking, crying without tears. Dry sobs. "But what am I going to do now?"

"What are you going to do?" Sonny wanted to slap him. "You self-centered bast— . . ." Sonny stopped himself. That was Charlie. Charlie couldn't help it. His free ride had just come to an end. He was going to have to stick out his thumb and hitch another one, and there weren't that many that came by these days. People didn't stop for Charlie anymore.

# Chapter Eight

# ANNIE

## 1904

July 20

Dear Diary,

This morning Captain Irene took me to the engine room. The men stared at me. Captain Irene didn't seem too happy about that. She told them to behave themselves, that I was a lady, and they were to treat me as if I was one of their sisters. I thought about John. Did he look at ladies like that? Did Joe?

But the engine room itself was a wonderful place, even though it was terribly noisy. I wanted to run away at first. It was so loud and booming, as loud as a tornado, or a train. The noise made the room seem crowded, like hundreds of people shouting at each other. But then I realized that no one was shouting. I held on tight to Captain Irene's arm. And then I heard the beat. It was like a heartbeat. It never stopped, not for an instant. The pilothouse was the boat's head, and now I was inside its heart. Giant rods moved constantly, pushing and pulling. They were dancing, and I found myself swaying to its rhythm. Steam filled the room. It was hard to catch my breath in the heat.

Irene says we will reach St. Louis by nightfall. I know Joe will be surprised. I only hope he's happy to see me.

Captain Irene has been busy all afternoon. I felt the change. So much excitement in the air. We are almost there. There's more activity on the river down here by the city. It's a good thing the river gets wider. There are so many boats around us, and I can't imagine how they manage not to bump into each other; but we haven't yet, so I suppose it's okay. It looks as though everyone in the United States and the world is coming to St. Louis, and they're all coming right here to my own backyard.

I think I'll thank the Committee when I see them. Father would never have brought me here if we didn't have to take care of all this rowing business.

That was a horrible thing to write. How could I be thankful for something that's making everyone so unhappy.

❧

July 20, Evening
Dear Diary,
We're here! St. Louis is a city of lights. Everywhere I look there're lights, on the land, on the boats, reflecting off the water. It's a wonder any one can ever sleep here with so much going on. People coming and going even after dark. But it sure does make you feel welcome. "Come in, the lights are always on" is what it seems to say. When I was getting on the train, I stood right behind a dark man wearing a turban that was wound so high it made him tower over everyone. I wonder if that's how tall his head really is. He must have been a snake charmer. Daddy told me not to stare, but I don't see how I couldn't. I didn't know this many people lived in the world.

Even the train was perfect. There wasn't a scratch on any of the wood, and the seats were perfectly cushioned in brand new leather. The brass fittings were so shiny I wondered how long it took to get them polished like that. Someone must truly love that train to take such good care of it. The most impressive part was the ride itself. It was so smooth I hardly felt that we were moving. But all that was nothing compared to when we finally arrived at the fairgrounds. I never thought it could be possible, but there were even more lights than in St. Louis. I wish it were already daylight, so I could go exploring. I don't think I'll be able to sleep tonight.

Our hotel is called the Inside Inn because it's right in the middle of the fairgrounds, and it's a very grand and fancy hotel. I think we were lucky to get in. It's only because Father is an important person that he managed it. John met us at the hotel, but Joe wasn't with him. I know I shouldn't be disappointed, but I was hoping to see Joe, so I could smile at him and let him know that everything is okay. John said that Joe's staying someplace else. Someplace else seems like a funny place to be.

I think that even if I had to go home right now and never got to see the fair, it wouldn't matter. Today has been the most perfect day.

## Chapter Nine

# NATHAN

*Winter*
*John Greer*
*1416 Concord St.*
*Quinley, Il*

*My dear friend,*
*By now you've probably been told that I am dead. I am not dead, and I do not know if you will ever see this. And I might as well be in hell seeing as this place has no water as far as the eye can see, and it's hot and dry and the wind blows the dust just like a good dry snowfall. I miss our talks and being out on the river. But I'm writing to tell you that I've finally gone and done it. Done what you might be asking yourself. I've met a woman. Yes, a real live woman. I can imagine my mother fanning herself and drinking huge amounts of hot, strong tea if she were to know. But the people here are different than what we were led to believe. I'm talking about the wild people, the native people. Maybe someday I will come home and deliver this letter straight into your hands, or maybe some trapper will find it long after we are all gone. In any case, I write. The people I am with hide themselves and they hide me. They are afraid that if someone knows I am here they will come to find me.*
*I can't pronounce her native name, so I call her Moon. That is because when I awakened delirious and in pain she leaned over me, and I thought I*

*had floated up into the heavens and was staring at the white face of the moon. She calls me Laughing Man. Imagine that. Me a laughing man.*

*Rest assured that I am not being kept as a prisoner. No, I can leave at any time. But I don't want to. I enjoy sitting by the light of the moon.*

*Your friend Nathan Barton*

# Chapter Ten

# JOE

## 1904

I got myself one of those blue, spun-sugar, fairy-floss confections and caught the train to the Ethnology Exhibit. That was the fancy scientific name for the people zoo, where the native peoples from around the world were on display in living exhibits; and it was where I had to go to get my assignment for the Anthropology Games. The train took me past the observation wheel. A flying porch swing is what Annie would call it. I wish I could take her on it. She'd love being that close to the stars. Just the other day she was telling me about a couple of fellows my own age who had built a flying machine in a place called Kitty Hawk. The sky didn't hold much interest for me. I'd never wanted for anything more than the river.

"I don't want to go! I don't want to go!" A kid across the aisle was in the middle of a temper tantrum. His mother couldn't have been much older than Annie. I wondered if the red stain on his white shirt was the problem. "You be quiet now," I heard his mother try to whisper, but it came out more like a hiss. "You be quiet now, or I'll let them eat you for dinner."

"Them" was the Filipinos that were being exhibited. Their reputation had grown. As far as I knew they only ate dogs, not naughty children, and the threat of them didn't seem to have any effect. I handed the boy the rest of my floss, and he stuffed it in his face. The mother smiled at me. I wasn't sure who I felt sorrier for, the mother or the kid.

The train took us past an Indian village filled with red, turquoise, and black tepees, and right next to them was an African village of mud and grass huts, and the Filipinos had their houses made of straw. Never build a house out of straw, I'd always been told. The whole fair was like a crazy quilt, disjointed bits and pieces barely stitched together. But after a while it made sense, as if this was the real world, being able to step from one country to another, from civilized to primitive in a train stop.

I joined the groups of women in lavender and white linen who strolled through the grounds, pointing and smiling at all the dark faces. A black woman sat on the dirt weaving long blades of river grass into a basket. She was nearly naked, only a few bright red strips of fabric covered the woman parts, the parts that I had never seen. I could tell that she was pregnant. Her black belly was stretched so thin that the black became gray. I squatted in front of her. I reached into my pocket and pulled out a red apple. Annie had sent us each a box of them. Fresh picked from the tree. I rubbed it on my shirt to give it extra shine, then I set it on the ground next to the half-woven basket. I stood up and backed away. I wanted to be sure she knew it was a gift. She picked up the apple and held it in front of her.

A small boy in a brown loincloth crawled out from behind her and grabbed the apple out of her hand. He took a bite out of it, then he ran behind his mother as if she were a secret hiding place.

"Is that you, Joseph? So you are real. I thought you might have been a spirit."

I turned around. It was the little black man from the river. I was surprised he'd recognized me. "Aday?"

"My friend." He smiled at me. His teeth weren't quite so yellow in the daylight.

"I'm here to sign up for the games." I didn't want him to think I was one of the gawking sightseers.

"Me too." He puffed out his chest and said, "I am a spear thrower." I couldn't imagine this small black man throwing anything very far. "And you?"

"Wherever they put me." Thunder rumbled in the distance. Even though I couldn't see the lightening, I knew it was there. "Storm's coming," he said.

Aday picked up some street dust and threw it at the sky. It was something my father would have done. We walked over to a low, wooden building that was tucked away behind some trees. It looked like a garden shed that had been converted to the administrative center for the special Anthropology Games. The boy with the apple followed us. I pretended I didn't see him.

"You have a family, Aday?"

"All men have a family."

I felt his eyes on me. Guess he didn't know staring was rude.

"I don't."

"That is nonsense. You cannot be a man without a family. Some woman carried you, some man taught you, and someone fed you. Where are they?"

That was the question.

---

I remembered the night before my father left. He sat on the front porch like he usually did after supper. He seemed more tired than usual. I had dried the last dish and put it in the cupboard. I didn't like washing much, but I liked drying. I sat next to him on the porch swing. The sun was down. The night hadn't cooled off yet, and the heat lightening put on quite a light show.

"I want you to have this." He handed me a wooden smoking pipe. "I carved this the winter I met your mother."

I'd seen him smoke it hundreds of times.

"What does the pipe remind you of?" he asked me.

"I don't know."

"Well, here, hold it. Let it talk to you."

He placed it in my hand. "It's not saying much."

"Humor me. What does it look like?"

I'd never noticed how delicate the carving was. The wind picked up from the west. It blew the dinner bell that hung outside the back door. "I don't see anything," I'd said. I never liked it when he played guessing games with me. He shrugged and handed me two pairs of shoes. They were the ones that he kept in a heavy, hand-carved box next to the silver that nobody ever polished. The first pair was leather Indian shoes, moccasins. "Your mother made these for me a long time ago. I think she'd like you to have them." I'd never seen my father wear them. I couldn't even imagine him without his heavy work boots.

Then he handed me the other pair of shoes. "These were your mothers," he said. I held them in my hand. It was hard for me to imagine that a grown woman could have feet that small. The leather was polished black and the soles had almost no mark on them, as if they had never been worn.

We sat for quite a while, the two of us and the shoes, and then he spoke, "I have to find her, Joe. I'm sorry."

How had I never noticed how unhappy he was? But then again he was always looking down the road, always looking west. In my ignorance I thought he was checking the weather, but he must have been hoping that maybe one day she'd appear, that one of the storms would blow her our way.

My father never talked about my mother's past or how he'd met her, at least not that I remembered. I didn't know anything about where she came from, but she did sing to me. I remembered that. She sang songs that I never heard anywhere else, songs that didn't have words I could understand, songs made of strange sounds that reminded me of the wind and the trees and the river.

"I still miss her, Joe. I miss Moon," my father said. "And you're old enough now, you know."

Old enough for what I wondered.

❧

Aday smiled and nodded at the people as they walked by. I didn't know how to explain to this strange little man I didn't know, this man who ran for days without stopping, this man who had been in a war that sounded like a wild animal on a continent far away. I didn't know how to say to this man that my mother left me when I was young.

I looked at the woman with the basket. Did my mother have children who hid behind her while she bent over her work? Would anyone here know her? Would they recite my history? Would they look at me and say, "You are the image of your mother"? It would be like Goldilocks waiting for me, hidden beneath a blanket. I would pull it back, "And here she is," I'd say. Only she wouldn't be an old woman with gray hair and her life behind her, but as I should have known her, as I wished I had known her, laughing and singing, always singing.

"Everyone has a family. You cannot be a man without a family." Those words burned into me. I turned back to Aday and said, "Then I must not be a man."

We walked toward the registration area. Lines of indigenous people stood in front of a row of tables. "Indigenous" was the official name given to the wild natives, like weeds that just won't go away. That's what we were, lines of weeds signing up to play weed games.

A well-dressed, young indigenous man stood behind one of the tables. His dark face looked even darker against the starched white of his shirt. The collar was too small, or maybe his neck was too big. He looked to be a few years younger than I was, maybe not even twenty yet.

"Next." He didn't even glance up to look at me when he talked, but read from the paper in front of him.

"Tribe?"

"Don't know. Consider me a floater."

"A joker, huh? I don't have time for this. Tell me your tribe."

I smiled. "Really, it doesn't matter."

"You can't be a floater. You have to be from somewhere. Otherwise why are you here?"

That was the blue-ribbon question.

"Because, they told me to be here. I handed him the letter. "And I really don't care where you put me, except I'm not very good at pole climbing, so don't put me there, and I'm better at pulling than pitching, so forget the spear toss."

He wasn't listening.

He read the letter and then looked up at my face, and then back at the letter, and then at my face.

"You're Joseph Barton?"

"Joseph Charles Barton, son of Nathan Forrester Barton, but my friends call me Joe."

He stood up. "Joe. Don't you remember me?" He opened his arms up wide as if that would jog my memory.

I looked at his face.

"Joe, it's me." He smiled, and I remembered the smile.

"Jake?"

He nodded.

Jake Redfeather, twelve inches taller and almost two hundred pounds heavier, but still the same old Jake.

⚜

I'd met Jake my first night at that godforsaken place they called a school. I was lying on my bed thinking about my father, wondering where he was, and what in the world he'd been thinking to send me away. I was plotting my escape, how I'd go off and find her first, find my mother, and then I'd find my father and bring her to him. Then he'd be happy and regret forever that he made me go away.

I had the pipe my father gave me hidden under my pillow. I was glad I'd thought to hide it. Anyone caught with tobacco was given the strap, no questions asked. But a pipe, that would probably have brought Miss Huffman herself out of the office. I shouldn't have brought it. I knew I should have left it home, but it smelled like my father. It smelled like sweet tobacco and wood.

In the bed next to me someone cried. It was a muffled sound, but I was awake and couldn't ignore it. I slipped out of my bed and knelt down on the floor next to him.

"Are you okay?"

"I miss my nana." He was so small that it made me feel more than twice his size.

"What's your name?" I'd asked.

"Jake . . . Jake Redfeather," he squeaked out his name as if he hadn't talked in weeks.

"Where is your nana?" I patted him on the back like my father used to do when I woke up crying in the middle of the night,

"Home," he whispered. And then I sang. I didn't know where the song came from. My father never sang to me; said singing was for birds. But it was a song that came out of my deepest memory. I sang words, but not really words. They were sounds that felt like they meant something, but I didn't know what it was.

"Na no ne na hwa ke ho."

Jake's shoulders stopped shaking

"No a we na no kue ka," the song felt strong inside of me.

Jake's breathing became steady and deep.

"Na no ne na hwa ke ho."

The door from the hallway opened and someone held a lamp. "What's going on here?"

I got down on the floor, so they wouldn't see me out of my bed.

"There's to be no talking after lights out. When I count to three it better be quiet in here." There was a pause.

"One."

I slipped back into my bed.

"Two."

I pulled the cover up over my head.

"Three."

The door closed. I could hear her outside the door, waiting and listening. The wooden floorboards creaked under her weight. And then I slept.

---

Jake walked around the registration table. He towered over me. The little kid had become a big, barrel-chested Indian.

"Damn, it's good to see you," I gave him a hug. "I have to admit, you're the last person I expected to see in this zoo."

"It is a zoo, isn't it?" He looked around. "But it's a money-making zoo.

They're really playing up these Anthropology Games. 'First of its kind, never before seen anywhere . . . See real live natives compete.' It brings in the tourists."

"Yeah, they're giving it more play than the real games."

"The real games?"

"See, you don't even know about them."

"Oh, I know about them, just don't see how they're more real."

Redfeather looked at the line of restless natives growing behind me.

"Look, Joe. I gotta finish assigning the teams. But I tell you what, I'll put you on my team. You can be an honorary Sioux. Can you meet me over at my place? I'm with my grandparents. Just find the Sioux camp and ask for Redfeather. Meet me at six o'clock."

I gave him one last hug and turned. Aday stood off to one side waiting for me. I'd forgotten about him. "I see you have a friend."

I looked back at Jake, his nose buried in paperwork. "I suppose I do."

# Chapter Eleven

# SONNY

## 2004

The conference room at the law offices of Pringle and Pringle reminded Sonny of a library, all dark wood and hush. Cases of old law books lined the walls. Sonny wondered if anyone ever looked at them. Charlie sat with his legs crossed, and he tugged on the ends of his mustache. The attorney was a young man who seemed hardly old enough to be out of law school. Sonny wasn't sure if he was a Pringle or not. He wore a bow tie, which seemed to be a quaint affectation. Maybe it was his way of saying, "You can trust me." He opened a legal folder and took out some papers.

Sonny knew he should be grieving, but he couldn't bring himself to feel anything. His father was gone, and he and Charlie were the only Bartons left. Not only were they the older generation, they were the last generation, since there didn't seem to be any more Bartons coming down the pipeline. It was obvious that he and Charlie were washouts in that regard. At least now he could leave town for good, sell the old homestead and wave goodbye to the river from thirty thousand feet. He'd always liked the view on the takeoff. And now there was no reason to ever to come back.

It was too bad about the house, but there was no way Sonny was going to be saddled with upkeep and insurance and liability and plumbing. And he knew Charlie wouldn't take care of the practical details. I'm not my brother's keeper. Is that how it went?

"I'm glad you were able to come together. There is one provision that needs to be taken care of before you can both have title to the house."

"Provision?"

"Yes, There is one small complication. It seems that your father did not own the house outright."

"What do you mean?" Sonny asked.

"It was your grandfather's house."

"Yes, but he's been dead for twenty years. The house went to my father."

"It seems that your father, Mr. Joseph Barton Jr., did not inherit the house free and clear. It was held in trust for your father's use during his lifetime only. The house was to then be left to you and your brother, but there was a caveat."

"What the hell's a caveat?" Charlie pushed the chair back and stood up. "This is bullshit."

"Charlie, sit down. Let him finish."

The attorney cleared his throat. He reached into his pocket and pulled out some throat lozenges. He'll never make a poker player, thought Sonny.

"There is one stipulation before any property can be liquidated."

"What's that?" Sonny asked.

"You and your brother are to enter into a rowing competition. You are to be in the same boat. You may have other teammates, but all persons on the team must be members of the East Side Boat Club. And the race must take place somewhere on the Mississippi River."

"Did I miss something? What race?" Sonny leaned forward in his chair.

"It didn't specify."

"This must be a joke. Nobody races on this river anymore. What if there aren't any races?"

"It states very clearly that if the two of you are not able to comply with the terms, then the house will be donated to a charity that benefits Native American orphans."

"Native American orphans? Is this a joke?" Charlie glared at Sonny. "This is your fault."

"Believe me, Charlie, the last thing I want to do is hang around here any longer than I have to. I have a life waiting for me." He turned back to the attorney. "This is absurd. You can't make a condition that's impossible to fulfill. Times have changed. This can't stand up in court can it, Mr. . . . ?" Sonny couldn't bring himself to say the name of a potato chip.

"Well, I can't say for sure, Mr. Barton. But it could tie up the estate for quite some time."

Tie up the estate. Their father must have known. Why didn't he ever tell them? Why didn't he prepare them? It was just like him. If you don't talk about something, it isn't real. Native American orphans. Was there even such an organization? The whole thing was ridiculous.

"Where the hell are we supposed to get a boat?"

"I'm afraid it doesn't specify."

"Well what the fuck does it specify?" Charlie stood up and grabbed the paper from junior Pringle.

"Sit down, Charlie. Don't shoot the messenger."

"I'll shoot anyone I damn please."

The lawyer took the paper out of Charlie's hand. "It just says that you have to do this, and you have to do it together. Let me read you the exact passage." He took a pair of reading glasses out of his pocket. Sonny doubted he needed them, but it made a good show, and even Charlie wouldn't hit a guy wearing glasses.

" . . . and lastly the house will be put into trust until such time as my grandsons, Joseph Barton III (Sonny) and Charles Barton, fulfill their destiny and race as a team down the Mississippi."

❦

"Well, Sonny, which one do you want, bourbon or scotch?" Grace put two bottles on the bar.

"I don't know. Does it matter?"

"Does it matter?" Frank put his arm on Sonny's shoulder. "You're worrying me, buddy boy. You're worrying me."

"I know it's hard to believe, Frank, but I've never actually tried the stuff. I went from beer to wine. Never felt drawn to the hard stuff."

"Now's the time. Let's see what you're made of. Grace, it's a special occasion, so none of the cheap rotgut. Let's have something from the good bottles."

"Let me just go ahead and set you up, and you can let me know where you stand. You're either a bourbon man or a scotch man. You can't be both."

He'd heard that before. You can't be both. You can't be a beer man and wine man. You can't be a country boy and a city boy.

Grace poured two shots of Glenfiddich from a triangular bottle. "This is a single malt, Sonny. It's as scotch as they get."

"Is that all?" He lifted up the shot glass. Seemed like barely more than a thimbleful. At least with beer and wine you get a full glass.

"Believe me, that's plenty."

Grace leaned forward on her elbows. "Don't take too much. Sip it."

Sonny pushed one of the shots to Frank and lifted the other. He inhaled the aroma as if were a glass of wine. It burned his nose. "This stuff smells like nail varnish with a wood finish."

Grace laughed. "Try it."

He put his mouth on the edge of the glass. It was smooth and cold. He tipped his head back and poured the liquid down his throat.

"Look at that, Frank."

The first taste burned the inside of his mouth and tongue. He coughed. A bittersweet taste lasted for a moment, and then it was gone. It just disappeared. He needed to sip a bit more to remember what it was that he'd just tasted.

She put another bottle on the counter: Jim Beam, the Gold Medal winner at the Louisiana Purchase Exposition. He couldn't get away from the damned 1904 World's Fair. Grace poured out two more. "This is bourbon, Sonny."

He sniffed. "This one smells a bit sweeter, almost as if it has a tinge of vanilla in it. That and some compost."

"It's not a wine tasting, Sonny." Frank picked up a shot glass and poured the whiskey down his throat. Sonny did the same.

"Damn!"

Sonny slammed the glass on the bar. "Aaaaaah."

He throat burned, his stomach burned, his head burned.

He smiled at Grace

Sonny looked at the shelves behind the bar. There was something about all the bottles, all the different shaped bottles. He never went to bars. Charlie was the one who went to bars. Sonny went to coffee shops. He picked up the smoky brown bottle in front of him. "Whiskey," he whispered. Whiskey . . . Old West saloons and gamblers and trappers and grizzly men panning for gold  . . . whiskey and whores and the Wild West . . . and the minutes passing by . . . and the cold breeze of the foggy morning . . . being passed out somewhere without a dog to warm you. "I guess I'm a whiskey guy, Grace." He belched.

"Okay, Sonny, now that we've got that established, I want to treat you to something really special."

Grace reached under the bar and brought out a purple felt bag with gold lettering and a gold braid tie with tassels. She loosened the tie and lowered the felt, exposing a bottle of amber liquid within. The bottle had shoulders and on its label a picture of a red crown resting on a purple pillow. She poured out a shot for Sonny.

"Go on," she said, "I think you'll like this. It goes down smoother and fuller, less bite, and the aftertaste is sweeter, much less bitter."

He took a sip. "You're right. That wasn't so bad."

"Well, it's the good stuff, and it's always reminded me of getting in a nice hot bubble bath.

Frank smacked him on the shoulder. "Looking good. We'll make a drunk of you yet."

"You know, Sonny," Grace pushed her hair back from her face. She looked flushed. "If you're really trying to get soused, I got a special I call Jim and Ginger you can chase that with."

He couldn't figure her out. She wasn't really a barmaid, she wasn't a career waitress, she wasn't a milkmaid, and she wasn't a Maid Marion—she was different.

"Hey there, bro," Charlie called from the doorway and walked straight over to the pool table. "Rack 'em up, Frankie. I'll play you." Charlie leaned forward, his beer belly brushing the top of the felt. A string of green and purple plastic fish lights hung over the table. Sonny wondered if they'd always been there.

Everyone seemed to move in slow motion. "Sweet Home Alabama" played on the jukebox. Sonny watched Charlie focus on the tip of his pool cue. He didn't look up, but kept his eye steady as he pulled back on the stick, and with the slightest movement of his wrist, he tapped the cue ball. A crack, and balls went every which way about the table.

The bar seemed to have a different look to it. Had someone changed the lights? Sonny looked at the other people in the room. The Evans twins played poker at a booth. "They take your money and your soul," he thought he heard someone say. He tried to imagine it. His money and his soul, were they the same?

"I gotta take a leak." Sonny pushed himself back from the bar. His head swam like the fish lights in a glass aquarium. Well this is a cliché, he thought. I'm staggering like a drunk. He made his way over to the toilets using the chairs along the way as support. This is why they have so much furniture, for handrails. He opened the door to the restroom and could barely push past the sink.

Through the closed door he heard them all laughing at him. He couldn't stay in this room forever. Five new rolls of toilet paper were piled up on the toilet. Someone had left a cigarette smoldering on the edge of the sink. He picked it up and threw it into the toilet. He looked up and saw himself in the mirror. Someone had etched "Fuck You" deep into the glass. He turned on the water and splashed his face. He had to go back out there before they came looking for him.

He opened the door. A rush of cigarette smoke filled his lungs. Sonny made his way back to the bar. An old television mounted in the corner was tuned to a very tall woman washing dishes. She made it look as if the greasy pan was a sex toy. Sonny felt warm.

Grace smiled at him. She poured herself a drink. "Bloody Mary?" he asked.

"A spicy virgin," she said. Her voice seemed to wash over the outside of him, matching the heat of the whiskey.

"Is it hot in here?" he asked.

A hoot of laughter broke out. Roy and Charlie came over and sat at the bar.

"Hard to believe you and Charlie are from the same family."

"I was watching you. When did you learn how to play pool like that?" Sonny asked Charlie.

"Like what?"

"Like you knew what you were doing?"

"Practice." Charlie turned away from him, back to Grace. "I'll take a Beam, and put it on Sonny's tab"

Sonny nodded.

Charlie downed the bourbon and walked back to the pool table.

"How are you doing?" Grace asked. "You're looking a little green."

Sonny felt Charlie stare at him from across the room. What did he want? Sonny never should have come. His head hurt. He didn't belong here. He didn't belong in this sorry, smelly place with a bunch of losers who did nothing all day except complain and talk big. He'd left for a reason. He couldn't stand the paralysis, and the mildewed wood, and the good old days that never were.

"Are you sure you're okay?" Grace put her hand over his. "You probably should have sipped that last shot, you know."

Sonny glanced up at his brother. Charlie was standing around with the guys. They were laughing at him, the computer nerd who couldn't hold his whiskey. And then somehow Charlie was transformed, and all Sonny could see was his kid brother, and Sonny was eight and Charlie was five, and they were with Grandpa Joe—squeezed into the red leather easy chair that only Grandpa Joe was allowed to sit in. Grandpa Joe was reading to them from *Huckleberry Finn*.

"Boys, there ain't nothing like being on the river, in a real boat, a boat that you got to use your own muscles to move, makes you feel like you're flying. Did I ever tell you about the Olympic race?"

"Yes, Grandpa."

"Can I be in the 'lympics?" Charlie asked. Grandpa Joe's face seemed to change in the firelight.

"Of course you can be in the Olympics, Charlie boy. You can do whatever you put your mind to. In fact . . ." Grandpa Joe stood up and Sonny and Charlie slid to the floor. Grandpa Joe walked over to the fireplace. A small American flag in a frame stood on the mantelpiece. Grandpa Joe picked it up. He seemed so big back then, a giant. "In fact, you two boys are going to be one of the greatest rowing teams in history. You're going to stir the ghosts up from the bottom of the river and set them free."

Their mother stood in the doorway, her hands on her hips.

"No more of your stories, Joe. The boys need to go to bed now."

Grandpa Joe nodded. "I know it boys. I can feel it in my bones. You're going to do something great."

<hr />

Sonny heard his brother's laughter. The haze in his head wasn't as thick as it had been.

Sonny called across the room, "Grandpa Joe said we'd do something great, Charlie."

"Grandpa Joe was an idiot. We can't compete in a race. He didn't mean it. We'll take it to a lawyer. No sane person would make us do this. It's nuts."

Sonny stood up. The plastic fish seemed to swim in circles. He walked toward his brother.

"Let's do it . . . just you and me, bro . . . the two of us . . . like the good old days. Let's race down the Mississippi and become bandits, riverboat bandits. Let's take over the Mississippi queen. Let's become gambling banditos. Let's be Injuns. Let's find a cave and paint our faces and . . ." He looked at Charlie. Somehow his little brother had acquired a beer belly and gray hair.

Sonny sank down to the floor. His legs couldn't hold him anymore. He wanted it to be like it used to be. He wanted to sit on Grandpa Joe's lap and imagine what it was like when the river ran free. There were sounds coming from him; he was sobbing out loud. He tried to cover his mouth, but they wouldn't stop. Nothing could stop them.

Grace came out from behind the counter and put her hand on his shoulder. "I think you're drunk, Sonny."

"Is this what it's like, Charlie?" Sonny moaned. "Is this what it's like for you?"

Charlie turned back to the pool table. He picked up the chalk and rubbed it on the end of the cue. "Four in the corner."

Grace put her hand out. "I'll take you home, Sonny."

# Chapter Twelve

# ANNIE

# 1904

July 21

Dear Diary,

Some men came to see Daddy today. They were all serious and formal in bowler hats and wool suits. Daddy called them "The Committee," but they just seemed like plain old men to me. It's odd to think that they can turn our lives so upside down. After all, they're no different than the men that hang around the barbershop. Just ordinary men that need suspenders to hold up their pants and someone to clean up after them. Ordinary men who blow their noses into monogrammed handkerchiefs. I can't figure out what made them so important. Maybe it's the gold. Each one of them wears a bit of gold, a watch, a ring, a lapel pin. Gold is okay, but I'd much rather have a glass bead, something with a bit of color in it, something purple or turquoise or red, something that I can see into and through to the other side.

Daddy opened a box and gave each one of them a cigar. I've noticed that this is a ceremony that men do when they get together. First they look into the box and examine the cigars. You'd think they were picking out the best chocolate cream. Then, when they've finally picked out the cigar they want, they wave it under their noses as if it was a lilac or a rose, something that smelled good and not like mown grass.

When the committee men were all looking pretty happy with themselves, Daddy cleared his throat and made his speech. "All I'm asking is that you just let the boy talk to you. You'll see, he's different." It was his politician voice, the one that got the men from the railroad to build their factory in our town. It's the voice that hardly anyone can say no to.

The man with the handlebar mustache smelled the cigar again before he answered. Maybe he wanted to make sure it hadn't changed or gone bad on him; that it was a real cigar. "It's not good to make exception, John. It we do it for one, then we'll have a whole slew of them telling us why they're different. But given that it's you asking, we'll give the boy a listening." Daddy thanked them for doing him this personal favor. He said that Joe was just like a son to him. Then one of the committee men said, "It's not good letting them think they're like us. Who knows, they might try to marry our daughters."

So what if your daughters wanted to marry them, I almost shouted. I was so upset I poked my finger with my sewing needle, and I let out a little cry. Nobody noticed. I wished it was the stupid man with the moustache that I'd poked.

As they left, Daddy shook their hands and then smiled at me. He hadn't smiled like that in a in a while, so I guess this means everything is going to be just fine. I can't wait to find Joe and tell him.

## Chapter Thirteen

# JOE

## 1904

I can't sleep in the same room with a lot of other guys. It feels too much like that boarding school with the rows and rows of beds filled with everyone else's dreams and other people's breath sucking the life out of me. With every inhale they take away a piece of my soul. I paid one of the other bodies a quarter to switch beds with me, so I could be on the end close to a window, but I still couldn't sleep. Whenever I could I snuck in a nap in the tall grass behind the bunkhouse. Mulhall barked instructions at the cavalry. From the loudness of his cursing I could tell they probably wouldn't need us savages for at least another hour. I closed my eyes and let the sounds of a fake battle wash over me. "Over there, you idiot, faster, faster, get out of the way." It was hard to believe my father had lived those sounds, lived through real gunfire, real savages, real wounds. I wondered what he'd think of me, playing at his life.

Something brushed against my foot. The damned cat seemed to think I was his own personal cushion. I kicked at the sensation.

"Hello."

So now the damned cat thought it could talk. I opened my eyes.

"Hellooooo."

I must have been dreaming. The voice sounded just like my sweet Annie.

"Joe, are you back here?"

The voice wasn't a dream; it was real. I jumped up and tried to shake the wrinkles out of my clothes. Annie stood right in front of me, dressed in the light blue dress that reminded me of a bit of sky. I ran my fingers through my hair, trying to smooth down the wild bits. I couldn't believe that Annie had come to the fair. Why hadn't she written and told me she was coming to the fair? Why hadn't John? She was more beautiful than I remembered.

"They said I'd find you hiding back here." She walked toward me, swinging a picnic basket on her arm. Leave it to Annie to bring me some food.

"Annie? I can't believe it's really you." My voice cracked. I needed some water. "Annie, what are you doing here?"

"Daddy brought me. To see the race, and I wanted to see you, Joe, make sure you're okay. You worried me." Annie opened the basket. "Are you hungry?" she pulled out a red checked tablecloth and spread it on the ground. We both sat down.

"You're wonderful, Annie. You know that?"

She took two plates out of the basket and laid them on the cloth. Then she took out the silverware and white cloth napkins. I loved to watch the way her hands moved. They were soft, oddly soft for someone who wasn't afraid to work.

"Guess what, Joe? We came here on the riverboat. It was wonderful. I stood on the deck and stared at that big paddle going around and around, and you would have loved it, Joe. We passed so many islands, and each one, I thought, Joe would love that one, I wonder if Joe's been ever been here before? . . ."

I couldn't take my eyes off her while she was chatting away. She opened the picnic basket. Annie made the best fried chicken, and I practically grabbed it out of her hand. They served beef slop and stale bread to the crew. I'd almost forgotten what real food tasted like. Then she took out some blueberry muffins. They were so fresh baked that the heat was still inside them.

Annie took a bite of chicken. "There were real live gamblers on the river boat, Joe, although Daddy told me I couldn't go near them. I had to stay in the ladies lounge. I'm sick of ladies lounges." She leaned closer to me, the chicken leg pointed at my chest. "What do you men do that we ladies aren't supposed to see anyway?" Then she tossed the bone into the shrub grass. "You know, I thought of you Joe, thought about how you talked about the gamblers and the riverboat captains, and how you wished you could ride on the riverboat all the way to New Orleans. I almost thought I'd see you there. I don't know why. I knew you were here, but it was as if you were with me."

Maybe I should just run away with her right now. Take her by the hand and hitch a ride on the riverboat. We could be anyone in New Orleans. We could be whatever we wanted to be.

I wanted to kiss her. And then I wanted to kick myself for wanting to kiss her. It wasn't a proper thought, not until we'd been bound together by God and Law for all our natural lives.

She lay down next to me on her back and looked up at the clouds. "Look, Joe. It's a rabbit."

I stared up at the big white cumulus cloud that hung over us. Looked more like a buffalo to me.

I let myself move a little closer to her, so close I could smell the lavender on her skin. "Annie, you smell so good."

"That's not saying much, Joe. I bet anything smells good compared to that group you've been hanging out with."

It was strangely quiet. I couldn't hear Mulhall or the sounds of Indians being massacred. "We should be getting back, you know. You probably shouldn't be away so long."

"I don't care, Joe, I really don't care. She was so close to me. I could feel my heartbeat pushing against my chest, it was beating so hard. I was afraid to move in case I'd scare her away.

She rolled over onto her side, leaned on one elbow, and looked straight at me. "I missed you, and I wanted to be here, and I was so glad that Daddy brought me here, to the fair."

A drop of perspiration, a drop of her body juice formed on her cheek. I could see the dark stain of it on her blouse and under her arm. I wanted to bury my face in the sweat of her. Her hair fell forward. I leaned over and brushed it back away from her face to tuck it behind her ear. I let my finger brush against the softness of her skin, let it slide down her neck, let it brush against the top of her collar. She barely moved. The two of us, it seemed, held our breath in that brief moment. Then she pulled away.

"Joe, I can't believe I almost forgot to tell you. I have some exciting news."

Her voice floated on top of the sensation of her skin. This is what was real.

She reached over and put her hand on my shoulder. Her touch was warm, as if the sun had found us in our hiding place. "Joe, I have something to tell you. Something good."

I heard someone calling out my name, Pinky, that was the joke, Pinky, that was me.

"Uh oh, Annie, I gotta go. Colonel Cummins himself is supposed to be here today for our rehearsal, and I can't be late."

"You don't have to do this, Joe. You don't really belong here." She pointed at nothing in particular. "You can come home with me. Daddy has come to make a fuss with the committee."

The memory of the touch of her neck seemed to addle my brain. I wasn't sure what she was talking about.

"He's got letters from the mayor and the city council and the pastor."

I liked this feeling of the two of us hidden in the tall grass. The sounds of the rest of the world were around the other side of the building, but we could just as easily have fallen down a rabbit hole, fallen into a different adventure. I liked to think that maybe this was what my father had gone after; that maybe my father and mother were even now lying somewhere with the same sun warming them. And my father held my mother's face in his hands, and they talked about their son, about their baby Joe and how big he must be by now, and maybe they'd go to see him. Maybe they were here and I didn't know it. Maybe they weren't that far away.

"Daddy has set up a meeting for you and the committee, for Saturday, and he thinks they will probably let you row."

"I'm not ready to row. I haven't been training."

"You're always ready."

How could I explain to her. I hadn't practiced with the team in weeks. They were a well-oiled machine, and if I jumped in now, I'd probably just rock the boat. I'd rock the boat, and then we'd all be swimming in that mucky lake. "They don't need me there. They need me here."

I could hear Mulhall telling someone to move their fat ass out of the way or they would get run over.

Annie sat up and looked down at me.

"What does that mean?"

"It means they're counting on me."

"I don't understand, Joe. I thought you came here to row, that rowing in this race was important to you. Don't you want to do that anymore?" She looked me straight in the eye. "What's happened, Joe? Has something happened?"

I watched two squirrels chase each other up the only tree.

"I gotta go, Annie." I stood up.

She grabbed my arm. Her grip was strong. Maybe she should be in the rope pull. "You'll come and meet Daddy, right?"

"It's not easy to find someone willing to be a body, Annie."

In the distance I heard Mulhall yelling at someone. I wanted to cover Annie's ears.

She didn't seem to notice his swearing, though. She was busy putting the dirty dishes and the leftovers back into the basket. Her head was bent forward, and I noticed the white of her scalp, a thin sliver of white like the river. I wanted to spend the rest of my life on that river.

"I'll come to the meeting, Annie. I promise. I'll be there."

---

"Where the hell you been, Pinky? I told you we got to look sharp for the Colonel." He looked over my shoulder as he spoke. I turned around. Annie stood on the edge of the path that led back out to the main fairgrounds. She waved at me and smiled before disappearing from sight.

All hope of slipping into the rehearsal disappeared. Every single eye was on me. Most of the guys had that knowing sniggering look that men give each other. The wink-wink-we-know-what-you've-been-doing look. I slipped in next to Redfeather.

"Sorry, sir," I brushed some of the dirt off my buckskins, not that it mattered much. In the distance we could hear a bugle, and a few minutes later five men decked out in full-dress army blues galloped into the show grounds.

Redfeather whispered under his breath, "That's him, Cummins. Chief Lakota is what he's called, the Great White Chief."

Mulhall ran back and forth in front of us shouting, "Get in your ranks. Get in your ranks."

The bugle corps led the way for the great man himself. Colonel Cummins was a hunter, an explorer, and a soldier. He was about the same age as my father. He might have even known my father. They might have passed each other on the untamed plains, talked about the weather and the price of corn, swapped adventure stories. Colonel Cummins rode up and down, and the horse kicked up a dust storm. The bugle corps lined up at attention facing us.

"Today is a big day, men. I have it on the highest authority that President Roosevelt himself may be in the stands to see you perform."

We all let out a cheer, and Cummins whooped along with us. I liked him. I could see why he was beloved by red and white and all colors in between, "Let's give the President the best damned show he's ever seen."

Redfeather turned to me. "Don't hold your breath. They've been expecting the old man every day for months now, and he hasn't made an appearance yet."

Cummins walked his horse over and stopped right in front of me and Redfeather. "You boys have something to say? Well, don't be shy, let us all in on it." He was an impressive figure up there on his horse. Everyone was dead quiet waiting to see what would happen to us.

I could see Mulhall out of the corner of my eye. He didn't look any too happy, and I wasn't looking forward to the punishment he'd mete out for us having messed up his parade.

"Well?" Cummins asked again.

Redfeather looked him straight in the eye and then let out an ear-piercing war cry.

Cummins hooted his appreciation. "Good show, but save it for the crowds. I tell you what. You keep up the good work, and I'll let you stay on, all of you. I'll take you all to Europe with me. What do you think about that?"

I didn't know what to think about Europe, but then I was thinking about all kinds of things I'd never thought about before.

We Injuns yelped like coyotes narrowing in for the kill, and the blue-coated soldiers hollered as if they were at a football match. Cummins smiled, leaned back on his horse so far that it reared up on its hind legs, then saluted us and rode off, followed by the bugle corps making a whole lot of dust and noise.

# Chapter Fourteen

# SONNY

## 2004

Sonny sat at the bar. Frank, Roy, Charlie, and the Evans twins all squeezed into one of the green Naugahyde booths. It was a perfect sunny day, but they huddled in one of the darkest corners of the room.

Sonny tapped a fork against the glass ashtray. "Okay, guys, listen up. I have an announcement."

"Quiet, everyone. We don't want to miss one of my big brother's announcements." Charlie clapped his hands.

Grace smiled at him, her hand on a beer tap. "Go on, Sonny. We're listening."

The stuffed badger stared down at him from the glass case, its paw-hand frozen mid-slash. Sonny still had nightmares about that badger, about it busting out of the case and tracking him down, stuffing him and leaving him in the case, his arm frozen for eternity.

"Hey, man, we're waiting." The cigarette in Roy's mouth bounced up and down when he spoke.

Sonny stared at the faces in the booth. What was he thinking? These guys were just a bunch of sorry-assed drunks.

"Look, man, if you got something to say, just say it, or turn on the music," Billy Evans chimed in.

Sonny ran his hand through his hair and took a deep breath before speaking, "I've entered us in a race."

Roy pointed his cigarette at Sonny. "What'd you say about my face?"

Sonny got off the barstool, strode over to the booth, reached into his pocket, and pulled out an advertisement. "Don't look so surprised. This is a boat club after all." He passed the flyer around.

*The Quinley Historical Society is proud to announce*
*The Great Mississippi River Days and Races*
*Sunday August 21ˢᵗ*
*Relive the Glory*

Five blank faces stared at him.

"Nice poster," Roy laughed.

"I've signed us up." Sonny slapped the poster down on the table. "We're an official team. The East Side Boat Club rows again."

"Is this a joke?" Frank asked. "What do you take us for?"

"Look, Charlie and I have to do this, and we need your help. It might be fun, you know, get in touch with our roots. Have any of you even been in one of those racing boats? The ones whose pictures are lined up around the walls?"

Roy wiped the foam off his upper lip and looked at the pictures as if seeing them for the first time. "I never even seen one of those boats round here."

Sonny looked over at Grace. She brought a pitcher of beer over to the table and a glass for Sonny.

"No, Grace. No beer for me. I tell you what, guys, I don't care what you say. Me and Charlie will do it without you if we have to."

"Yeah, right. I think you forgot something, my dear brother." Charlie blew smoke rings that floated up to the ceiling. "We don't have a boat."

"Yes, we do. We've got a whole fleet of boats."

"Yeah, yeah, in your dreams."

"No, right here."

"Here? No way. What're you smoking?"

"I'll show you."

Roy looked at Sonny. "This better not be a joke, 'cause if it is you're gonna wish you'd stayed in California. That you never showed your sorry ass in these parts again."

"Just follow me. You'll see."

"We don't follow no one." Bob Evans eased himself out of the booth. "And you can definitely count us out of your little adventure. Let's leave, Billy." For a moment Sonny thought Billy might defy his brother. But the earring battle had taken all the fight out of him.

Charlie, Frank, and Roy were left. What a motley crew. The three beer bellies squeezed out of the booth.

"Okay, bro, take us to this imaginary fleet, but make it quick, I got things to do."

"Can I come?" Grace already had her apron off and the Back in Five sign out on the bar.

"Sure, the more the merrier."

Sonny led them down the stairs and around the side of the building. Sonny could just make out the remains of the broken asphalt path. The neighboring land used to be part of the club, but it had been sold off decades earlier for the grain elevator. They were thick in the commercial section of the river now. At one point someone had planted bushes to shield the club from the industrial onslaught, but they'd grown so thick that there was barely enough room to walk by.

"Where the hell are you taking us?" Roy wheezed, "It's a goddamn jungle."

"Stop bitching. We're here." Sonny stopped in front of a door. It had been painted blue once, bits of dried-out paint hung like splinters from the wood. He turned the handle and pushed in. The hinges creaked, but the door opened easily. He took a flashlight out of his pocket and led the way into the room.

"What is this place?" Grace stood next to Sonny.

"I think it's an old root cellar." The air was cool and moist.

"It's creepy." Charlie stopped in the doorway.

"Well go in or get out of the way. You're blocking the door," Frank said as he pushed by Charlie. Roy followed.

"This don't feel right, Sonny." Roy threw his cigarette down and ground the tip with his foot.

"Just look." The flashlight made shadows of the floor-to-ceiling wooden racks.

"What are those?" Grace pointed at three large canvas shapes that seemed to breathe in the moist air.

"It's like a fucking tomb in here, Sonny. What the hell is this place?" Roy pulled a cigarette out of his pocket. "This better be good."

"It is a tomb." Sonny stood next to the shelf with the shapes and pulled back an edge of canvas. "It's a boat tomb."

"It's creepy and it smells. Just like a place you'd find."

"Are you saying these are boats? Where the hell did these come from?" Frank asked.

"They never left. They've been here all this time. Just forgotten."

"Well, how'd you find them?" Grace huddled next to him. Her skin was cold to the touch.

"I noticed that old asphalt that didn't seem to go anywhere, and I followed it."

That was only a half-truth, because he'd been looking for the asphalt. It was all so different than it used to be. He wasn't even sure if it was a real memory or a dream or a movie he'd seen, but he remembered his father and Grandpa Joe. It was one of the few times his father had been at the boat club, which he usually referred to as "the waste of time." Sonny was in the tree swing. He watched as his father and a few other men carried the boats up the path. Grandpa Joe shouted out helpful orders like Watch it! Careful! Don't drop it!

It had been a cloudy day. The air felt cold with a winter storm on its way. Like Rip Van Winkle, their world had changed.

"You're not thinking that we're gonna use these?" Roy took another cigarette out of his pocket. "No way. You're not getting my ass in one of those."

Sonny grabbed the cigarette out of Roy's hand. "If you want to kill yourself with those things, that's your business, but keep it outside."

"I don't have to stand for this, old friend. Who the hell do you think you . . . ?"

"How long do you think they've been here?" Grace pushed herself between Roy and Sonny.

Roy turned toward the entrance. "A long time. Hell, I can't even remember the last time anyone in this place used a boat without a fucking motor."

"So, are you guys in?" Sonny asked.

"In what?" Frank asked.

"We got enough here for a team, four rowers and a coxswain. You could be the coxswain, Grace."

"That sounds a bit risqué, Sonny. What exactly does a coxswain do?"

Sonny could feel her smile in the shadows. Flirtatious banter was a lost art, and he'd never been comfortable with it. He lived his life in a black-and-white world of programming language zeros and ones. There was no place for innuendo.

"I think the coxswain keeps the crew in line."

"That I can do."

# Chapter Fifteen

# ANNIE

## 1904

July 21

Dear Diary,

I saw Joe this morning and my insides are all turned around. I would have liked to spend more time, but he had to go to his practice or rehearsal. He's an actor now. He doesn't want to talk about the games or home or anything else. I was able to convince him to at least meet with Daddy. But he was changed and I am changed. I let him touch me in ways that I shouldn't.

On the way back from meeting with Joe I saw a strange woman on the street. Her face was painted white and her mouth was a deep red, like a clown's face. Her hair was piled up on her head and held in place by a single stick. I couldn't imagine a stick holding up so much hair. Could I do that to my hair? The woman shuffled as she walked, and the dress she wore was wrapped tightly around her, all the way down to her golden slippers. Her feet were so tiny; I couldn't imagine how they held her up. And the dress itself was like a painting, the color a deep red, and it was embroidered with pictures of birds, white birds with long necks, like hers. She had the most beautiful long, white neck I'd ever seen. But then all the women I know cover up their necks.

I wanted to open my collar, but I didn't have the nerve. I wanted to let my neck feel the air, maybe then I'd feel like a bird, too, maybe then I'd become a bird. The woman looked down as she walked by, but she smiled at me from under her eyelashes. She seemed to know more about me than I could ever know. I wondered if a man had ever kissed her neck.

## Chapter Sixteen

# JOE

## 1904

The door to the tepee wasn't really a door, not like in a normal house. It was more of an opening with a flap. A cowbell hung on the outside. I wondered if that was traditional, if they had cowbells out on the prairie. I doubted it. The flap was open. I wasn't sure if I was supposed to ring the bell, shake the flap, stamp my feet and howl at the moon, or just say hello.

A small girl played with glass marbles in front of the opening. Her hair was braided around a red ribbon. A woven band of fabric was wrapped around her forehead and a feather tied to the bottom of her braid hung down her back, making her hair look even longer.

I knelt next to her.

"Do you live here?" I asked.

She nodded.

"Is Jake in?"

She shrugged her shoulders, then she pulled me by the arm. Before I knew it, I was sitting in the dirt right next to her. She handed me a green glass shooter and drew a circle in the dirt. I felt someone looking at us from inside the tepee, but I didn't get up.

The little girl poured all the marbles into the middle of the circle.

She took her shooter, flicked back a finger, and let it loose. She knocked a marble out of the ring and giggled.

"Okay," I said, "you got one. You're good."

I picked up my shooter and flicked it at the circle. I missed.

She giggled again and knocked another marble out of the center. Someone tapped the cowbell. I looked up. A gray-haired woman stood at the door.

She motioned for me to come inside. I handed my marble to the little girl. She took it and shot it toward the center, knocking another marble out of the circle.

"Thanks." I tapped her on the top of her head and walked into the tepee. The smells of leather, sweet tobacco, and sour milk filled the space. It took a few seconds for my eyes to get used to the darkness.

An old man sat cross-legged on a blanket. The woman who had motioned me in sat behind him to his right.

He pointed to an empty space on the floor, and I sat down.

"I'm looking for Jake," I said, although he hadn't asked what I was doing there.

"I'm his grandfather." I looked more closely at the old man, trying to see my friend.

It was strangely quiet. The sounds from the fair didn't seem to make it inside, as if they needed light to carry them.

The old woman offered me a hot drink. I wasn't sure where it came from. It just appeared—a conjuring trick, or maybe there was another room that I couldn't see or a hole in the ground. I felt as if I was back in Mrs. Macavey's parlor. Mrs. Macavey, with her tight bun that stretched the skin on her face until it looked like it might tear, would have all us heathen boys into her parlor to read us scriptures and serve us shortbread cookies. This woman had a tight bun like Mrs. Macavey's, except Mrs. Macavey's hair was pure white, and this old woman had steely gray hair. Mrs. Macavey could beat me in a staring contest, and this woman didn't even look at me when she served me. But even though she didn't look at me, I felt she saw right through me, as if she knew every chicken's egg I'd ever stolen and every stone I'd thrown at a passing carriage.

"I'm glad you made it." The old man paused. "Welcome to my grandmother's bones."

I looked around thinking maybe I was going to see a skeleton. I must have looked confused because he laughed and made a broad sweeping gesture. "This tepee, this place, the tall straight poles, the painted hide, all of it is my grandmother's bones."

He leaned back, put his pipe in his mouth, took a deep inhale, and blew a smoke ring.

The gray-haired woman brought over a tray with a pipe on it. I pulled my own pipe, the one my father had carved for me, out of my pocket.

"That is a nice pipe," said the old man.

"My father made it."

"May I?" He held out his hand, and I gave him the pipe. He rubbed his finger over the carved wood. Then he held it up to his ear, listened, and nodded. "Your father does nice work." He put a pinch of tobacco in my pipe, then handed it back to me. "Do you follow the Way of the People?"

"Which people?" I asked.

He shook his head while he rocked back and forth. "Then, you must follow the Jesus Way?"

The Jesus Way. When I first went to the school I heard all the Indian kids whispering about spirits and other things that I couldn't see. It didn't take long for them to realize that that spirit talk just got them into trouble, but Jesus talk got them out of chores. Eventually they stopped even the whispering.

"Everyone walks a path. Which one do you follow?" he asked again.

"I've never thought about it before."

"There are two paths we travel in our lives, the one that our feet walk, and the one that our heart walks. In your world, the Jesus path is one of words and deeds. Where does your heart walk?"

"On the river." The words seemed to jump out of me. "On the river," I repeated.

"That is not the Jesus Way." He motioned for me to put the pipe in my mouth, and then he lit it. I inhaled. I wanted to cough, but I held it back. I'd never actually smoked the pipe. Mostly I just carried it around. I thought I heard him laugh, a quiet inside kind of laugh.

"Your father had a different path. We all have different paths."

My heart pounded against my chest, like I'd been running hard. It was probably the tobacco or whatever it was he gave me. "You know my father? Have you seen him? Is he well?" I knew that was impossible. This man couldn't possibly know who my father was. I hadn't even told him my name.

The old man shook his head and smiled. His face seemed to crack from all the lines in his face. Someone else looking at him would see trails and roads, and others would see trees and branches. I saw a fluid, ever-changing face, a face of rivers and creeks and canyons.

"I know lots of men like your father. They spend their whole lives looking for their paths, looking for home."

I took my mother's moccasin out of my pocket. I always carried it, just in case. "Do you recognize where this might be from?" He leaned forward and shook his head. Then he called the old woman over. She took the moccasin from my hand and turned it around and around. She said something to him, and they both smiled.

He looked back at me. "The woman says this is a very nice moccasin. Well made. It has heart in it. But she cannot tell which people made it."

It was hot in the tepee. I stood up and felt as if my head was going to fly up through the little smoke hole at the top of the tepee. I stooped over. "I should be going. Tell Jake I couldn't wait."

The old man closed his eyes and nodded. There was a commotion outside. The flap opened and Jake Redfeather came in, bringing sunlight and a bit of chaos. "Hey, Joe, I'm sorry I'm late." He hugged me.

"I've been talking to your grandfather." The old man smiled and blew out a ring of smoke. Redfeather kissed him on the cheek. "Grandfather, this is Joe. I told you about him, you know from the school."

The old man nodded, "Ahhhh. I remember, now. You were kind to my grandson."

"I'm sorry I'm late, Joe, but I went and signed up for the Wild West Show. I'm going to be working with you."

My friend would make an imposing warrior all dressed up with bows and arrows and war paint. He was definitely chief material.

It was that in-between time of day, not light, not dark. The smells of food, wood smoke, and horse manure. When I was a boy my father would ring the dinner bell. That meant I had ten minutes to get myself home and to my seat at the table. "We have to sit together at least once a day," he'd say. And then there was always the third seat, the empty seat with the placemat laid just in case she came back in time for dinner.

The little girl with the marbles jumped up when she saw us come out, and she ran right up to me. She took my hand and walked with me to the end of the row of tepees. Her hand felt small and warm in mine. Redfeather was already far ahead. I said goodbye and sprinted to catch up with him. I felt something heavy knock against my leg, something that hadn't been there before. I stuck my hand in my pocket and pulled out a brown suede bag. The little girl had given me her bag of marbles.

# Chapter Seventeen

# SONNY

# 2004

"Okay, you take this side."

"No, back up."

"It's heavy,"

"No it's not. Just hold on."

"I can't."

Roy lurched, then Frank tripped and the boat fell on the grass.

"You dropped it, you idiots."

"You call us idiots again and I'll drop you." Roy pointed a finger at Sonny's chest. "

"He's right, Sonny. Just chill a bit." Beads of sweat rolled down Frank's face. He was breathing heavily.

They haven't lifted more than a beer mug in years, thought Sonny.

"Okay. Sorry. This whole thing is making me tense." Sonny looked around. "Anyone see Charlie?" Charlie always managed to be someplace else whenever anything needed to get done.

"Don't have a fit. I'm right here." Charlie looked like a giant bird. He balanced the oars over his shoulder, each one over twelve feet long. "Look what I found. I'm pretty sure we're going to need these."

"Shit, man, look at those things." Roy shook his head. "How the hell are we supposed to row with those things?"

Charlie dropped the oars on the ground next to the five canvas mummies. No one moved. Now what? Sonny stood still and bowed his head.

"This is really stupid, Sonny. Just unwrap the damn things. They're probably rotten anyway and full of who knows what, so let's just get it over with and get back inside. I'm freezing my nuts off."

"Quiet, Roy. Sonny wants to say something." Grace nodded at Sonny.

"Thanks, Grace," he paused, "I just wanted to thank the ghosts of all the old oarsman for leaving us their boats."

"Thank the fucking groundskeeper for putting them away, Sonny boy." Charlie laughed.

Sonny ignored him, then he nodded at Grace and knelt down. Someone had wrapped them well. They looked like a family laying there on the ground, one big happy family: Papa boat and mama boat and baby boat. "Okay, let's go for it."

Sonny held his breath. He was almost afraid to look. Right now they were perfect. Right now they could take the boats and put them on the river and row away and win honors and medals and be successful and great. Maybe that was all they needed. They could stop now and still be winners. Out of the corner of his eye he saw Grace and Roy, Charlie and Frank. "It's like Christmas, isn't it guys."

"Maybe. Get on with it, Sonny." Roy looked at his watch.

Sonny ignored Roy. He felt like a grave robber about to raise the dead.

Charlie sat in front of the smallest boat and stared at it.

"Are you okay, Charlie?"

"You can't make us be something we're not, Sonny."

A riverboat sounded its horn.

"I'm not trying to make you into something you're not, Charlie." He didn't want to fight with his brother. Everything was always a fight, a struggle. All he wanted was for his brother to say thank you. Just once.

Grace peeled the canvas back from the small boat. Soft chunks of wood stuck to the fabric. "Oh, Sonny, this one's rotten. The flooding must have got to it."

Frank stood in front of the bigger boat. "This looks like it was a six man, and it looks like the flooding got to this one, too."

He pulled the canvas away. "No go, Sonny, this one's a loss. Not even good kindling here."

"Roy rubbed his hands on the front of his jeans. "Oh well, it was fun while it lasted."

Charlie got up. "Okay, that's that. Good job, Sonny."

Frank, Charlie, and Roy headed back to the bar. "Grace, are you coming?"

"Sonny?" Grace waited.

"Let's just finish it off, okay?" Sonny took a deep breath and pulled back the last canvas. There were no bits of rotten wood sticking to the fabric. He pulled a little more. The paint still had sheen to it. "So far, so good."

Frank and Charlie turned back and stood over him. "Well, take it all off. Just unwrap the damn thing."

"Sonny never could just unwrap a present. He always had to make it into an event."

Sonny ignored his brother. He folded back the canvas as if it covered a sleeping baby.

"It's perfect," Grace whispered.

It was perfect. Somehow this boat had survived. Sonny ran his hands over it. The wood was smooth and hard. No soft spots. No rot. No smell. And it was a four man, with a coxswain's seat for Grace.

# Chapter Eighteen

# ANNIE

## 1904

July 23

Dear Diary,

This morning Joe took me around the fair. We didn't talk about the committee meeting or rowing or anything like that. We didn't talk about much of anything. Joe was my own personal tour guide, and I'm glad of that because this place is huge. I think if I could stay here for two months I wouldn't be able to see it all. I love the palaces the best. That's what they call the grand buildings that house all the different exhibits from around the world. But they're not just exhibits, and that is what is so surprising and special. They've set up factories and stores, so that you can see how things are made. You can buy just about anything you could ever imagine. They even have a glass works that spins fabric out of glass. I didn't get to try any of it on, but I saw it with my own eyes. Joe took me to the Ethnology Exhibit. He said he wanted me to meet Redfeather. On the way over there, he stopped and talked to all sorts of people and showed them some old moccasins. He told me that his mother made them for his father, and someone must know the workmanship or something like that, someone must be able to tell him what tribe he's from. I can't imagine how anyone could know where those dirty shoes came from, but he keeps asking. I think it must be easier for me with my mother in heaven and all. At least I know where she is.

I stopped to watch two old Indian women who sat on the ground. They were sewing leather pouches. That's what it's like here at the exhibition. We get to watch how the primitives do things. Not that her sewing was much different than mine. One of the women smiled at me and nodded. Then she said something in a language that didn't sound like any language I'd ever heard before. She said something to her friend, and they looked at me and smiled. They had that look of giggling girls, even though they both had leathery skin and more wrinkles than most of the grandmothers that I knew.

I reached into my pocket and pulled out a button. I held it out for them to see. They both peered into my hand. I nodded at the older woman, and then I held the button out to her thinking that maybe she'd like it.

She put the button in her mouth and bit into it. Imagine that, biting into a button as if it was a gold coin. She smiled at me and said thank you.

Then she reached into her bag and took out a small piece of hide, but it wasn't like animal hide I'd ever seen before. It was as pliable and soft as velvet.

She asked me if I'd like it. She gave her friend a funny look when she handed it to me, and I'm not sure if they weren't making fun of me, but I took it anyway. It was a perfect little square, and it made me think of one of the baskets hanging from the observation wheel. That's when I got the idea to make a quilt for Joe, something that he could take home with him from this place and wrap around him. I think the old woman could tell I saw something in the bit of fabric. She started handing me so many scraps, some hardly bigger than the tip of my finger. I gathered them up and put them in my bag. We finally got to the place where Redfeather lived, but no one was home. Joe told me to rest and later on he would take me to the Pike. But I can't rest. It's all so wonderful.

## Chapter Nineteen

# NATHAN

*Cold*

*John Greer*

*My dear friend,*

*I miss my old life. It's hard for me to write this 'cause my fingers won't move in this bitter chill. Moon and her people don't seem to feel the cold, not as I feel it. They have blankets and furs and animal hides to keep warm, but they don't do it for me. But maybe it's because I know what it is like to sit beside a fireplace in a solid house that keeps the wind out and the warmth in, maybe that's why I'm cold to my bones.*

*Moon made me a pair of shoes out of animal hide, it is odd walking around and feeling the shape of the earth under my feet. And I cannot get used to the layers. I am hardly able to move I have so many pieces of clothing layered on my body. All I do is wait. Wait for something to happen. They have lots of chores to keep them busy all day, ceremonies and daily tasks that seem to take hours. One of the men gave me a knife and a piece of wood. I'm starting to see things in the wood, faces and shapes of animals. Maybe I'm going mad.*

*At least Moon Woman spends time sitting by me. She has tried her damnedest to teach me her language, but I just can't seem to learn it. I think I know why. I think they speak wind, and I, my friend, only understand river. I am teaching her English, though, and she is quite good at it. I plan to bring her home with me one day if she will come.*

*The wind doesn't stop howling out here. It's like a pack of coyotes chasing their meal across the prairie. They tell me I have to wait for spring. Perhaps it won't be too late. Perhaps I will still be able to kiss my mother and introduce her to the moon.*

*Your friend Nathan Barton*

## Chapter Twenty

# JOE

## 1904

I wasn't ready for the guys on the team to see me yet, so instead of going straight out the launching pier, I hung back in the shadow of an elm tree. I'd had to bribe Mulhall with a bottle of Jack Daniel's Tennessee Whiskey to let me out of the rehearsal. I couldn't stand the stuff myself, but it had just won some big prize at the fair, and Mulhall was pretty pleased with the gift. I seemed to have inherited the Indian's weak head, and I couldn't drink more than watered-down ale without passing out.

My team was already out on the lake. I recognized Greer's voice as he called the strokes good, strong, and loud. There were a lot of other coxswains yelling out to their crews. Counting out in languages I'd never heard before, enough foreign talk that it sounded like the tower of Babel out there on the lake. I knew Greer was under a lot of pressure to pull it all together without me, but I had to admit they looked good. Somehow old Izzy Johnson had upped his game, and he had a nice solid rhythm in his stroke. Greer must have put the fear of God into him, or maybe he told him that if he didn't shape up they'd give him a dunking. By the looks of that lake, nobody wanted a dunking. A green slime of algae covered the surface. You wouldn't want to get your whites in that mess.

The first time I'd been dunked I hadn't ever rowed with a team before. The East Side Boat Club didn't exist back then, at least not as an official club.

It was an idea mostly. Greer and Tucker liked messing around on the river, and they discovered racing while I was away at the school. Dr. Greer had the idea to build a boathouse for them so they could go and practice whenever they wanted and not to have to go all the way to the West Side Club.

I had just turned sixteen when Dr. Greer came and got me out of the school and brought me home. I'd only been gone for a year, but I felt like a stranger to my old life. Maybe that was because of where I'd been, or maybe because we'd all gone from being boys to near men. In the year I'd been gone, my friends' voices had changed, a couple of them were shaving, and they'd taken up a new sport, one I'd never seen before.

"Go down to the river, Joe," Dr. Greer had said. "That's where someone your age should be. John and Bill are down there. They've got a new boat."

I thought he was talking about a fishing boat, but this wasn't like any rowboat I'd ever seen, with the bench firmly attached to the sides of the boat and room enough for plenty of gear. This wasn't a boat meant for lazing around on the river with a fishing pole. This was a racing boat—long and sleek and unsteady. A catfish could probably roll it.

The boat was tied up to a makeshift wood dock that was attached to an oak tree. Johnson knelt down and held the boat steady.

"Hey, Joe," Greer called out when he saw me. "Glad you're back."

"Yeah. Good to see you," Tucker said and slapped me on the back. "Want to try it?"

"It's a bit different than what I'm used to."

"I'm sure you can handle it, Joe."

I put my foot into the boat shell and reached over to steady myself. That was when Johnson let go. He never confessed, but I'm sure he let go on purpose, and that he added a little push for good measure. The boat tipped and I did a somersault over the side and somehow managed to land with my head up. I felt the muddy bottom churn around me. The river was damn cold, but it was shallow enough so I could stand. The mud oozed between my toes. I forgot how good the mud felt. Greer, Johnson, Smith, and Tucker stood on the dock and laughed a doubled-over, go-in-your-pants kind of laugh.

I felt like a fool, though, falling out of a boat. I wanted to stick my head in the mud. But John reached over and held out his hand. I grabbed it.

"Welcome to the team, Joe. Welcome to the team."

⚜

The guys pulled in next to the dock and got out. They pulled the boat up out of the water and lay the oars inside. "Thirty minute break and don't be late," I heard Greer say, and then he saw me.

"Hey, Joe." He called as he headed toward me.

"What are you doing here? And how in tarnation did you get here? They've got us so far out it's a wonder we're still in the United States of America." Tucker slapped me on the back. He didn't usually say much, but I could always count on him, freckles and all.

"I took the train." The lake was a good ten miles from the main fairgrounds, but the train ran all day long. "You guys are looking good."

"Not as good as if you were here." They surrounded me. This was my real tribe. I don't know what I'd been thinking. What I'd been all worried about. Nothing had changed. I was still me. They were still them. We were still us.

Smith pointed at the lake. "This whole race is a sham if you want to know the truth. They're letting some young kid be coxswain for the Frogs"

"Yeah," Johnson shook his head, "and they won't even let you compete.

"It's a farce," Tucker chimed in.

It may have been a farce, but I knew that it was still the biggest event of their lives. They wouldn't walk away from this chance just to make a point or a statement. They'd compete because that's what they did. It's what I would have done.

"You know, Joe, I don't think they even gave this event much thought." Smith was our deep thinker. "They just tacked on the Olympics to the fair, you know." It may be a farce and an afterthought, but I was still going to miss out, and we all knew it.

They were good guys, and they meant well. "Let me see what you got. Maybe I can't row, but I can give you some pointers, if you want me to."

Greer didn't seem to hear me. He was looking back over his shoulder and around the shoreline. "Did you see Annie and my father? They were here just before we went out, and I thought you might have seen them."

I shook my head. "I must have missed them." Greer put his hand on my shoulder.

"You know, Joe, Annie is pretty sweet on you."

I did know.

I waited around until the guys went back out on the lake. I stood on the shore and watched the boat as it grew smaller and smaller and then disappeared around the bend in the lake. I could run after them, try and keep up. I could put on my father's moccasins. I could run and not make a sound like an Indian, maybe run as fast as Aday, as fast as the wind. But my boots were walking shoes, good solid walking shoes. Maybe I should let them take me. Which way? The Missouri River was nearby. I could just keep on going west. I could follow Louis and Clark, follow my father. In the distance a train whistle sounded. The return ticket to the fair was in my pocket. I'd promised Mulhall I'd be there for the six o'clock show, and it's important to keep promises.

# Chapter Twenty-One

# SONNY

## 2004

Grace leaned against the counter and stared out the kitchen window. "You know, Sonny, where I come from you can't look out a window without seeing the neighbor's laundry hanging from a line on the porch. I could practically read the labels on the clothes. The yards were full of rusted fenders, old tires, and broken screen doors."

"I can't imagine that," said Sonny. "We always had space. Maybe a bit too much space. In the middle of winter I used to wish the neighbors were a little closer, when it was just me and Charlie and nothing to do."

"I didn't realize how much more you could breathe here, barely ten miles from the Walmart, ten miles from the fast-food drive-ins, and ten miles from the funky motels." She turned toward him and said, "I can't believe you grew up in a place like this. It's like a storybook."

"It's not all it's cracked up to be."

"I guess that's what we all think about where we grew up."

"And you?"

"I've always been in a city. That's why I came here, to get out of the city. But I guess I didn't . . . not really. I haven't strayed too far from the action." She lifted the teakettle off the stove and filled it with water. He pointed to the cabinet where his mother had always kept the tea. She seemed to belong in a kitchen like this, a big airy room with lace curtains and refrigerator magnets.

"You would have gone crazy out here. The only bright spot was Grandpa Joe, and he died when I was sixteen. After that it was pretty dismal. I got out as soon as I could."

"And Charlie?"

"Charlie just got out in a different way."

"At least you have a place to come back to." The kettle whistled. Grace stood still for a moment, stared at it as if she wasn't sure what the sound was, then turned down the flame and poured the steaming water into two matched mugs. "I mean, we moved around so much, my mother didn't keep anything. Said she got tired of packing and unpacking, that we'd just always travel light. I used to think that was a good thing, used to think that somehow we were better than other people because we didn't let 'things' rule us, but now . . . I don't know. I think I wish I had something."

Sonny watched her pick up the old kitchen witch, a cloth witch on a broomstick. The dust had collected in the cobwebs, somehow appropriate for a witch. It was another one of his mother's things that no one had ever thrown away, as if she had been the last to go instead of his father. Sonny realized there was almost nothing of his father around, not even a ghostly presence. "It's the opposite here. We've got so many damn things. . . . It's going to take forever to sort it all out. Maybe I should torch it, let it burn."

"Someone here was a collector."

"That was my mother. She never got rid of anything. I bet you ten dollars that if you open that right-hand drawer you will find a small bag with all our baby teeth in it."

"She kept your baby teeth?"

"Every last one. At least the ones she knew about. There were a couple that got away. I lost 'em somewhere out there. . . ." He pointed toward the barn and fields.

Sonny opened the drawer, and right where he said it would be was the flannel pouch filled with teeth.

"Why did she keep them?"

He opened the bag and emptied it into the palm of his hand. He'd gotten a quarter for each tooth.

"Maybe she thought if she kept my teeth she'd always have me just as I was, a cute little thing."

Grace smiled, "I can't imagine my mother keeping my baby teeth. I don't think she even kept my phone number."

Charlie stumbled into the room. "Goddamn lawyers. Think they know everything." He pointed at Grace, "What the fuck is she doing here?"

"I brought her. She's helping me."

"I see." Charlie winked. "Got any beer?" He opened the refrigerator and stuck his head in.

"No, Charlie. There isn't any beer."

"No worries. I have one in my car."

"Charlie, you idiot, you shouldn't be driving around with a beer in your car."

"Why not?"

"You're never going to learn are you?" Sonny didn't want Charlie here. He didn't want to be the big brother, didn't want to be the father, didn't want to be the patriarch that worried about everyone. He wanted to be the little boy finding the quarter under his pillow.

Charlie ignored him and sat at the kitchen table. "So, Grace, You know. I really don't get why you're here."

Sonny stood in front of his brother. "I asked her to come and help me sort through stuff. You got a problem with that, Charlie?"

"No. No problem. I forgot, you always liked to play around with the ladies."

"Oh, shut up, Charlie." Grace said.

"Well, it's true, Sonny. You can't deny it. You don't know my brother, Grace. He's a love 'em and leave 'em kind of guy. Ain't it true, bro?" Charlie grinned at them both. His teeth were tinged brown. It looked as if he hadn't been to a dentist in years.

Sonny wondered if he passed by Charlie on a crowded street if he'd even recognize him. The alcohol and cigarettes had made him old. "You know, Charlie, I think you better just get out of here. You're obviously not here to help, and I'm not in the mood for your special brand of humor."

Charlie leaned back and put one foot up on the kitchen table. The cane-backed chair creaked from his weight. The bottom of his boot was caked with mud and straw. "You can't throw me out of here, Sonny. It's my house, too."

Sonny pushed Charlie's foot off the table.

"Not for long, Charlie."

"What the hell is that supposed to mean?"

"Maybe I should leave," Grace turned to go.

"No, don't go, Grace. Charlie's leaving."

She put her hand on his arm. "Sonny, it's okay."

But it wasn't okay. Sonny turned and opened the back door. "Let's get out of here, Grace. I'll show you the old barn."

It used to be the reddest barn in the county, red with white trim. Now it was nearly all bare wood, faded to a purple white, bleached from the sun, a few flakes of maroon remained, something to pull away in moments of boredom. His father had managed to keep the roof patched just enough to keep it dry, but after Grandpa Joe died no one bothered to keep it red. Bit by bit the acreage was sold. His father had built a small chicken coop close to the house because his mother didn't like going out into the barn. Too much rat shit, she always said. Sonny knew it wasn't the rat shit. It was the past.

The barn door creaked when they opened it.

"Is it safe?" Grace held onto his arm. "Are you sure the roof won't fall in?"

"Very funny."

"I've always wondered why people didn't convert barns into houses more often."

"Too drafty and cold. Believe me you wouldn't want to pay the heating bill in the winter."

"Maybe, but there's something wonderful about all this space."

The rope that he used to climb on when he was a kid still hung from the center beam. This had been their winter playground—his and Charlie's and anyone else's who braved the snowdrifts.

The place smelled like dust instead of horse. Sonny motioned for Grace to follow him. "Grandpa Joe had himself a room in the back. After my parents were married and me and Charlie came along, he pretty much lived out here. When my mom died he moved back into the house, but this was where he came to get away from it all. He told us when he was out here he was working, so we had to leave him alone." Sonny reached up and brushed the rusty horseshoe that was tacked over the door. "I couldn't do that when I was a kid."

It had been a tradition. Whenever they came out to the barn, Sonny would jump up and touch the horseshoe. One day he was babysitting his little brother, Charlie. "Just take Charlie with you," his father said. "Look after him."

Sonny didn't want to look after his pesky little brother. "I want some luck, too," Charlie pulled on Sonny's arm. "Get me some luck." Sonny leaned over, forming his hands into a stirrup so he could give Charlie a boost. Just when Charlie was about to brush his hand on the horseshoe, Sonny swerved to the side so that Charlie couldn't reach it. Charlie cried. It seemed like Charlie was always crying.

"Sorry, bro, guess you're not big enough."

Sonny hadn't heard Grandpa Joe come out, but there he was in the doorway looking down at Sonny. He didn't say anything, but he lifted Charlie up over his head, higher than Sonny had ever been able to reach, and held him steady until Charlie touched that horseshoe more times than Sonny could count. After Grandpa Joe put Charlie down, he looked at Sonny. "It takes more than touching a damn horseshoe to bring you luck, boy. You got to take care of your family."

Sonny opened the door and walked into the room. Grace was right behind him. "I'll be damned. It hasn't changed a bit." The room was just as he remembered. In the corner under the window was a small kitchen, consisting of a two-burner stove top and an old refrigerator. The furniture was simple: a single bed, a small writing desk, and a wooden cedar chest. In the far corner stood a wood-burning stove, and next to the stove was a wicker rocking chair.

Sonny walked over to the cedar chest. The initials "JB" were carved into its lid. Sonny ran his hand over the surface. Someone had stenciled ivy over the sides of the chest. It had faded from green to brown, as if the ivy had died from lack of water and light.

Sonny tried to open the chest. The hasp was frozen closed, its hinge rusted.

Grace knelt in front of it. "It's like a treasure chest, a buried treasure."

"It's not buried. It's sitting out here in plain view."

"No, it's buried," she said. "Lots of things are buried right in front of our noses."

Grandpa Joe would have said something like that.

"Come on, we can work it loose." The light caught a faint blue streak in her hair. "Wait a minute." Sonny walked over to the kitchenette and opened the cabinet under the sink. "Grandpa Joe believed in WD–40. He kept one in every room, and look, it's still here." He held the bottle up as if were a trophy. He twisted the cap off the dusty bottle, poured a drop of oil on his finger, and rubbed it on the hinges, then he dabbed some more oil on the hasp. "This way we won't break anything." He worked the hasp back and forth letting the oil seep into the tight spots, until he felt it loosen. The creak of the hinge sounded like a trumpet call, trumpets and drum roll. Sonny opened the lid.

Grace leaned forward. "Wait." She put out her hand. The tattooed feather on her forearm pulsed.

The two of them sat there for a moment, their heads together. Sonny inhaled the smell of cedar, leather, and sage that emerged from the opening.

"Grandpa Joe," Grace bent her head and closed her eyes. Her hair was parted down the middle in a straight line. Sonny wondered how she got it so even. "I never knew you, Grandpa Joe. I've only heard about you and seen your picture, but if you're still here, please know that we aren't meaning any disrespect by opening your chest. We promise to cherish your treasures and keep them safe . . ." She opened her eyes and looked at Sonny.

"Don't look at me," he said. "I don't believe in ghosts."

" . . . and I'm looking forward to meeting you."

She took her hand off his arm. "Okay."

Sonny lifted the lid of the chest all the way open.

He reached in and lifted out a leather-bound book. "I remember this," he said. "It was Grandpa Joe's favorite book. He always had it with him." *Huckleberry Finn*. Sonny opened the cover, inside was an inscription, "From one river rat to another."

Inside the book was a pamphlet from the 1904 Louisiana Purchase Exposition and on the cover of the pamphlet was a picture of an old Indian with the inscription:

> *To Pinky,*
> *Thanks for the show.*
> *Geronimo*

Sonny stared at the famous face. It was craggy and weathered and seemed to be staring at something in the distance that Sonny couldn't see. It was a stock photograph. Geronimo had probably signed thousands of them.

"To Pinky. That's an odd name."

"Who's Pinky?" Grace asked.

"Don't have a clue." Under the book was a patchwork quilt. Someone had pieced together a Ferris wheel. Assorted bits of fabric made up the baskets that seemed to swing, their movement captured in the darks and lights of calico. It was sewn against a background that was itself a piecing of backgrounds, patches sewn together as massive buildings all superimposed on top of each other. And around the outside, like a frame, was a blue silk river.

Grace lifted the quilt. She held it up to her nose. "It smells sweet."

Sonny took it from her. She was right. It smelled like apples and cedar wood.

"Look at this." Grace lifted a leather pouch out of the trunk. She opened it. "Marbles. Glass marbles. I've always loved playing with marbles."

He reached into the chest and pulled out a wooden box. It was filled with letters tied in a pink ribbon.

"I think there's something else, Sonny, a scrap of paper." Grace held up a small piece of paper. Sonny took it out of her hand.

"Careful, Sonny, it is awfully brittle, and everything in this box is so precious."

Her cheeks were flushed. He wanted to touch them, feel her heat. He looked at the pile that lay in front of them, a lot of old stuff. "Things aren't precious, Grace."

"They are when you haven't had them."

He realized he didn't know anything about her. Except that she had appeared in his life, and he was suddenly afraid that she might just spread her wings and fly away.

The paper had been folded so long it had almost dried shut. "I'm afraid if I open it, it's going to crumble."

"I can try." Grace reached for it.

"No. I'll do it." Sonny didn't know what was on the paper. Probably a shopping list, but he didn't want any one else to be responsible if it was destroyed. He laid it on the desk and coaxed the folds open.

"Sonny," She knelt on the floor next to him. "It's a map, Sonny. Look, it's a treasure map."

He looked down at the half-opened paper; on it was a drawing of something that looked like a lower arm and a fist, with a single extended finger pointing downward. Above where the elbow would be was an oddly shaped crescent moon, and on the tip of the moon was an X with the letters "BI" written on the side.

"Grandpa Joe was always making treasure maps. It was one of his favorite games, burying trinkets around the property for us to dig up. Must be left over from that, but I don't recognize this place."

"But maybe this one's real." The white of the paper reflected in Grace's eyes.

"You didn't know him, Grace. It probably marks the spot where he caught a giant catfish or found a wild strawberry bush. He didn't have a treasure to bury. If he did, he'd of bought himself a new boat."

"Maybe he meant to go back and dig it up and just got too old. Or he forgot. Too bad there's no one around to ask anymore. Did your parents ever tell you any stories?"

"No. They never talked about much of anything except the weather and how Mrs. Angelino must have an in with the judges at the county fair 'cause she was always winning first prize for her strawberry jam."

Sonny had never cared much about strawberry jam, and he never actually met Mrs. Angelino, but if they'd talked about a family treasure he would have listened.

The door swung open.

"What are you guys up to?" Charlie lurched into the room. He tripped over the rocking chair and landed on the ground next to the cedar chest.

"Damn." He sat up and rubbed his shin. "You know, I forgot about this place, how big it is and all. Hell, a guy could live out here." He stood up and opened a door in the corner. "I'll be damned—there's a toilet. No wonder the old coot hung out here so much. What are you guys doing?"

"We're looking through some of Grandpa Joe's old stuff that no one ever got rid of."

"Well, just remember anything you find is half mine you know. No stealing the family treasures. What you got in your hand?"

"It's nothing, Charlie, just one of Grandpa Joe's silly old maps."

Charlie grabbed the map out of Sonny's hand. "Well, I'll just take that."

Sonny didn't argue. It was one more thing he didn't have to pack up or throw away.

# Chapter Twenty-Two

# ANNIE

## 1904

July 24, Later

I met Joe's little black man today. Joe was so proud to introduce him to me. He said we didn't have time to do all the exhibits on the Pike, but he wanted me to see the Anglo-Boer War Concession, so I could see his friend. I was surprised Joe was calling him his friend, him not being white and all, but then everything about Aday is different. He's not like the colored people that live in our town. He looks me straight in the eye when he talks to me, and he speaks in riddles. I think it's because he doesn't speak English very well. And he has a funny name. "A day" Joe called him. It doesn't sound like a proper Christian name, not even a proper heathen name, if you ask me. Not that I know a lot about heathens.

Aday doesn't like to wear shoes. He just carries them around his neck as if his shoes were a necklace. And he is perfectly comfortable walking around in short pants and no shirt. I found myself staring at his chest mostly because it was such a skinny little chest. He seems like he is still a child, but I know he's a grown-up person. Joe says Aday is one of the fastest runners in the world. I find that hard to believe, looking at him and all. Joe says that he used to run for days carrying messages for the British, so they could know what was happening and crush the Boers, and that's why they brought him to the fair for the exhibit.

I'm not sure why everyone is so fascinated with all this war play. But I suppose boys like their toy soldiers and all. I told Joe I think it's silly playing at war and cowboys and Indians. He told me it was so they could keep the past alive.

I see now why John is worried about Joe. I have to admit that I'm also worried. I don't understand why Joe spends so much time with the little man and with that Redfeather person. Redfeather sounds like a bird name. Maybe it's just because I'm hot and tired and it's hard to breathe here. I would have liked to have gone on the Siberian Railway, but Joe said there wasn't time. He had a show to do, and he had to get me back to the hotel. I would have liked to see his show, but he's meeting with the committee tomorrow. That means he'll be rowing with the team again, and everything can go back the way it was.

# Chapter Twenty-Three

# JOE

# 1904

I'd left early, so I wouldn't be late. I didn't want to keep the committee waiting. I had my doubts about the whole meeting. Even though Dr. Greer was an important man in our town, a man who kept us all out of the grave as best he could, and a man that even the mayor consulted about almost everything, I wasn't sure he was going to be important enough for the committee. I wasn't even quite sure how they got to be "The Committee," they just were. And they made the rules. I know the ancient Greeks didn't have rules about half-breed American Indians. They didn't even know about American Indians, but the committee was in charge now, and they were big on rules.

My hands felt sticky from the ice cream I'd just eaten. It was served on a hot waffle cone, a brand new invention. But that's what it was like at the fair. Everything was new. I couldn't go anywhere without seeing the newest product and invention. I wanted to wash my hands, but I saw Dr. Greer in the distance. A woman walked next to him, not with him. She was wrapped in a blue cloth that did not cover her arms and legs, and she carried a child in a sling with the babe's face turned inward. Dr. Greer didn't even seem to notice her, but he saw me and waved. He was always well dressed. I'd never seen him without a collared shirt and wool coat, even in the middle of summer, even when he'd been out all night with a sick patient. He said that people deserved respect, and that the person looking after them needed to take the time to dress up proper. Dr. Greer had been like a father to me and just about everyone else in the town.

It was Dr. Greer who came and rescued me from the Indian school. I don't know how he knew how miserable I was, but one day after I'd been there a year I got called into the office. Redfeather and I had been in the schoolyard kicking a ball back and forth.

Mrs. Huffman stood off to one side and waved at me. She never walked out in the middle of the playing field, never came close to the dirt. She always stood on the sidelines and watched. She was always watching.

"Joseph Barton. Joseph Barton, please come here. Joseph Barton, there's someone here to see you."

Dr. Greer stood next to her, a big smile on his face. "I'm taking you home, son. Go pack your things."

I turned around to wave, but Redfeather was gone. Recess was over, and everyone else had gone back to class. Mrs. Huffman didn't let me say goodbye to anyone, not even Redfeather. Over the past six months we'd shared everything, and then he was just gone. I didn't have much. All my possessions fit in a wooden chest at the foot of my bed. We all wore the same uniform during the day, and the clothes I'd arrived in were too small for me. I folded them like Mrs. Huffman had taught us. I put them on Redfeather's bed. They'd probably fit him; he was still a scrawny kid. Then I reached under my mattress and pulled the wooden pipe out of its hiding place, put it in my bag, and never looked back.

Dr. Greer smiled when he saw me, he put out his hand and I took it. I hoped I wasn't too sticky. "I'm glad you're early. Big day, Joe, big day."

"Yes, sir."

"Are you ready?"

I nodded and wiped my hands on my pants, and then we went inside the Administration Building. The building was massive. A brick building that felt as if it had been around forever, as if it had sprouted out of the ground. People lived in their wood houses, but I noticed that institutions dwelled in red brick.

It was cool inside. I hadn't expected that. Bricks always made me think of heat, brick ovens, brick fireplaces, hot bricks at the foot of my bed. But it was the silence that surprised me the most. I hadn't realized how noisy it was outside in the fair until I came into the silence. Like a church, even quieter than a church; like a library, even quieter than a library. It was power. Power was quiet, power was silent, and power was like the river making its own way, no one controlling it. The committee had to have a building like this, to keep it all in, not let it out, not let anyone else know that so much power and silence was behind the thick wooden doors, inside the brick walls.

Dr. Greer put his hand on my shoulder. The weight of it felt like a heavy wool blanket.

"I just want you to know, Dr. Greer, that I appreciate your coming here to help."

"Your father was my best friend, Joe."

Dr. Greer and my father, they'd been friends; friends that fished for catfish, friends that climbed into dark caves and carved their initials into the stone, friends that built tree forts, friends forever.

A young man in a white linen suit came up to us. He had a thick black mustache that was shaped into handlebars. I'd heard mustaches like that were the fashion in the big city, but they hadn't yet caught on in our little town. Good thing, because I hadn't ever been able to grow much of a beard.

"The committee can see you now." He led us down a long carpeted hallway. I couldn't take my eyes off the moustache.

He opened a door and showed us into a room with five men seated at a large table. Each one of them seemed to be reading from a paper in front of them. The room felt like an elegant dining room, and one day it probably would be. I wondered what was going to become of all these buildings. So much effort and time and money went into them. What could they possibly do with it all when the fair was over?

"Are you Joseph Barton?" I wasn't sure who was speaking because no one stood or raised their head.

Dr. Greer nudged me, "Yes, sir, I'm Joseph Barton."

"You understand why we are meeting with you, don't you?"

"Yes, sir."

"Well?"

"Well, what, sir?"

"Well, son, why do you think we should make an exception and change the rules for you?"

Dr. Greer nodded at me, his head bobbing up and down in encouragement. I looked at those stern men and Dr. Greer. And suddenly I wasn't sure why they should change the rules for me.

"Well?"

"For the team, sir. They need me."

As soon as I said them, I knew my words sounded forced. My reasons had nothing to do with the team, not really. The team could go on without me. It was vain of me to think that I alone could save them—that without me they were nothing. They were a team, and somehow they'd make it work.

"Well, son, I've seen the team practice, and frankly, I don't think they look too bad."

Dr. Greer interrupted, "This boy has never known his mother. He was raised as white as any of us."

"But he went to that Indian school."

Dr. Greer waved at them, as if the words or idea was an annoyance, a fly to be swatted out of existence. "Bah. That was just some silly decision his father made. He was under stress. Obviously, something was wrong. Look at what happened." He paused and looked at each one before he spoke again. "I told his father that the boy could stay with us."

"Yes, but he didn't." A round gentleman who wore a monocle and spoke with an English accent looked up from the papers in front of him. "That is the point, Dr. Greer. He didn't. He was housed with the savages and probably learned from them."

"But the whole point of these schools was to make young Indians more like white people, to educate the *savagery* out of them."

"But if he wasn't a savage to begin with, why did he have to go there to become more . . . ," the Englishman paused and rolled his tongue around his mouth, as if he had a bad taste, " . . . civilized."

Dr. Greer looked over at me as if to say help me. I had never seen him look like that before. He was the man who always knew what to do, and now he was looking to me for help, and I couldn't help him. I lifted my head and looked my inquisitor straight in the eye. "You're right, sir."

"What did you say?" He put down his pencil and looked at me. For the first time I think he really saw that I was there.

I stood up a little straighter.

"I said, you're right, sir. I don't belong with the team. I belong with the savages." As soon as I said those words out loud I felt a wave of relief. It was as if I'd been holding my breath for weeks, ever since I got the letter. Suddenly I could breathe again. I looked over at Dr. Greer.

"I'm sorry, sir."

"Well, then," said the gentleman with the monocle, "I think that is settled. There is nothing more to discuss." He took the monocle out of his eye and cleaned it with his handkerchief, "So, my boy, which game are you going to participate in?"

"Tug of war is where they put me."

"Hmmmmm, tug of war. Very good. We're finished here. Thank you for coming, Dr. Greer, but as you see, it wasn't necessary."

Each one of the committee members picked up their pile of papers and walked out a door at the back of the room. I felt as if I was witnessing a play. I was surprised they didn't bow before they left the stage.

The room was silent except for the steady beat of a grandfather clock. Dr. Greer watched the men from the committee leave the room, and then he looked at me. It was a look I'd seen before, the look that used to make me and John want to hide down by the river all day, the look that told us he wished he had a paddle, and he wasn't going to use it to row a boat. I didn't blame him. I would have given me that look, too.

"What was that all about?" He didn't raise his voice.

"I'm sorry, sir."

"Sorry? What does sorry have to do with anything? I went out on a limb for you. We all did. What am I going to tell them?"

I could imagine them. All the people back home, the men in the barbershop and the women in their sewing circles. They might not be sitting behind tables with stacks of paper and hushed voices, but somehow they all seemed the same.

"Tell them I was turned down."

"But you didn't even try."

I didn't want to argue with him. This was Dr. Greer, John and Annie's father, my guardian. And he'd been my father's best friend. He was a good man. I tried to imagine him and my father as boys fishing on the river—lazy boy days building tree forts and catching frogs. I don't think Dr. Greer had ever been more than ten miles from the Mississippi his whole life. Not like my father, who'd been to the edge of time.

"It wouldn't have done any good. They'd already made up their minds."

"You don't know that, boy." Boy. It's how he would have spoken to John. I know he thought of me as his son. I was his son. My father had left me to him, a pretty sorry inheritance. "I miss him, too, sir. I miss him, too."

"And what is that supposed to mean?"

I never got to tell him. The young man with the handlebar moustache came running in, "Dr. Greer, come quick. We need you, there's been an accident."

We ran outside. A huge crowd was already gathered in front of the building. "Make way for the surgeon. Move out of the way." I followed Dr. Greer. Moustache forced a path through the gawkers, and we followed close behind him. The crowd pushed behind us as we made our way to the center of the circle, and there on the ground lay two men. I recognized both of them. One was Mulhall and the other McKay, a loud-mouthed cowboy. Mulhalls' leg was bleeding, and he was swearing harder than I'd ever heard him swear at us out the field. The other guy lay flat on the ground with a bloody knife in the dust next to him.

I couldn't take my eyes off McKay. I wasn't sure if he was alive or dead. He lay very still, and he seemed peaceful, like us bodies on the field. Dr. Greer knelt down next to him. Two days earlier Mulhall had fired McKay for drinking and picking fights with the Indians.

A policeman looked at McKay and then at Mulhall. "What happened?"

"He just came at me," Mulhall pointed to his leg. "Out of nowhere, he ran straight at me and started swearing. I tried to fight him off. He . . . ." For the first time Mulhall didn't have the words. "I didn't have a chance."

"He's right. We saw it." I couldn't tell who was talking. But the faces around us all nodded in agreement. "The man just came at him."

The policeman took notes.

"He attacked me," Mulhall repeated.

Dr. Greer had his head close to the man's chest. He motioned for us to be quiet. I held my breath. We all did.

Then we heard a groan, and the body seemed to come back to life. We let out a collective sigh.

Dr. Greer looked at Mulhall's leg again. "We need to get you over to the infirmary."

"I'll help him, sir." I stepped forward.

Dr. Greer nodded at me and turned his attention back to the other man. I held out my arm, and Mulhall grabbed onto me. A few of the other onlookers helped me get him to his feet. He couldn't put any weight on the one leg, and his pant legs were soaked in blood. Someone offered me a dirty bandana, which I pulled tight over the wound. It was better than nothing.

"Ow."

"I've got to do this sir, to slow the bleeding."

"Just hurry up."

"Put your arm around my shoulder." He did as I told him.

"Thanks, Pinky. Damn, I'm cold." It was a hot day and his teeth chattered when he tried to talk. "I knew that guy was trouble. Don't know why I didn't have him hauled off weeks ago. Ain't nothing worse than a drunk cowboy, unless it's a drunk Injun."

"Yes, sir." I had my arm around his waist. It was all I could do to keep us both from falling. He seemed to be getting weaker and weaker as we got closer to the infirmary. I should've waited for a stretcher.

Just as I thought I couldn't go another step, we arrived. Someone saw us come up, and a couple of men ran out to help me. "You'll be okay now, Mr. Mulhall," I said. "These men will take care of you."

"Mr. Mulhall. No one ever calls me Mr. Mulhall." One of the men helped him into a wheelchair. Mulhall held onto me as they lowered him down. My nice clean suit was covered in blood. He held onto my arm and wouldn't let go, even though the men carried him away. "You know, Pinky," he said, "my boy had red hair, too."

# Chapter Twenty-Four

# SONNY

## 2004

Sonny lay on the bed he'd slept in for over eighteen years. It was his birthday. "Happy birthday to me," he sang. The room hadn't changed since he'd left and gone off to college. The varsity pennant that he'd received his senior year for debate team hung on the wall, as did his poster of Peter Fonda in *Easy Rider*.

The glow-in-the-dark stars were still stuck on the ceiling. They had long ago faded to nothing more than another chore to be done, something else to clean up. He remembered when he and Charlie had created their cosmic universe.

"We don't need them to be like the real thing," Sonny said. "We can make them be whatever we want. We can make up our own constellations. And we'll have secret names for them that only we know, just you and me."

Charlie had jumped up and down on the bed as Sonny carefully arranged the stars into a constellation and named it. Badger was at the center of their sky. His five-starred paw protected them at night.

Birthdays had always been the major holidays in their house. "That's because of your Grandpa Joe," his father said once when Sonny asked what the big deal was. "He likes his cakes."

Sonny and Grandpa Joe came back to the house after their paddle on the river. No one had even noticed they were gone. There was so much to get ready for the whole town to come to wish Grandpa Joe a happy ninety years old. Ninety. Sonny couldn't imagine being ninety, living nearly a century.

Grandpa Joe had held Sonny's hand. "Aaaa, look at the flame." It was a huge chocolate cake, nearly as big as a wedding cake. On top of the cake was one large candle stuck in the middle of "Happy Birthday Grandpa J." The lettering faded out at the ends, but the blue-frosted silhouette of a paddler hunched over his oars was unmistakable.

"Here, Joe, let me help you." Mrs. Franklin, their housekeeper at the time, had on her party apron, the one with the white starched eyelet. The one she would only wear if she didn't think she'd be getting it dirty. "Make a wish." She leaned forward ready to blow as soon as the wish was made.

"No." Grandpa Joe pushed her away. "Don't blow it out. Let it burn."

"But you've got to make your wish. Everyone has to make a wish."

"Wish schmish. Go ahead, Sonny, you're getting to be a man now. You go ahead and take my wish. I don't need it."

Sonny closed his eyes. He tried to make a wish happen, but he wanted it to be a good one, and all he could see when he closed his eyes was the river and Grandpa Joe.

"Go ahead, Sonny, make your wish, but let it burn."

Sonny reached over and pulled the burning candle out of the cake. Chocolate icing stuck to the bottom.

Sonny took the candle and carried it away from the crowd. He wasn't ready to make a wish yet. He'd save it. He took a cup from the cabinet, put the candle in it, and set the candle on the table. It was still burning when he kissed his grandfather good night.

※

Sonny glanced at his watch. It was two thirty in the afternoon. He was supposed to meet Charlie for a birthday drink at the club around five o'clock. It was early, but he knew that if he stayed where he was he'd never get out of bed and go out. When he got to the club, there were no cars in the parking lot, not even Frank's Corvair. He should have realized that no one showed up there until after three—used to be they didn't show up until five, the traditional quitting time. The factory whistles would blow, and everyone would show up for the evening. But these days they got started earlier. Sonny walked up the steps and opened the door. It wasn't locked. He wondered if it was ever locked. Like a church, always open, always ready for the next supplicant, the next convert. Grace was there. Vivaldi's *The Four Seasons* blasted on the sound system. He didn't know it could play anything other than rock and roll.

"Hi, Sonny, you're early." She turned the music off.

"I'm looking for Charlie. Have you seen him?"

"It's a little early, even for Charlie."

Sonny climbed onto one of the bar stools. His back was to the big picture window, and he faced the glass case filled with stuffed wildlife. The badger stared down at him. Local legend was that Grandpa Joe had caught that badger. Sonny changed seats so he could look out the window.

"It's my birthday," he said to Grace.

"I didn't know. Happy birthday," she smiled. "I'd sing, but it might ruin your day."

He laughed with her. Maybe she'd smile some more.

"So tell me, Grace, what brought you to this town?"

He couldn't imagine anyone coming here intentionally. People left. They didn't move in, as was evidenced by all the for sale signs that looked as if they'd been there a very long time. No one was buying.

She smiled. "A guy, what else?"

That said it all, he supposed.

"Woman follows man."

"And?"

"And it didn't work out."

"Is he still here?"

"I doubt it."

"But you don't know."

"It doesn't matter, Sonny." She pulled out a wet cloth and wiped down the counter.

She wore a necklace with a piece of turquoise set in what looked like a silver hand.

It swung back and forth as she moved her hand in a circular rhythm. She hummed as she wiped. "Hush a bye, don't you cry, go to sleep my little baby."

"What's that song?"

Just something my grandmother used to sing to me.

"Tell me about your grandmother?"

Grace paused for a moment. "You know, I don't remember much about her. I remember I called her Nana. I remember my Nana Ida, with whiskers on her chin and the waist that wasn't there. I seem to remember her in layers, with the old nana superimposed on the younger one who was always old to me. The younger nana was the one with the apron around her waist as she took the chocolate cake out of the oven, the best chocolate cake, the one we called "Nana's chocolate cake." Grace took a glass out from behind the bar and looked at it in the light.

"There's a spot there," said Sonny.

Grace put the glass down. "There was that nana, and then the later one whose speech slurred when she talked and who smelled of urine and garlic. They are layered one upon the other in a three-dimensional time picture, a morphing almost. I remember the young nana never sitting down at a meal because there was always something to be done."

Like you, Sonny thought. Always moving always doing something.

"And the old nana lost in her chair at the head of the table when the house was gone and the kitchen was no longer hers. I remember the young nana whose gray hair was kept in place with a hair net, and the older nana whose wisps of yellowish white hair were so thin you could see the gray of her scalp. I remember the lipstick that melted out of the cracks around her mouth. I remember my young nana running up and down the stairs in the old house—the stairs that we loved to slide down on our bottoms, over and over, and she wouldn't ever care—and the old nana with her walker shuffling along until she couldn't shuffle anymore."

Sonny put his hand on hers. She looked him in the eye. "And then I remember that I never went to see her anymore, that I went on without her, and that she died, and I didn't cry."

Sonny leaned over and kissed her on the cheek.

"What was that for?"

"For your nana."

She wiped her cheek with the back of her sleeve and took a deep breath.

"So, Mr. Sonny, what would you like for your birthday?"

He stared out the window. He loved this window. He realized that it was this window that he took with him to California. It was this window that he looked through when he looked at anything. Everything he ever saw was through this frame. "I think I'd like to go out on the river."

She took off her apron.

"Okay."

"What do you mean okay?"

"Let's go."

"Where?"

"To the river."

"Now? I don't know where Charlie is. I need to find him."

She rested her elbows on the counter and leaned forward.

"You know, Sonny, you can't fix him."

Sonny watched the barges on the river. It was like a busy highway, so much commerce, so much industry. "When I was a kid I wanted to be a captain on one of those towboats. That's what they call them, even though they push the barges. I wanted to be able to sit up real high and look down over the whole river. I used to think that if I looked hard enough I'd see all the way to New Orleans. I wanted to take all those big heavy metal barges and be the one that steered them."

"Why didn't you?"

"I was twenty-five when Grandpa Joe died. No need to hang around, so I left."

"So you went to the ocean."

"The ocean is nothing like this river. The ocean is just big. It doesn't have the same kind of personality. It doesn't make you feel safe; it doesn't feel like the arteries carrying blood. You can predict the ocean. You can predict the tides. Hell, you can even predict the hurricanes. But you can't predict this river—at least you couldn't back then. A few good beavers and the river can change.

Grace reached into her pocket and pulled out a pack of gum, Juicy Fruit. Grandpa Joe used to chew Juicy Fruit. He and Sonny built houses out gum wrappers. They used Doublemint for the grass, Beemans for the roof, and Juicy Fruit for the frame.

Happy birthday to you, happy birthday to you, happy birthday, dear Sonny, happy birthday to you.

"My Grandpa Joe told us he cried when they built the dams."

"Oh?"

"Said it was like trying to put the river in a shoe. Said if they didn't look out, the whole place would get bunions."

Grace laughed. He liked the way her eyes crinkled up when she laughed.

"I guess my Grandpa Joe was big on metaphor."

"Let's go, Sonny. I can get us a rowboat. Let's just go. Let's do this, for your birthday."

He looked out the window.

A row of empty barges was lined up on the other side of the river. Someone had managed to tag a few of them with the Picasso art of a street gang. He used to think it was beautiful in a primitive kind of way, those thick geometric patterns that appeared out of nowhere on a highway overpass, a bridge, and even here. They didn't have gangs here when he was younger, although maybe they would have called him and Charlie and Frank a gang.

Sonny pulled the boat up close to the shore. His hands hurt. He knew he wasn't supposed to grip so hard. It had been a long time since he'd been out on the river. A balmy wind came out of the south. The south wind brought humidity and hot jazz up the river from New Orleans. He relaxed his grip and looked at the water. The ripples caught a patch of sun and reflected it back at him, a fire in the water and a face—his face, her face, some face, a friendly face calling, "come to me, come here, jump in, jump in." He pulled himself into the shadow of the tree and the face disappeared. He maneuvered the boat back into the pocket of sun. There was something here, something that he needed to grab a hold of. He dipped his hand into the water. It was colder than the air. He pulled his sleeve down over his hand, grabbed the oars, and steered the boat into the current. He looked at Grace. "Are you having fun?"

She nodded. "I am. I really am. You know, I've lived here for five years, and I've never been out on this river, never even put my toe in it. I was afraid of it. Don't know why."

"A lot of people are afraid of this river."

He gripped the oars and pulled harder, backward and forward rolling. He should have brought a CD player. Rhythm, he needed rhythm. Grandpa Joe had talked about the rhythm of the river. Grace leaned over the side. Her hand trailed in the water creating a small wake of its own. With every pull the oarlocks creaked. With every pull his body creaked. Him and the boat, they both needed grease, some WD–40. How many WDs were there? Maybe sixty, maybe infinity. Who knew what it took to take away the pain, the resistance? He pushed his legs against the bottom of the boat, and pulled the oars into his chest. He threw his head back and looked at the sky. A wisp of a cloud floated above him, kept pace with him. Forward, back, forward, back, push, pull–he felt as if he raced the cloud.

"What's that?" Grace pointed at a sign on the bank that looked like a street lamp.

"Mile marker." He watched Grace. Brown-eyed girl, you're my, brown-eyed girl. All the lonely people, where do they all come from? Push, pull, lap, gurgle—the river, the cloud, the mile marker and the rhythm of the wind. He stopped rowing and sat still. He was tired. He hadn't worked this hard in a long time.

"Do you want me to take over?" Grace asked.

He shook his head no. A large motor yacht sped by; its wake rocked them. Grace gripped the sides. Sonny dipped his hand in the water. A lavender film of oil covered the brown. Lavender, not quite purple, not quite pink, not quite blue—it was a smell more than a color. "Just put some lavender oil in his bath. That's what Annie used to do." Grandpa Joe had stood in the doorway of the bathroom. His father had a hand in the bathwater, feeling for the temperature. Sonny hadn't asked who Annie was. "It cures everything 'ceptin the influenza. Nothing cures that." Sonny shivered. The heat inside him made the hot summer's day feel like the middle of winter.

"Leave him be, Dad, he's going to smell like a sissy," his father had said. "Lavender is for ladies."

Don't let me smell like a girl; don't let me smell like a girl. Sonny pulled himself into a ball. Grandpa held out the bottle of bath oils. It smelled half-sweet, not like roses or lilacs, more like his dad's breath after he'd had his evening drink.

Grandpa Joe poured in the oil. "Just put him in that. Let it soak out the fever." Dozens of small beads floated like river barges, nose to nose in the bath.

Sonny looked at Grace, then he lifted the oars and turned them so they rested inside the boat. It was a skill, bringing the oars in so they didn't get water all over you. He was good at it. Had always been good at it. He could row as silently as an Indian. He tossed the extra life jackets into the space between the seats, then lowered himself down. He motioned for Grace to sit next to him. He put his arm around her, and she let her head lean on his shoulder. He closed his eyes and let his head rest on hers. He was no longer racing the cloud. He was no longer racing anything.

Sonny stared at the pile of money on the table. "What's this, guys?"

The Evans twins looked like Tweedle-dum and Tweedle-dee in Harley jackets. "The pot. Are you in?"

"What's the game?"

"No game," said Frank, "Straight bet. These guys say we won't make it."

"What'd you say?"

"I put down a twenty that says we will."

"I'll bet that they need to tow us back to shore." Roy threw another twenty in the pot.

Frank wrote the bets on a piece of paper.

Sonny pulled out his wallet. "Thanks for the vote of confidence, Roy. You're supposed to be on our team."

"Doesn't mean I can't hedge my bets. I'm going along for the party you promised me, a blow-out beer blast if we cross the line."

"Yeah, a triple kegger. Grandpa Joe is buying," Charlie slurred his words.

"Can I get you boys something else?" Grace asked.

"Coffee for him." Sonny pointed at Charlie.

"Don't coffee me, brother. I can hold my liquor."

"Ease off, Sonny." Frank picked up the bills and sorted them into piles of singles, fives, tens, and twenties. There was nothing over a twenty. "Leave him alone, already."

Sonny looked at the pot. "How much is here?"

"Looks like five hundred."

Five hundred dollars. It wasn't really a lot of money. Not like winning the lottery or anything. He stared at the guys. The Evans boys grinned. Frank chewed the side of his mouth. Roy counted the pot. Charlie sulked.

"Okay, I'm in." Sonny threw a twenty on the table. "We cross the line."

"What about you, Charlie?" They all looked at Charlie.

Charlie put his hand in his pocket and pulled it inside out. "Thanks to Grandpa Joe, I got nothing."

"It has nothing to do with Grandpa Joe, Charlie. It's all about you."

"Hey, you two, don't start that crap again."

Charlie pushed his chair back and stood up. "I ain't starting nothing," he said, glaring at Sonny. "Just get yourself out of my face."

"Charlie, I'm sorry." Sonny wanted to shake his brother. What should I do Grandpa Joe? He looked at the old pictures on the walls. What should I do? Maybe I should just walk away. Maybe that was the right thing to do, just walk away and let the old place fall into the ground, get plowed over, get foreclosed for nonpayment of taxes. Grandpa Joe hadn't thought of that, hadn't thought that maybe they'd just let it go and the state would get it. Maybe he thought that Sonny and Charlie would be tied together forever.

"Maybe we should just throw the old boat in the dumpster."

"It wouldn't fit," said Frank.

It wouldn't fit, thought Sonny. He could chop it into little bits, and then it would fit. He could rip it apart with his bare hands. But he wouldn't. He knew he wouldn't. Grandpa Joe's soul was etched into that old dried wood, like the Virgin Mary's face on a grilled cheese sandwich. Some things you just don't throw away. "I really am sorry, Charlie."

"Oh hell." Charlie sat down. "I'm in. Sonny, lend me a twenty."

# Chapter Twenty-Five

# ANNIE

## 1904

July 26

Dear Diary,

Daddy came back very upset from the meeting. He wouldn't talk to me about it at all. He just said that Joe had disappointed him and something about bad influences and other things I didn't understand. That's when I got the idea to find Mr. Redfeather. No one knows I went there, not John, not Joe, not Daddy, especially not Daddy, but I thought that maybe Mr. Redfeather could talk some sense into Joe, that maybe it wasn't really too late. I got on the train that runs all through the grounds and got out at the Anthropology Exhibit. I like that word, "Anthropology," sounds like apology.

I was trying to remember my way to the place where Joe took me, where Redfeather lived, but I hadn't been paying too much attention at the time, and there were tepees everywhere. That's what they call them, "the upside down cones." They make me laugh, the way they look like a silly garden, a place where you might find elves and gnomes.

I stopped and asked an old woman the way. I didn't know if Redfeather was a common name or not, maybe there would be a lot of Redfeathers. I noticed that the old woman's skin was different than the skin of the old white women I knew. It was a dark red-yellow, almost like a dried apple. I wanted to touch it, to see what it really felt like. She smiled at me. I'd never seen a smile like that before. She smiled with her whole face, not just her mouth. I must have shouted out the words "Jake Redfeather" because she took a step backward. Then I said it again just to be sure that she understood me."

"You want Jake Redfeather," she said to me in perfect English. It was very formal and distinct like. No one I know speaks as well as that woman did.

I asked her if she knew him, and she pointed to a group of children playing.

I saw the group of children. They surrounded a very large man. He towered above them, almost like the top of the tepee himself with the children ringed around him.

I smiled at the woman and thanked her. Then I reached into my pocket and took out a coin. The smile left her face. It was as if all the rivers had run dry. She turned away.

I couldn't take it back.

Mr. Redfeather is one of the biggest men I've ever seen. The top of my head barely comes up to the top of his shoulder. Four or five little Indian children climbed all over him as if he were a tree. They hung from his arms and his waist, and he had one boy on each of his shoulders. It made him seem ever taller than he was, like a three-headed giant. I pushed my way to the middle of the crowd. Some of the children had their hands out, as if they were expecting something from me. I didn't have anything, didn't know I was supposed to, so I put my hand in my pocket and pulled out some sugar cubes. I always like to have sugar cubes for the horses. The big man nodded at me and told me to go ahead. So I threw the sugar away from me, and the children chased after it. Then the big man leaned over, so the boys on his shoulders could jump off and chase themselves some sugar as well. I asked him if he was Mr. Redfeather.

Then he said to me, "I'm not used to being called mister, but yes, that's me. I'm Redfeather."

I must have looked pretty silly then, because no words came. I wasn't sure why I was there. Seeing him was all I really wanted, seeing this man who came out of Joe's past. But there I was, and he seemed to be expecting something from me, so I held out my hand and said to him, "I'm Annie." He didn't take my hand, and then I wondered if I'd done something very rude, if maybe they didn't shake hands, the Indians, but I was wearing gloves, so it should have been okay.

"Joe's Annie?" he asked me. Hearing him call me that made me feel good. I am Joe's Annie. Then he smiled at me, turned to the children and spoke to them in a language I didn't understand. I couldn't tell where the words or sentences were supposed to be, they all sounded like nonsense words to me, but the children seemed to know what he was saying because as soon as he finished talking they waved at him and ran off to play someplace else.

He led me over to one of the tepees and opened the flap, so I went inside. I hope my daddy never reads this because I can't even imagine what he would say if he ever finds out that I went into one of those all alone with a man, let alone a heathen man, but I never even had a second thought about it at the time, that's how kind Mr. Redfeather seemed.

There were no chairs to sit on, only backrests on the floor that were covered with animal skins. Those skins looked so fresh that I was a little worried the animal itself might still be somewhere nearby. What amazed me though was how neat it was inside. Even the legendary Mrs. Macavey would have been impressed. But then again, it had to be neat because the space was so small. There wasn't room to leave anything lying around. It reminded me of living in a boat cabin on the river.

When Mr. Redfeather dropped the flap to the outside, it was hard to tell where I was. There were no windows, and the room was so round it made me feel a bit dizzy. Animal skins hung on the inside like tapestries or paintings. And it was warm. Almost too warm. He motioned for me to sit on the ground. I couldn't. I didn't want to offend him, but I didn't bend like that. That's the problem with corsets and petticoats. Getting down to the ground wasn't easy, not that I do it much, so I had to stand. He shrugged his shoulders and sat down. I'm glad he did, otherwise my neck would have hurt from having to look up at him.

He didn't say anything; he just sat there waiting for me to say something. I couldn't think of anything to say, so I said to him, "Joe tells me he knew you when he went away to school."

That was a good start because Mr. Redfeather nodded and said that was right, they'd been to school together. Joe doesn't talk much about it, I said.

"Not much to tell," he replied, then pointed to one of the backrests and asked if I wasn't sure I didn't want to sit down.

I'll admit my feet hurt, but I didn't sit. I heard the children laughing. I wanted to go outside and watch them play. There was a musky smell inside the round room. I should have brought some lavender. That would have been better than sugar cubes.

He didn't rush me, didn't even look at me while I was finding my way inside my thoughts. He just sat nice and still and waited. The kids must have run off somewhere because I didn't hear them anymore. I didn't hear much of anything, the skins muffling the outside sounds.

"Mr. Redfeather," I finally said to him, even though he told me he wasn't a mister. "Mr. Redfeather, can you please send Joe back home?" That wasn't what I meant to say, but it's what came out.

"I'm not sure I can send Joe anywhere" is what he said.

"Can you try?" I asked him. That's all I wanted was to know that he would try.

Then he reached into a white fur bag that hung from the backrest. He pulled something out of it and handed it to me. I'd never seen anything like it before. It was made of glass beads, feathers, and bits of polished green stones.

He told me it was a wedding necklace. I'm sure I blushed. But I couldn't take it from him, so I told him so, I said to him, "This is beautiful, Mr. Redfeather, truly beautiful. But, it's much too valuable, I can't take it."

"It's not valuable" is what he told me back. "It's only got sentimental value, and that won't buy anything. But I'd like you to have it, you're supposed to have it."

# Chapter Twenty-Six

# JOE

## 1904

Redfeather and I were on cleanup duty. That meant checking the field for broken glass or other trash.

"So, you going?" I didn't even have to ask Redfeather what he meant. I knew. Today was the crewing event out at Creve Couer Lake. "Don't think so. Got too much to do here."

He took the rake out of my hand. "Get out of here. I can do this. You don't have to hang around. He looked at the field, "This is a big day for you."

How big is a day? Bigger than a lifetime. More than twenty-four hours that was for sure.

"Mulhall'll have a fit if he finds I snuck off."

"If you're not there when they compete, you'll never forgive yourself."

"I'm not the one that needs forgiveness," I said.

Redfeather wagged his finger at me, as if he was my mother. "Stop feeling so damn sorry for yourself. It's just a stupid race. It doesn't mean anything. It's a show. A big show. You win; you lose. What does it matter?"

Some crabgrass grew in the dirt. Hard to imagine that any living thing could survive all the battles that took place on that field. The charging horses, the rolling bodies, the war cries. I put my hand around the base of the plant and pulled. Only the top came off; the roots were deep in the dry soil.

"Just go." Redfeather took the weed out of my hand. "Just go."

I put on my crispest white linen suit and white boating hat. I thought twice about the hat. If the wind picked up, I didn't fancy chasing the damn thing all over the state of Missouri, but I wore it anyway. The full-length mirror in the wardrobe room made me look squat. I could almost pass for one of the committee members, nice and round in the middle. I saluted myself and made my way over to the train station. Because of the races, they were running more trains than usual, but even so it was crowded on the platform. A steady stream of people made their way to the event. I let myself get carried away with them, let myself drift on the current. No one gave me a second look. I fit right in with the ladies in parasols and the men in their bowler hats. The shoes I wore hurt my feet. I'd gotten used to the soft leather moccasins of my costume and the stiff leather of civilized shoes took some getting used to. But I liked the feeling it gave me. Everything was back where it belonged. I could have ridden the train for free, being part of the exhibits and all, but I reached into my pocket and pulled out a coin. One of the biggest draws at the fair was the Hereafter Exhibit. It portrayed a fire-and-brimstone Hell, and a harps-and-angels Heaven. People paid their nickel to experience the afterlife right in the middle of Missouri. Creve Couer Lake was my own little bit of heaven and hell. The Heaven I couldn't get into; the Hell I paid my nickel to visit.

"Excuse me," said a young man in a blue seersucker jacket as he pushed past me. He was going for one of the seats. I let him by. The rest of us managed to make it on the train, but there was standing room only. I didn't mind. I was planning on standing anyway, so my suit wouldn't get all rumpled. The train was thick with people and the scent of the ladies. All the perfumes mixed together, and I began to feel a bit sick. I wasn't used to being in such a small place with so many people. Those of us who were standing swayed together as if we were at a revival meeting. They probably could have fit more of us on the train if it wasn't for the ladies' hats, silly things that stuck out in all directions. One lady's fake fruit got caught up with another's fake bird. Most of the women had them tied under their chins with giant bows. At least they wouldn't blow too far in the wind.

I stood in front of the man in the seersucker jacket. He stared at me. I tried to ignore it. I wasn't sure what he was looking at. Maybe I hadn't washed off all the war paint.

"I know you," he finally said.

I looked at him. "Don't think so."

He sat with his hat in lap, his hands folded around it. "You look familiar to me."

Then I realized I did know him. How could I forget the moustache? He was the clerk who'd ushered me into the room where the committee was meeting. He was the committee's errand boy.

"I'm sure we've never met." I turned away, so he couldn't watch me, couldn't see that I did know him.

"Creve Coeur!" the conductor shouted into the crowd. "Next stop: Creve Couer." Next stop. Only stop. Seersucker stood up and pushed his way to the front. I held back. There was no reason to jump into the fray, and I didn't fancy having some woman's hat feathers in my mouth.

By the time I got off the train the platform was empty, except for a few people milling around looking at the program and maps of where to go from here. Seersucker leaned against a pole. I ignored him and walked in the direction of the lake. He ran and caught up with me. My stride was longer than his, but he managed to stay right next to me.

"I do know you. You're that damn Indian turncoat, Barton."

I stopped and let him stumble a bit past me.

We were alone on the path. I could hear the announcer in the distance. I was sorry I'd missed the carrying in of the boats from the boathouse. I always loved that bit of ceremony, when the boat looked like a sea creature with legs as it crawled toward the water. The guys usually didn't want me to be under the boat, since I was a good six inches shorter than the rest of them, and the boat got all lopsided when I was carrying. They always made me the paddle man. "Just wag the tail, Joe." And I did. I was a damn good tail wagger.

"Look, Mr. . . ." I didn't know his name. I want to see the race about to start any minute."

"You can't hide behind that suit, you know."

He put his arm out and stopped me from moving forward.

"What's that supposed to mean?"

"It means I know who you really are."

The train whistle blew.

On the top of the train station the weather vane spun around in circles. It needed oiling. Maybe I wouldn't be late. Maybe they'd postpone the race. It was always a tough call when the weather changed and the water got rough.

I tried to push my way past him, but he grabbed me by the sleeve. "Hey."

"Stand here and face me like a man," he said.

I looked around. There was no one I could call to help me. "What do you want from me?"

"I want you to just turn around and go back where you belong. After what you did, turning your back on your team and all. You don't belong here."

I did belong. They were my team, each one of them. John was probably wearing the flask I'd given him—the flask filled with good luck water. Hopefully, he'd remembered to change out the Mississippi for Creve Couer, for broken heart water, but I gave it to him. Me.

"I just want to watch. Let go. You're wrinkling my sleeve." I couldn't shake him loose. He was surprisingly strong, like a river leech. I took my free arm and pushed against his shoulder. He wouldn't let go. I kicked him in the knee and then leaned into him. He lost his balance and fell backward, but he still wouldn't let go of my sleeve. My momentum, our weight, his tenacity, gravity all conspired together and down we went, him on the bottom and me landing right on top of him. "Help," he shouted into my ear, "help."

A uniformed man ran out of the train station. He took one look at us and blew on a whistle. "What's going on here? Stop it, you two."

Seersucker was crying. That looked bad. "Arrest this drunken Indian, at once."

The officer put out a hand and pulled me to my feet. "Sir?"

"It's nothing. We fell."

Seersucker reached into his pocket and pulled out an identification tag. "I tell you, I'm with the committee. This man attacked me. Do what you have to do."

A roar of horror erupted from the direction of the lake. They only roared like that when someone caught a crab and ended up in the drink. It was bad. Too damn bad.

The uniform gave me a look. I shrugged my shoulders. "Sir, please come with me, and I'll take your statement."

Seersucker stood up. He was covered with dirt. I pulled a handkerchief out of my pocket and handed it to him. At least my suit was still white.

# Chapter Twenty-Seven

# SONNY

## 2004

Sonny tucked the cigar box under his arm and approached the front door. The houses in this neighborhood had stoops instead of porches. He almost tripped over a mud-covered pair of yellow gardening shoes. A handwritten sign was taped to the door: IF YOU KNOCK WE CAN'T HEAR YOU. Sonny rang the bell. The chimes resonated like a pipe organ throughout the house.

He heard a voice, a brief pause, footsteps, and then the door opened.

A small, round woman gave a squeal and threw her arms around him. He was surprised at how strong she was. She stood back and looked up at him. Her hair was pulled back into a tight ponytail, the blond faded to an almost gray at the temples. "Well, Sonny, I was wondering if you were ever going to get your butt over here to say hello."

"Hi, Jane." Sonny gave her a kiss on the cheek and walked in. "You're looking good."

"You're still a liar. You know damn well I'm looking older and fatter, and you're probably counting your blessings that I never said yes to you."

Sonny hated to admit it, but she was right.

She smiled. That hadn't changed. Jane's smile had always been her real power.

"Is he home?"

"Of course he's home. The damned club doesn't open for two more hours. Where else would he be? He's watching some game, but he might turn off the tube for you."

She led him down a hallway lined with bright oil paintings, still life studies, and black-and-white charcoal figures. "Who's the artist?" he asked.

"Me."

The initials "JJ" were legible at the bottom of each picture. Jane Johnson. Sonny couldn't get used to her being a Johnson, being Frank's wife. Jane was the first girl he ever kissed. He suspected she was probably the first girl all of them ever kissed. But she went for Frank. Of all of them, Frank was the one. Sonny always wondered why.

"Nice work."

"Well, when you don't have any children to take your time, you've got to fill the space with something. I paint." She opened the door to the basement. "He's down there. It's his place." She smiled and squeezed his arm. "And Sonny, thanks for doing this, the race and all. It's good for him."

Sonny stood at the top of the staircase, "Frank?"

"Hey, Sonny, come down." Sonny heard the voice of the television announcer. Baseball. It was still baseball season.

"Who's winning?"

"Not the Cubs."

"The Cubs never win."

"No, but I can always hope."

"I think you'd be better off rooting for the other team."

"You know, Sonny, if I rooted for someone else, they'd probably lose. Better to just stick with one jinx."

Frank sat with his legs up in a Lazyboy recliner. The basement smelled like mildew, and plastic board made to look like oak covered the walls. In one corner a wet bar was covered with boxes of model airplane kits, bits of plastic, and different types of glue. Sonny heard the swish of the washing machine in the next room. "Nice place you got here, Frank."

"It's the pits, but Jane doesn't like the TV going all the time. She can't hear it when I'm down here."

Sonny sank into the couch. It was classic 1970's brown and yellow, and the cushions needed to be replaced.

"Hello, I've brought you something hot out of the oven," Jane came down the stairs carrying a tray with cookies.

"Thanks, honey." Frank brushed her hand as she placed the tray on the table.

"I'm just going to leave you boys." Sonny watched her walk up the stairs.

"It's hard to believe you've been married twenty-five years, Frank. Twenty-five years is a hell of a long time." Sonny bit into the cookie. It was soft and chewy, just how he liked them. "Shit, Frank, this is good."

"Yeah. Jane knows her cookies."

They chewed in silence. On the television someone hit a line drive. Frank didn't notice, and Sonny didn't tell him.

"You know, Sonny, seems like you selling the house is kind of final, the end of an era. I always thought you'd end up back here somehow."

"I'll come and visit." Sonny took another cookie off the tray and took a bite.

"No. You won't. No one ever does."

"I'll still have ties. Charlie will still be here."

"Like that matters to you."

"What's that supposed to mean."

"Nothing, forget it. Would you like something else, coffee? I'm sure Jane will be happy to get it."

It was hard to imagine getting a coffee without going to Starbucks and ordering a river mud latte.

"No, I'm good."

Sonny looked at Frank. Jane kept him well groomed, his shirt was pressed so the collar laid flat, unlike Sonny's that curled under from too much washing and drying. It still came to a crisp point. His hair was neat and even, no straggly ends around his neck.

"Can you keep an eye on Charlie for me, buddy?"

"I can't promise much, Sonny. You know Charlie."

He did know. But he had to ask. In the next room the constant churning had stopped. The laundry was done. "Hey, Frank, I found something that you left at my place."

"I didn't leave anything at your pla— . . ."

Sonny handed him the cigar box.

———❦———

Sonny and Frank must have been eight years old when Frank's mom had dropped him off at their house to spend the night. It was the first time Sonny ever had a friend for a sleepover. Frank clutched a red tin cigar box to his chest. Sonny thought it must hold his toothbrush, but when they got up to Sonny's room, Frank opened the lid and let the cowboys and Indians fall onto the floor.

"Wow," Sonny said, "look at these." He picked up one of the cowboys who was so bowlegged that if it had been a real person it would have been a cripple. But the cowboy needed to be bowlegged so that his stiff legs could fit around the plastic horse. Most of the Indians had bare chests and pigtails, but one had a fancy headdress, like a peacock in full feather.

Charlie, Sonny, and Frank set up their scene. They wouldn't let Charlie play with the men on horseback. The horses were for the older boys. Sonny had the Indian chief on the small black-and-white horse. Frank had the cowboy and the large, white stallion. The Indians had bows and arrows; the cowboys had rifles. The Indians didn't stand a chance. Since Frank had brought them, he got to be the good guy; he got to be the cowboy.

The three of them were so immersed in their game that Sonny didn't even remember Grandpa Joe coming into the room. It happened so fast. There they were, flat on their stomachs carefully arranging the fields of dead plastic Indians, and Grandpa Joe came right at them. He shouted, "No!" Sonny had never heard Grandpa Joe raise his voice before. Then Grandpa Joe swung his foot and knocked over all the men, brown black, red—it didn't matter; they were scattered around the room.

"You are never to play that game again. Never. Do you hear me? If I catch you so much as thinking about playing that game, you will be grounded for the rest of your lives."

Sonny was sure he didn't mean to, but Grandpa Joe kicked Charlie when he kicked the plastic men. He didn't kick him hard, but Charlie ran out of the room crying almost as loud as Grandpa Joe was yelling. Frank and Sonny lay there on the ground, not moving at all, just in case Grandpa Joe decided to scatter them as well.

⁂

Well, I'll be damned." Frank ran his hand over the Imperial Club cigar tin. Frank opened the box. "I can't believe you kept these." He took out one of the figurines, a blue, bow-legged cowboy, and put it on the table. It looked silly standing there. "We never did finish that game did we?"

Sonny reached into the box and pulled out the Indian Chief. The red of the headdress had faded to a faint pink, but the face was unmistakably a warrior face. Sonny placed it on the coffee table nose to nose with cowboy.

"No, Frank. We never did."

## Chapter Twenty-Eight

# ANNIE

## 1904

July 30

Dear Diary,

Today was the big race. I know the boys are all disappointed. Coming here was supposed to be something greater. Greater than what? I'm not sure, but boys are like that. They need to take on the world, I suppose. It just so happened that a lot of the world hadn't made it for the games—too far to travel and all that. Most of the other competitors came from right here in the United States, but I think it's still exciting. Daddy hasn't mentioned Joe at all, none of them have, not since the big meeting. It's as if they're pretending that Joe couldn't be here for some other reason, as if he was home taking care of business or sick or something. That's their attitude. There is so much they don't say. I wonder if they have a diary. I wonder if they tell their thoughts to anyone.

I looked for Joe at the race and didn't see him. Once, I thought maybe I'd caught a glimpse, but it was probably just wishing him that made him seem to appear. I couldn't imagine him not coming to watch. I wonder if he was able to turn himself into a spirit. I've always heard that Indians and others like them can change themselves and become a spirit. Maybe he was a fish in the lake. Maybe he was a bird. Maybe he was a cloud that brought the rain that made it hard for anyone to see.

The boys didn't win because Johnson caught a crab, and Joe wouldn't have caught one. That's what everyone was thinking. Joe wouldn't have caught one.

At least Johnson didn't fall in, that would have been even more embarrassing. They were all trying too hard. They'd been in front the whole way, and my throat hurt from yelling and shouting and cheering. That's how exciting the race was. And then we saw it, the skip skip, the little splash of the water, and the boat swung to the right. I knew what that meant because one day I'd followed John and his friends to the river. I was the pesky little sister. John was always asking me if I didn't have anything else to do, saying that they were doing guy stuff.

As if messing about on the river with their boats and all was important. As if it was work. This was their work, and my work was supposed to be back in the stuffy house with no one to talk to, scrubbing the dirt off their clothes. I just told them my chores were all done, even though they weren't.

They let me carry the big oar. Joe said that was his job, but he'd let me carry it if I promised to stay out of their way. It was like carrying a small tree it was so long and hard to balance. But the boat was beautiful. They called it a scull. I don't know why. Skulls always makes me think of pirates and buried treasures.

We stood around for a while watching the boat bob up and down. Finally John asked Joe if he'd told Johnson they were having a practice.

Joe was a bit defensive, "Of course I told him. I told him twice just to be sure he heard me."

Me, John, Joe, and Bill Tucker stood around. I felt a little silly because I could have been home doing my chores after all. Standing around looking at a boat and not being in it seemed a waste of time. Then Joe pointed at me. "What about her?" he said. I couldn't believe it. He was pointing at me. I held my breath so as not to spoil anything.

Tucker laughed out loud and said, "But she's just a girl."

Then Joe smiled at me and said, "That don't matter. She's Annie."

I was Annie. He knew, even back then, Joe knew.

John picked me up under my arms and eased me into a seat right in the middle between him and Joe. "This here is your seat, Annie. You're number two. You gotta remember that. When I say 'two in' that means you row with us, and you just match my stroke okay. Try to get your paddle in when mine goes in. That's all you have to do. Got it?"

I'd watched them enough times, so I was pretty sure I could figure it out. Like Joe had said, I was Annie. I was no silly primping girl.

So we pushed off and got ourselves into a nice, easy channel without a lot of current, so we could practice on a smooth spot. Joe was behind me, and his voice was loud in my ear. "Good job," he said, because I was doing it, getting my paddle in just when I was supposed to. I was working hard at it, at matching John's stroke. And then, John started counting faster, and I'm not sure how it happened, but my paddle didn't make it high enough and the water caught the paddle. The handle just flew back at me and knocked me right out of the boat. The boys said it was called "catching a crab." That's what they told me, after they all finally stopped laughing.

That's how I knew what it was when I saw it. Anyone who knew anything about rowing knew, and the crowd let out a cry all at the same time. Johnson ducked down and tried to hold his oars steady so they wouldn't catch anymore, but it was too late. The other boats pulled out ahead. Our boys got back on course, but they couldn't catch up, there just wasn't enough time.

My arm still hurts from where Daddy held on so tight. I just wish they wouldn't blame Joe.

## Chapter Twenty-Nine

# NATHAN

*Spring*

*Dear John,*

*Hopefully you will see me long before you see this letter. She's coming with me. I can tell that she's nervous. She's never been away from her family, "I choose you. You are my man" is what she said. I am her man. And she is my woman. We are meant for each other. I cannot honestly see myself with anyone else. Not after what I've been through.*

*Moon has washed my wounds in a way that no white woman could have or would have. It's hard for me to explain. I think maybe because she has felt the pain of loss. I know I don't have to justify my choice to you, but that is what will be expected, I know. I am practicing for my mother, who will not understand, but I can't stay away forever, and that is the choice isn't it? So I make my excuses in a letter that I doubt you will ever see.*

*I think this place is getting to me. I hear the faces in the wood laughing, and everywhere I turn there's a cow patty in my path. I can't step over them, they're so thick on the ground. Some are dried out, but some of them are still fresh, still steaming with the body heat of the cow—those are the ones to watch out for, you know what I mean? No, you don't know. You got to watch out for them because when it gets so cold those steaming patties look good and warm and something to be cuddled up next to, like a warm body.*

*I'm rambling friend, just rambling. I'm bringing her home, and all the highfalutin rationalizing isn't going to make a hill of beans difference. I don't want to leave her, and that's that. I've gotten used to her body, and I've gotten used to her touch, and I don't want to take a chance on some prissy-faced white woman who probably sleeps with her clothes on. So she's coming with me, and my mother and everyone else will just have to put up with it.*

*Nathan Barton*

## Chapter Thirty

# JOE

## 1904

I ended up in a six-by-eight-foot cell. Just me, with a cot and a piss bucket. I hoped I wouldn't need to use either of them.

"I didn't attack him," I continued to protest. "He wouldn't let go of me, and he pulled me down on top of him."

"That may be the case, sir, but being as he works for the committee and all, I couldn't call him a liar." My jailer was a round man who took pride in his buttons. I could see my reflection in them, and I didn't look too good. He'd been good enough to send a message off to Redfeather, but I had no idea when he'd get it or how long I'd have to wait. I'd been given a slice of cold meatloaf and a cup of bitter coffee, so at least I wasn't going to starve.

There wasn't much to see through my small barred window. The jail backed up against some scrub bushes and the lake was behind us. I wished I could have seen them compete. "Have you heard any results, yet?"

Buttons looked at me. "You got a bet on or something?"

"Or something."

"Well, all's I know is some kid blew the fours. Team was ahead, and he just plain blew it. Glad I didn't have any money on them."

The fours. "Any names?"

"You just shut up, now. You're a prisoner."

I heard the whistle, and the long slow exhalation of steam as the train came into the station. Buttons stood up and stretched. "You wait here. I'll be right back."

There were loud voices and some shouts.

"You just wait. You just wait," I heard Buttons and some other voices, then the door to the jail burst open and there was Redfeather. He just about filled the whole doorway.

"Joe. Are you okay, Joe?"

I didn't answer him, because I was too surprised. Right behind Joe was Mulhall looking madder than a teased bull.

"Are you okay, Pinky?" he echoed Redfeather.

"I'm fine." I looked at Redfeather. "I didn't get to see the race."

"I'm sorry," he said as if it was his fault. But I knew he meant it.

Mulhall pulled out his wallet with a few bank notes prominently displayed and his identification. He slammed them both down on the desk in front of Buttons. "You can release this man right now. He's one of the Colonel's men. You had no call to arrest him."

"It's okay," I said from behind my bars. "He didn't have much choice."

Mulhall looked at me. "Where's the other guy?"

"They let him go."

"There's going to be hell to pay for this."

"It was all just a big misunderstanding, sir." Everything was one big misunderstanding.

Buttons looked at Mulhall's credentials and the cash offered. He took the money and stuffed it in his pocket. "Well, I suppose it ain't my fault if somehow the paperwork just went missing, somehow."

Mulhall put his arm around Buttons. "Not your fault at all, sir, not with all the thieves and gamblers hanging round these parts."

Redfeather jumped in. "Don't think that man will want to come all the way back out here to see what happened, do you?"

"No, of course, not," Mulhall winked at me as he lifted the keys from the hook behind Button's desk.

Buttons looked up at Redfeather, "I'm just going to step outside for a few minutes and get myself some fresh air. You all have a good day."

Mulhall unlocked the cell door, and I stepped out. The air was sweeter on the other side, easier to breathe. Redfeather gave me a big hug, and Mulhall put his arm around my shoulder.

"I didn't know you had it in you, Pinky. Never took you for more than a body."

"No, sir." I wasn't about to argue with him. I don't know if anybody would believe me that I hadn't actually done anything.

"Don't let it happen again." He put his wallet in his pocket and laughed.

"I won't, sir."

We walked outside into the dusk. The races were long over and most of the crowds had already made their way back to the fairgrounds. Mulhall, Redfeather, and I walked in silence. I didn't expect to see anyone I knew, so when I heard someone call "Joe," I assumed they were calling someone else.

"Joe, Joe Barton," I turned. It was John. He was alone, no Tucker, Smith, or Johnson. "Johnson blew it."

I didn't answer him. There was nothing to say.

"We could have used you out there, you know."

"I'm sorry, John. They've got their rules. They weren't going to bend them for me, no matter what anyone said. They weren't."

Mulhall and Redfeather stood off to one side.

John turned to them, "This is your fault, you know. This wouldn't have happened if it wasn't for you."

"Now just wait a minute, you pansy-assed . . ." Mulhall started toward John with his fists in the air. John took his own boxing stance. I stepped between them.

"John," I looked him in the eye and said, "this has nothing to do with them. It's me. It's just me."

"We could have used you, Joe." For a minute I thought he was going to punch me. "I don't get it, Joe." He lowered his fists and turned to go.

"John," I called after him.

He stopped.

"Do you remember when I had to go off to that school, the summer my dad left?" He didn't turn around, but I saw his head nod from behind.

"You told me that you thought it would be fun to be an Indian for a while. That it would be fun to be able to wear animal skins and carry a bow and arrow."

"We were kids, Joe."

"For me, it's real, John."

"Well, when you grow up let me know."

## Chapter Thirty-One

# SONNY

## 2004

Sonny leaned against the sink behind the bar and watched Grace fill it with hot water. "Dishwasher broken?"

"No, I like to hand wash the glasses. It's my little ritual." She picked up a glass and inspected it in the light. "See? No spots."

No spots. Sonny doubted anyone noticed.

She put the dry glass on a tray and leaned forward, her elbows on the counter. "So tell me, Sonny, what do you do out West?"

She reminded him a bit of Grandpa Joe, when he'd look Sonny straight in the eye and say, "So what do you want to be when you grow up?" What did he want to do? What did he want to be? Back then growing up wasn't real. Growing up was imagination and dreaming. He could be anything, a fireman, a pilot, a sailor, a king, even a prince charming. And here he was all grown up and still didn't know what he wanted to be. He knew what he did, but that wasn't what he wanted to be. He looked at the animals behind the glass. The owl stared at him.

"I got lucky," he replied. "I fell into computer programming and got in on the ground floor with some software and now . . . now I don't have to work too much."

"Ever been married?"

"If a computer counts, then sure."

The lights flickered for a second. The wind whipped outside. He heard something crack, maybe a tree branch, maybe the sky.

"Storm's coming," Grace said.

He'd almost forgotten about storms, at least the Midwest kind. He'd forgotten about lightening and thunder and sitting around the kitchen in candlelight. Was this why he'd left, too much uncertainty and chaos?

She put her hand on his.

The door blew open.

"Hey, Grace. Hey, Sonny. Set us up with a couple of beers, would you? Hell, it's blowing like crazy out there." Roy and Frank and Charlie walked in. Sonny smiled to himself.

"I was wondering when you guys would show up."

Roy looked at his watch, "Yeah. Five minutes late and she's calling search and rescue. Had to stop and get some cigarettes." He glared at Charlie.

"Hey, Sonny, I saw you got a for sale sign up at your place." Roy perched on a stool.

"It don't mean nothing." Charlie went behind the bar and poured himself a drink. "Just a lousy sign."

"You interested in buying it, Roy?"

"Me? Hell no. If I had a house, I might need to get myself a wife. Although I do hear Jenny Mitchell's just got herself divorced again."

Jenny Mitchell, everyone's high school dream girl.

Sonny looked at the clock and stood up. "I don't think anyone else is going to come in here tonight. I think it's as good a time as any to work on our training."

"Training? We can't go out on the river in this weather? You'll get us all killed, or worse."

"Yeah, you might get your sorry asses all wet. Don't worry. I'm not going to make you go outside. We can practice right here."

Grace took off her apron and walked over to the pictures that hung on the wall. "Okay, I'm game. As long as we don't have to wear those silly outfits."

Roy hiked up his pants. "Nobody said anything about outfits. I'm not wearing no outfit."

Sonny grabbed a chair and set it out in the middle of the room. "Okay, now, everyone get a chair, put 'em in a line, like a train. That's it."

They sat in their seats, looking like a bunch of overgrown school kids waiting for the teacher to tell them what to do. "Grace. You got to turn your seat around and face us."

"This ain't going to work, Sonny," Charlie said.

"Well, it's the best we got, so just shut your face and sit in your seat."

Charlie put his hand in the air, said "Whoo-Whoo," and pulled down on an imaginary rope.

Sonny looked at his team. "We're going to need some oars."

"Well, I'm not going down to that old shed in this storm." Charlie crossed his arms tight against his chest.

"I wasn't asking you to go down there." Sonny looked around the room. "Here, use these." He handed each of them a pool cue. "And don't poke anybody's eyes out."

They stared at him, waiting. Sonny took a deep breath.

"Okay, so as far as I can tell, we've got to practice working together, pulling as one, getting the paddles in the water at the same time, pulling together and releasing together, no one dragging and braking."

Roy pushed the back of Frank's seat. "Guess that means we're going to have to let Frankie boy here off the boat. Hell, that gut of his is practically an anchor."

"Look who's talking about guts."

"Boys, boys, be quiet and listen to Sonny," Grace admonished and clapped her hands.

Boys, they were a long way from boys.

"Okay, so I think we need to distribute this weight a bit more evenly. Roy, you sit in the middle. Frank, you go right behind him. Grace, you're good where you are in the coxswain's seat. You'll be calling the strokes. Charlie, I want you up front, and I'll take the stern."

"Listen to him with the fancy boat words." Charlie got up and walked over to the bar. Roy followed him.

"Charlie, Roy, stop messing around. Get over here. Get back in your seats."

"The sooner we do this, the sooner he'll let us get back to the bar." Frank got up and took Charlie by the shoulders and sat him down.

Roy followed.

Grace took her place.

They were quiet, now what? "Okay, guys. Frank and I will put our cues out to the right . . ."

"Starboard," Grace piped in.

"Starboard, schmarboard." Roy waved is cue in the air.

"Frank and I have our cues to the starboard. Roy and Charlie are to the left," Sonny looked at Grace and said, "that would be port."

She smiled and nodded her head. She was so adorable.

"Okay, grab your cues like this." Sonny put his two hands on the handle of the cue stick as if it were a paddle. "Now, let's just push them back and forth, holding them out to the side, like this."

"This ain't like rowing. I only got one paddle, feels odd," Roy shook his head. "It doesn't feel right."

"You'll get used to it, just keep your hands together and keep it low. Don't forget, they're going to be locked into place with oarlocks. It's not a canoe. Okay, Grace. You start counting."

"What am I supposed to count."

"One-two out, three-four in, one-two out, three-four in. Something like that."

"Now, Frank, you keep your eye on Charlie and try to match his stroke. I'll match Roy. Let's just work on staying even."

"We need some music, Sonny. You guys have no rhythm."

"Just sing for us, Grace. Sing anything."

Grace looked at him and then smiled, "Row, row, row your boat . . ."

Outside the wind whistled. Sonny imagined the feel of it on his face. The chair creaked as he leaned forward and back. Grace set the pace. "Merrily, merrily, merrily, merrily . . ." Her voice faded away, and he felt his body take over.

"Good job, guys. Keep it up. We're doing it. Almost there."

"Almost where, you idiot. We're on chairs," Charlie laughed.

Sonny closed his eyes, push pull, in out. He could feel the oar as it hit the water, hear the slight splash. "Just keep singing, Grace, a few more strokes, just a few more, keep it going."

"Life is but a dream . . ."

Creak. Crack. "Ow."

The river faded and Sonny opened his eyes. The back of Roy's chair was on the floor, and Roy's head was in Frank's lap. The old stuffed badger seemed to be laughing at them. "Get him off of me." Frank pushed Roy on to the floor.

The front door swung open. The Evans twins stood in the doorway. "What the hell is going on in here?"

Roy rubbed the back of his head. "Grace, I need another beer, and Sonny's buying."

## Chapter Thirty-Two

# ANNIE

## 1904

July 31

Dear Diary,

I will never understand boys. We were all in the hotel lobby, me, John, Tucker, Johnson, and Smith. Daddy had already gone to his room, and I can't help but worry about him because he's looking so tired these days. He seems sad when he looks at me and tells me that he just wants me to be happy. I think he's talking about Joe.

Anyway, he went to bed and the rest of us stayed in the lobby reliving the race. Poor Johnson, I don't think he wanted to relive it. Everyone was trying hard to be nice to him, but he knew everyone was thinking about him catching a crab in the big race. Well, it shouldn't have happened, and everyone knew it.

It almost felt like we were at a funeral, sitting around not knowing what to say about the dead person, not knowing how to make the live ones feel any better. If we'd still been kids I might have run up to Johnson and given him a tag-your-it hit, and then we'd all go off and play hide-and-seek until no one remembered that anything was wrong. But then again, we weren't kids anymore, and something had gone wrong.

I sat in my corner under the light working on my quilt when a few of the guys from the winning team came in. Smith muttered under his breath something like, "Oh no, look who's here. It's McKay and his crew." McKay was obviously the leader. He reminded me of John. I tried to keep my head down, so as not to seem like I noticed them, but it was hard not to look. There were four of them, and they all wore their medals around their necks. I wanted to go see one of the medals up close, but I didn't dare.

"So look who's here. It's the loooosers. Shouldn't you loooosers be in bed by now?" McKay wasn't being a good winner.

My brother John is never one to let a remark like that pass by, so he stood up and met McKay head on. They looked like a couple of billy goats about to lock horns.

"You know we can beat you any day. If it hadn't been for the committee taking out our best man, we would have left you in our wake. You won on a technicality, McKay, so don't go getting all puffed up about it."

John shouldn't have said that. Even I could have told him that was not a good thing to say.

"We won fair and square." McKay poked his finger at John, which was not a good idea because John can't stand it when people point their fingers at him. Besides McKay was right, they had won fair and square. After all Johnson had gone and caught that stupid crab. For a minute, I thought McKay and John were going to start a fight. They were making fists and circling each other. They were practically bumping into the furniture.

"You'd have been drinking spray from our wake if Joe had been able to row." John pointed back at McKay.

"Oh, yeah?"

"Yeah."

They were being silly boys and should just have a rematch I thought, but somehow the thoughts were more than thoughts. I mean, they came out in words. Everyone got quiet, and John and McKay stopped and stared at me. In fact, everyone was staring at me. I felt a bit uncomfortable, but I liked it, too. Right about then a man dressed like a kind of policeman walked into the room. He stopped inside the door and looked at the boys. "Is everything okay in here?" he asked. John put his arm around McKay's shoulder. "Everything's just fine, just fine. We're just reliving the race." The man nodded and walked off. Then John lowered his voice and said to McKay, "How about it, McKay? How about a rematch?"

McKay looked at John as if he were a bit crazy. "Why would we want to do that? We already won the medal? We're not giving that up."

"It's not about the medal," John said to him. "It's about who's the best. Isn't that what these games are all about? Who's really the best, without the committee and its arbitrary rules." He paused for a moment. Even my breath felt loud, the silence was so thick. "I'd like to know, wouldn't you?" When I looked around the room, everyone in there was nodding in agreement, even McKay. He held up the medal, "We're not giving these up, you know."

"Fair enough. So what do you say?" John stuck out his hand.

"I say we'll still whup you good, that's what I say." McKay took John's hand.

"Let me buy you a drink as a pre-consolation prize." They were all headed out to the men's smoking lounge when John looked back and saw me in my chair. He came over and gave me a hug. It had been a long time since he hugged me like that. "Thank you, Annie. That was brilliant" is what he said to me. He thinks I'm brilliant. It's good to see John smile.

# Chapter Thirty-Three

# JOE

# 1904

I sat on a log and looked at the empty battlefield. I wondered what it would become when the fair was over. I knew that many of the buildings were being taken over by the university, but this was just a big piece of dirt. Maybe it would become a sports field, or maybe a farm, or maybe just some empty lot. I picked a piece of grass that grew nearby and put it my mouth. Grass chewing was my big vice. I'd bite on the crunchy tip so I could get the juice from the root to squirt into my mouth. I was a bit surprised that I could still find myself a nice juicy piece after so many horses, so many feet, so many battles had worn it all away. I wondered if Dr. Greer ever chewed on grass, or the skinny man with the spectacles who wouldn't look anyone in the eye, or Annie? But then again, I didn't want to think about Annie.

I heard someone walk up behind me. It was Greer. I could recognize his walk just by the sound, the way he shuffled, not quite clearing the ground with his right foot, dragging it a bit. John always complained about his cheap shoes, how the damn toes wore out so easily. He'd blame it on the leather, or the dog. Damn dog must be chewing on it again, he'd say. Pick up your feet I wanted to shout at him, but you didn't shout at John Greer. You didn't even suggest. He was Dr. Greer's son. He would be an important man someday. Besides, he was Annie's brother and my best friend.

"Hey, Joe, I've been looking for you."

"Really?"

"I'm sorry I was so hard on you about not rowing and all."

"Me too."

He stood and looked around the field. "Looks empty, doesn't it."

I nodded.

John kicked at the dirt. It almost felt as if he were kicking me, and I wanted to hit him. I wanted to knock him down and cover his crisp whites in dust. Battles seemed to come more easily for me those days. Then I began to laugh. It started out small, almost a hiccup, but it ended up a full on chuckle, and it got bigger and harder and deeper until it was a full-on belly laugh. I made the mistake of looking over at Greer, and then he started. The two of us, we sat on that log and we couldn't stop. Everything was hilarious, Johnson catching a crab, me in a jail cell. The laugh seemed to come out of the ground up through us both.

It took a few minutes for the laugh to run its course, and then we were gasping for air as if we'd just rowed the fastest race of our lives.

Greer got himself settled down first. He put his arm around my shoulder. "Look, Joe. I'm sorry. We're all sorry."

"Well, it's over and done."

"Not really. That's why I came here."

"What's that supposed to mean?"

I looked down and noticed an ant climbing up my shoe. If I walked away would it ever find its way back home? How far would it go before it just gave up.

"We all want to do it again. Have our own race. It was Annie's idea. And the other teams are all willing, including the Canadians and the winning team. Nobody thinks it really counted for much because you weren't in it. You can't call yourself champions if you didn't race against the best."

"You mean, you're going to row another race just so I can be in it?" I put my hand in my pocket and felt the smooth carving of my pipe.

Greer nodded.

"It seems like an awful lot of effort."

"Not really. The boats are all still on the lake. It will be no trouble at all." He grinned at me. "We gotta go. We're supposed to meet there as soon as the moon starts to come up. It's full tonight."

"We're doing this at night?"

"We didn't want anyone trying to stop us, so no officials, no fuss. This is just for us, for all the guys. This is for real."

I flexed my arm; the rowing muscles felt stiff. "I'm out of practice you know."

He patted me on the back. "You'll do just fine, Joe. You're the best."

I took a deep breath. "Okay, count me in."

"Well, we better. That's the whole point."

❧

By the time we got to the lake, all the boats were lined up. The moon was already high, and its light reflected off the lake.

Greer, Tucker, and Smith wore their river clothes, not the fancy white ones we'd gotten for the Olympic Games, but our practice uniforms, the ones that were a muddy river brown and green.

Smith handed me a shirt. "Here, we brought one for you. We thought maybe you'd forget to bring your own."

I had forgotten. Johnson stood off to one side. The poor guy looked miserable. I went over to him. "It could have happened to anyone, you know."

He tried to smile, but it came out lopsided. "No, it couldn't, but you know, Joe, I'm almost glad it happened."

I looked at the teams all lined up by the dock. I patted Johnson on the back. "Thanks."

Greer climbed up on a tree stump and looked down at everyone milling around. It was an impressive crowd. He pulled out his megaphone.

"Okay, teams, here are the rules. If you look over there, you'll see we have lanterns hanging on all the finish buoys. First one to cross the line wins." We couldn't see the lanterns from the dock because of the bend in the lake. "Just make sure you stop before you hit the other side." We all laughed. "Everyone to your boats."

The lake had a reddish-silver cast in the moonlight. It was still warm, my favorite kind of summer night, balmy, like a balm you rub on your skin to take away the pain. In a few months, the lake would freeze over and people would be ice skating on its crusty surface, but that night, it was perfect.

"You call it, Joe," said Greer.

"Thanks, I'd be honored."

I loved to call the strokes. It was my song. It was my na ne noo song, my lullaby. It was the song that beat in my body.

We all got in the boat, almost forty feet of narrow rocking motion, me, Tucker, Greer, and Smith. We were used to its roll and knew how to shift our weight so that it barely moved, not like the first time I got in one of the boats and tipped right over.

We sat there for a moment. We needed all four of us to be one. If any of us were just a tiny hair's breath off in rhythm, if one of us dug the paddle in too far, or struck the water a moment too late, we would cancel each other's movement, and we would go in circles. That was always a good one to see— some poor souls going around and around in circles, getting sucked into their own personal man-made whirlpool.

This moment was what it was all about. This is why we had all come here. It was our moment of prayer, our church, the time for our own private conversation with God.

While we rowed out to the starting position, no one spoke a word. We didn't have to. Each of us was hunched forward, our arms cocked, our legs pulled in. We were ready for the push and the pull. GO! We shot forward, slicing through the water like a knife. The race wouldn't last long. That's what made it all so precious. For those few minutes, everything had to work as one.

Stroke, stroke, stroke, stroke. We turned the bend. I glanced over my shoulder and saw the lanterns bobbing up and down. We rowed toward the lights. Each boat had its own rhythm, its own stroke, its own heartbeat. I heard a chorus of voices and realized that some of the tribes were there. Redfeather must have called them. They were lined up along the racecourse in their canoes. Canoes and rafts and rowboats. I wondered where they'd all come from, all these boats, all these people. We were so far from everything, out in Lewis and Clark country, the gateway to the West. There were no rules out here. No one could be left out, and no one could be left behind.

Stroke, stroke. The oars barely splashed as they sliced into the water. Not a drop of wasted motion. We were almost there. I could sense the air changing, smell the grass on the other shore, hear the wind in the leaves, feel the shadows of the trees. Whichever boat caught the rope was the winner. It was that simple. You couldn't throw out your chest like a runner at the last minute. You couldn't make your boat catch that prize except by being faster. There were no tricks.

I couldn't think about the end. I couldn't think about the rope. This was God, one mind, one spirit, one body. But I didn't think those thoughts then, not during that moment. I wasn't thinking about anything. I was Greer, I was Tucker, I was Smith, and I was the boat. One pull, one push, one mind. I felt the tug as the bow of the boat hit the rope. There was the slightest pull and then release. We'd done it. We'd won.

Tucker and Greer let out a whoop of victory. I looked up and saw all the people on the shore. The crowd was not as big as it had been just days before, but it was our crowd, our people, my people, Larson, Redfeather, even Annie and Dr. Greer. And off to one side waving the American flag was Aday.

## Chapter Thirty-Four

# SONNY

## 2004

Charlie stood outside the house. Sonny could see him through the curtains. He just stood there, not moving.

Sonny wondered where Charlie was sleeping these days. He hadn't spent a night in the house since their father had died. Maybe he slept in a hole by the river, or maybe he didn't sleep. Maybe he just rolled from one party to the next. If they weren't brothers, Sonny wouldn't care. If they weren't brothers, he probably wouldn't even talk to Charlie. Maybe he'd give him a dollar as one stranger to another, as one man to a beggar. Why couldn't he just forget that they had shared a room and climbed trees together? Charlie wasn't that person anymore. This Charlie was someone else, and Sonny couldn't remember when he changed.

Sonny opened the door. "Are you coming in?"

"Not sure," said Charlie. He reached into his pocket and pulled out a pack of cigarettes. He carefully tapped the bottom of the pack and let one slide out. He put it in his mouth. There was a deliberation and theatre about his actions. Sonny found it amusing. Charlie worked hard at being the bad boy.

"Well, when you finish your smoke, come on in."

Sonny walked back into the living room, but he left the front door open. Then he sat on the red chair. He hadn't decided what to do with the chair. It was hard to imagine not ever being able to sit in it again, but shipping it back to California seemed silly. Grace had taken all the books. He was left with sorting through all the rest of his parents' lives.

A hint of smoke wafted in through the window. Charlie knew how much Sonny hated cigarettes.

"Hey, Charlie, get in here. We need to decide what to do with all this stuff."

He heard Charlie shuffle into the house. At least he'd put his cigarette out before he came in.

"Look at this."

"What is it?"

Sonny handed Charlie a leather pouch embroidered with Indian beadwork.

"I found this in Grandpa Joe's trunk out in the barn."

Charlie pulled the pouch open and let out a low whistle. "Cool." Then he turned the pouch upside down. Dozens of glass marbles rolled across the floor.

"Charlie, you idiot, look at this mess."

"Don't call me an idiot, Sonny."

Sonny picked up one of the glass balls and held it up. An amber-and-brown cat's eye seemed to stare at him. "I wonder where he got these? I've never seen a marble like this before."

"Who knows where anything in this mausoleum comes from. It's all about the great Grandpa Joe. All hail the old man. All hail the hero." Charlie saluted, then sat down on the floor in front of the fireplace. "Let's see if you still got the touch."

"Okay." Sonny got down on the floor. His knees hurt. When did his knees start to hurt?

He and Charlie had spent a lot of time in that spot in front of the fireplace when they were kids—in the winter when the snow was knee deep and they couldn't get outside; or when the rain pounded so hard it felt like the mighty river itself was in their driveway, as if they were underwater creatures; or in the summer when the humidity was unbearably high. It had been a long time since he'd sat on the ground.

"I wanted to show you something else I found. It was in a drawer with some old photos. It's a chart of the river, from the 1950s." Sonny reached over to the table where he'd laid the chart and spread it on the floor. "It's amazing. Look here. Grandpa Joe seems to have written all over this thing."

Charlie leaned forward and looked at the map, "Races, fishing spots, who knows what else he'd be marking. They probably don't exist anymore. The river got 'em like it gets everything."

He sat up and took a pack of cigarettes out of his pocket.

"Not in the house, Charlie, please."

Charlie put the pack away. "I was thinking, Sonny. We don't have to sell. I could live in the barn in that old room, rent out the house. It's not a bad place. Warm in the winter, cool in the summer."

"Way too much upkeep, Charlie. I can't afford it, not from a distance."

"Come off it big brother. You can afford any goddamn thing you want."

Charlie swept the marbles into a pile in front of him, "You know, Sonny, you could have loved our dad just a little bit more."

"What's that supposed to mean?"

"Look at this place. Look at everything around us. Look at the damn club, for Christ's sake. Frozen in time, like all those animals. Gives me the creeps. We couldn't go out on Sundays until you called. Dad and me, we'd sit here in this room waiting for the phone to ring. But not in that chair, oh no, no one could sit in that goddamn chair that might as well have had a plaque that read 'Grandpa Joe Barton, may he rest in peace.'" He stood up. "We couldn't even sit in that stupid, old, moth-eaten chair."

Sonny flicked the brown cat's eye marble at the pile. "You can't go on like this, Charlie, you know that."

Charlie kicked the pile of marbles left on the floor. "I'm sorry, Sonny, but I really don't want to play with you." He pulled a cigarette out of his breast pocket and lit it. Then he picked the river chart off the floor, put it under his arm, and left.

One less thing to get rid of, thought Sonny. The cat's eye marble had rolled across the room and stopped against the box of old pictures. There were so many pictures. He hadn't recognized most of them: pictures of a boy with chocolate all over his face, pictures of a boy on a tricycle. At first he hadn't been sure if it was him or Charlie, until he realized that there were no pictures of Charlie by himself. Even when Charlie was a baby, the pictures were always of Sonny and Charlie: Sonny holding Charlie, Sonny feeding Charlie, Sonny changing Charlie's diaper. And there were lots of pictures of Grandpa Joe and Sonny: Grandpa Joe with Sonny in the boat, Grandpa Joe with Sonny at the tree fort, Grandpa Joe with Sonny at the fair. There was only one picture of his parents, their wedding photo. His mother and father were all stiff and formal, neither of them smiled for the camera. And then there was a picture of Grandpa Joe standing next to a little black man. Both of them waved American flags.

❧

The sweat from Sonny's palms made the steering wheel slick. He was early. He knew he was early. Grace was probably still getting dressed. It hardly took any time to get from his house to her apartment, but he didn't want to sit by himself any longer than he had to. When he was a kid, going into town had always been a big event. He'd have to wash his face, comb his hair, and put on his good shoes—the stiff, black leather ones that he hardly ever wore, so that by the time he did put them on to go someplace they were so tight and uncomfortable that he could barely walk. He liked those trips, though. They usually meant a trip to the soda fountain and a real banana split.

He looked at his watch. It was still early, and he didn't want to seem too anxious. "Are you asking me out on a date, Sonny Barton?" she'd said. Then she smiled and wrote her address on a club napkin. "See you at seven. 620 Elm Street." He doubted there were many elms anymore. Dutch elm disease had taken its toll.

⚜

He pulled up in front of Grace's house. She lived in one of the Grand Old Houses. A red brick Victorian, the windows and eaves framed with ornate wood. "Fancy curlicues" was what his Grandpa Joe had called them. Sonny liked the architectural detail and wished they still designed houses like that, but no one did because it cost too much. Unfortunately, the Grand Old House had been converted into apartments. Five mailboxes were attached to the outside of the door.

Sonny got out of the car. He checked his reflection in the window, licked the palm of his hand, and slicked back his hair, even though it seemed silly. Grace had seen him knee deep in Mississippi mud. He looked up at the house. A little girl sat playing jacks on the ground. He was surprised kids still played that game. He stood and watched as she bounced the ball and picked up a jack. Bounced it again and got two.

"Hi," she said without taking her eye off the ball.

"Hi." He looked around and didn't see a parent. Apparently no one had told her not to talk to strangers. "Are you supposed to be out here all by yourself?"

"Are you?" she asked.

Smart aleck kid, he thought and stepped around her. The lawn was overrun by crab grass. The girl stood up and skipped ahead of him. He wasn't used to kids, had never been around them much. None of his friends back in California were married or had kids. Odd, he hadn't noticed that before.

She opened the front door and yelled out, "He's here. He's here."

How did she know anyone was waiting for him?

"Sonny, is that you? Come up! Emily will show you."

"Emily?"

The little girl smiled at him. She was missing some teeth, but he recognized the smile. It was Grace's smile. Why hadn't anyone told him? But why should they? Probably everybody else knew. There was nothing to tell, nothing to talk about. Absolutely nothing. Grace had an Emily. Grace had a child.

"Right this way." Emily held out her hand and pulled him behind her, as if he were the child. Her grip was stronger than he expected.

He looked up. There was something very familiar about this house. This was the house that used to have the poker room up at the top. It had been a private retreat for the men in the town. No women were allowed up there, or so the rumor went. Grandpa Joe had brought him here a long time ago. He couldn't even remember how old he had been, just that he and Grandpa Joe were going someplace special, someplace just for men.

⁂

Grandpa Joe knocked on the door. A black housemaid answered. She didn't say anything to them. She simply took their hats and hung them on the hat stand that stood in the entryway.

"Wipe your feet, boy," Grandpa Joe said.

Sonny did as he was told. The entrance hall felt crowded. Pictures and mirrors covered every inch of wall space. A grandfather clock stood at the end of the hallway. Directly in front of them was a steep stairway. Grandpa Joe started up the stairs. Sonny stood at the bottom. "Come on, Sonny, we're going up."

The clock chimed the quarter hour. Its deep tone echoed in the small space. Sonny looked up. He'd never seen such a tall stairway before. Their house was all on one level. He followed his grandfather. They continued past the first landing. He paused and looked down a long hallway. All the doors were closed. He heard women's voices coming from behind one of them, but no one came out to see who had arrived. The house smelled sweet.

The stairway narrowed as they climbed. Sonny turned around and looked down. It seemed they were going to climb as high up as the clouds, and then the stairs ended. Grandpa Joe stopped in front of a door at the very top. He knocked twice, paused, and then knocked three times. It was a secret knock.

The door opened and they walked in. The room was thick with cigar smoke and sweat. An octagonal table filled the whole room. Five men sat around the table, each one with a pile of neatly stacked poker chips.

"Who's this?" asked a man who looked like a dried-up turtle. "Don't tell me that's Sonny? Hell, he's getting to be a quite a young man."

"Why, he looks just like you, Joe," said another man who had a thick white beard.

"No, he doesn't look a bit like me. I think he looks just like Annie's brother, John." Then, Grandpa Joe turned to Sonny. "I'm talking about your Great Uncle, Sonny boy. Joustin' John was what we called him back in the day, 'cause he knocked out the competition with his oars."

"You were the only one who could beat him," said Turtleneck as he shuffled the cards.

"I sure do miss him," said Grandpa Joe. He patted the table in front of him. "Okay, Smithy, deal us in."

———※———

Emily opened the door and ran into the room. Sonny knew it was the same room he'd been to with his grandfather, the Poker Room. The smell of cigar smoke was gone, and there were no old men or piles of poker chips. The octagonal room with the table was now a living room. A hall led to a galley kitchen, and there was another door that probably went to a bedroom, but it was closed. The whole place was so small that there was hardly enough room to walk without bumping into a piece of furniture or a wall.

Grace held out her hand and said, "Welcome." Then she motioned for Emily to come to her. She put her hands on Emily's shoulders. "I see you met my daughter, Emily."

"You know, Grace, I had no idea you had a daughter." Of all the people he'd met she seemed the least likely to have a child. Maybe it was because of the tattoo. Maybe he thought women with tattoos didn't have children. Maybe it was because Grace always talked like she had no roots, and children were roots, at least that's what he'd always thought.

"Oh, didn't you?" She made a sweeping gesture with her hand. "Make yourself at home. I'm going to take Emily downstairs. I'm lucky, my landlady, Mrs. Pritchard, watches Emily whenever I work or go out."

"I want to go with you," Emily said, grabbing Sonny's hand.

"No, honey, Sonny and I are going to go out now, and you can't come with us. Be a good girl."

Emily squeezed his hand and then her grip loosened. He wasn't sure what he would have done if she'd resisted. He waved as she walked out the door and down to the landlady's place. Grace smiled and said, "I'll be right back."

⁂

He walked over to the one of the windows. Grace touched him on the shoulder. She smelled like mint. "It feels like you're on top of the world here." They were high enough, so they could see the sunset over the houses and trees. There were no mountains to block the horizon here. He felt as if he were in the pilothouse of a riverboat.

"Sometimes I think I'd like to open my window and just walk out. Walk from treetop to treetop and never bother to come down. It's good up here. Somehow the air is different."

"I guess it's because you can see where you're going."

Grace turned away from the window and walked toward the door. "And you can see where you've been." She turned off the light. Sonny stood for a moment, then he turned and followed her out the door.

# Chapter Thirty-Five

# ANNIE

# 1904

August 11

Dear Diary,

Daddy and I spent our last day on the Pike. We went and saw Creation today and Hereafter and Deep Sea Divers. The divers looked like sea monsters with their big suits and helmets and hoses coming out of their bodies. They needed the hoses so they could breathe under water. I wished I could get in one of those suits and see what it felt like. Whenever I go swimming, I always wish I could stay longer under the water, maybe even live there like a mermaid. I wonder if there are mermaids in the river? It's so quiet down there, quieter than any place else I know. We got to see the divers through a big window, and they swam around and floated and found treasures. I liked it even better than Heaven. I could see the ropes pulling the angels, so I knew they weren't really flying, but the divers, they were flying under the sea. And I got to see Jim Key, the famous spelling horse that can do his arithmetic better than a lot of folks I know. And we saw the place where the baby Jesus was born, not really because it's far away, but they made a copy of it. Not that I wasn't thinking about Joe the whole time.

It's hard to believe that we're leaving soon. I wanted to go watch Joe in his tug of war, so he could know that I was rooting for him, but Daddy wouldn't let me. When I asked if we could go, he got all stiff and formal and distant and said that this native business was all a lot of nonsense, and he didn't want to make it seem important by going to watch them in those heathen games. I wonder if he knows how much I care about Joe? I reminded him of Kaskaskia. He laughed at me, pinched my cheek, and called me a silly girl. But these stories must come from somewhere. Who could make up something like that? After all, they say Kaskaskia was destroyed by a father, just like my daddy. All those people cursed, the town eaten up by the river, the dead bodies lifted from their graves, and the living just drifting away. I believe it. I think it must have been real, because feelings are so powerful—Daddy's disappointment, my sadness, and Joe's pain. When it gets big, it has to go somewhere. I'm afraid it could happen to us, and it scares me because I'd hate to be responsible.

# Chapter Thirty-Six

# JOE

# 1904

Aday and I sat in the stands waiting for our events, me the tug of war, and him the spear toss. I'd managed to nab us a couple of seats on the bleachers that were still in the shade. It was too damn hot out there in the sun. A tall pole was set up in the middle of the field for the pole-climbing competition. It was hard to imagine that there were trees like that, straight up, no branches, nothing to hold onto, no place for a bird to build its nest, or for a boy to build a tree house. But they managed to climb it, the men in loincloths. A few fairgoers walked by on their way to someplace else.

Aday stood up and stretched. "I run. That is what I do. But they want to see me throw the spear, so I will throw. I will put on a show for them." Aday leaned closer to me and whispered, "But, tell me this, Joseph Barton, why do your women carry those weapons around? I see them everywhere." I looked at two women who strolled by arm in arm, each one dressed in starched white muslin.

I laughed. "You're joking, aren't you? Those aren't weapons, Aday. They're called parasols."

"But why do they carry them if they're not weapons?"

"To protect them from the sun."

"That is the problem with this modern civilization of yours. The Sun does not attack. The Sun is our friend. It feeds us and warms us. Those silly women cannot do anything when they hold those things. Their hands are useless."

Aday jumped up and tossed his spear in the air, then he caught it, and spun it as if dancing with it. He was already putting on his show. Way off in the distance a band played. I could barely hear it. The moist thickness of the air carried the sound not to our ears but to our bodies.

Aday moved to the sounds, and through his movement the music became louder until I felt that I was watching an ancient dance, not just the playful movement of a man from the other side of the world who was putting on a show.

A Filipino group walked by. "Igorot" was the official name. It sounded like ingot, like gold. They were certainly gold for the exhibition. I couldn't believe the crowds that flocked to get a look at these odd-looking primitives. The Igorots ate dog meat in a ceremony that was supposed to help them become better headhunters. Sometimes they offered the meat to male spectators. I couldn't imagine eating a dog or cutting off someone's hands for a trophy. Knowing they did these things made them seem somehow less than human.

A young boy ran through the crowds of people shouting, "Tug of war in fifteen minutes."

"That's me." I stood up. "I better go."

Aday grinned. "I wish I could see this. All you savages pulling and tugging at each other. Too bad real wars aren't fought that way, my friend." Aday threw the spear high into the air.

"If you catch a bird with that, I'll eat it raw."

"Be careful what you say, my friend. Birds come in many shapes and sizes."

I walked across the field. It was hot and humid. I wished I could jump in the river and cool off.

A little boy in a white sailor suit pointed at me as I walked by. Don't stare," I heard his mother's say.

Did she think I ate dogs, too?

Redfeather and Crooked Nose stood around the large mud pit that had been built for the event.

"Looks nice," Redfeather laughed.

"How deep is it?" I asked.

"Who cares," said Crooked Nose. "We're not getting in it."

A crowd gathered in the stands.

⁂

Mulhall was in charge of organizing the tribes for the tug of war. He held a whistle in his mouth like a cigar, and when he spoke it created a lisp to his already thick speech. He drew circles on the ground with a stick, as if he were choreographing a battle reenactment, but there wasn't much strategy in a tug of war.

"Four to a team. First up, Sioux against Apache, and if you win, you get a nice American flag to take home." An American flag just like the ones that were sold everywhere. I wished it was a stuffed doll or something, at least I could give that to Annie.

"Where should I go?"

Mulhall looked at me. "That's a silly question, Pinky, you go with your tribe."

"I don't have a tribe."

The Sioux, the Arapaho, the Apache, the Cheyenne, they were all present and accounted for. I was supposed to be a floater. There wasn't much to float on around there. He stared at me so long I thought maybe he'd forgotten I was there, then said, "You can watch with me." He turned back to the others, "One more thing," he said, pointing at the stands, "they're looking for a good show, so when you're at the pit remember to yell a lot. Give 'em your best war cries. Now go!" Redfeather and the other Sioux ran off yelping and whooping.

"Save it for the event," Mulhall called after them, but no one heard.

A teenage boy came out on the field. He carried a green armchair upside down so that it practically covered his head.

"Put it over there," Mulhall shouted at him and pointed at a tree. He turned back to me. "The old man is coming to watch." I didn't need to ask. The old man was Geronimo.

Mulhall took a cigar out of his pocket and lit it. "Everybody wants a piece of the old man. The committee thought that if he was here it would bring the crowds in."

Geronimo moved slowly, using a walking stick as he made his way across the field to his spot under the tree. At least he was in the shade.

"Why isn't he dressed up in his chief outfit?" I asked.

"They won't let him." Mulhall took a bandana out of his pocket and wiped the sweat off his face.

"Who won't let him?"

"I guess all those same old white men who didn't let you row your boat."

Geronimo looked ordinary sitting in his chair under the tree in his brown felt hat and black suit jacket. He looked like any tired old man.

Mulhall limped when he walked. We hadn't talked about the stabbing, but I could tell he still hurt. "The old man goes a little crazy when they dress him up like an Indian or a warrior. Acts like a madman. I haven't seen it, but that's what I heard."

Mulhall put his arm around my shoulder. "My money's on the Sioux, Pinky. What about you?"

I wasn't sure I'd want to bet against the Apache. They had that determined look. An age-old rivalry. "I don't gamble, sir."

Redfeather and the other Sioux were dressed in their finest tribal costumes that looked as if they'd been made special for the event, the headdresses had feathers running down their backs, but I could tell something was wrong. Redfeather and the one they called Gambling Man were having an argument. The Apache stood off to one side, and if I didn't know any better I'd have sworn they were laughing.

"What the hell . . ." Mulhall stood up. "Pinky you wait here." He hobbled down to the field. Gambling man pushed Redfeather. Redfeather was about to jump all over him. Mulhall blew his whistle and got between them. Seemed like he was just in time, or we would have ended up with a boxing match instead of a tug of war. It probably wouldn't have mattered to the crowd. Gambling Man said something to Redfeather in Sioux, then he turned and stormed off the field. Mulhall looked in my direction and motioned for me to come down.

Redfeather ran to meet me. "We need you, Joe."

"What happened?"

"Gambling Man didn't want to get his clothes dirty."

I looked off in the direction that Gambling Man had gone. I wondered if maybe he'd put a little too much money down on the outcome.

"Anyone got some war feathers for Joe?"

"Here." Redfeather reached up and pulled some feathers out of his headdress and gave them to me. "Use these."

I stuck them behind my ear. I wasn't sure they'd stay on for long, but it didn't matter. I was now an official Sioux, one of Redfeather's brothers.

Redfeather patted me on the back. "We're going to put you in the middle. Just dig in your heels and hold on. Whatever you do, don't let go of the rope."

The rope was coarser than I had expected. It already hurt my hands, and no one was pulling yet. The stands filled up, and people started cheering. I wasn't sure who or what they were cheering for. They probably just wanted something to happen. It was hot, and they'd been promised a show.

"Maybe we should give them a rain dance," someone joked.

"Ready," Mulhall was on the sidelines standing next to the official judge, "set, now."

"Pull, pull, pull, pull," someone yelled. We were a team. The rope cut into my hands. I couldn't grip it hard enough because it cut and slipped at the same time. It burned, like whiskey. Maybe I should have had some whiskey. Why would anyone think this was fun? I felt myself being pulled forward, felt my weight shift, and I dug my heels in more.

"Hang on, Joe"

"My hands are slipping."

"Can't let em slip, just hold on."

"They're sweating."

"Hold on, pull, hold, pull, hold,"

Redfeather was right behind me. Hold, hold, pull, hold. Redfeather mumbled under his breath. I could feel the shift of weight. We were all leaning, tipping. I felt the slight change in momentum. Felt the infinitesimal give.

"Step, take a step, dig it in, don't fall."

I shifted my weight so I didn't fall backward against Redfeather.

I heard the shouting all around me as a background roar.

"Don't fall."

I didn't want to fall. I wanted the other team to fall. I felt the veins in my arms pulse against my skin.

My sweat soaked into the rope.

"Step back."

We each took a step back.

"One more."

We moved as one. Step, pull, step, pull. The rope went slack, and down we went, like a row of dominos. But the Apache had gone down first, down into the mud.

We all got up, us Sioux, yelping and hollering, while the muddy Apache didn't say a word. Redfeather slapped me on the back. He had a big old grin on his face. "You make a damn good Sioux, Pinky." We walked toward the shade to wait for our next round against the winners of the second pull. A photographer called to me as I walked by, "Hey, you, the old man wants you."

"He wants me?" I figured they had mistaken me for someone else. "Yeah, you. He wants you."

Geronimo smiled and motioned me toward him. Redfeather and the others walked ahead.

"Here, hold this while I have my picture taken." Geronimo handed me his umbrella. The face of a bear and the head of an eagle were carved into the handle. It reminded me of the carving my father used to do.

I stood off to one side as Geronimo posed with a bow and a couple of arrows nestled in the crook of his left arm. He was smaller than I had imagined him, and his face was deeply lined. He stared out into the distance, not at the camera, not at the person behind the camera, not even at me, but out past the fake battlefields beyond the top of the Ferris wheel, past the Mississippi.

The man behind the camera gestured to me. "Come over here."

I walked closer. A crowd gathered around us. People always surrounded the old Indian. It's okay to crowd around a dying lion, when you know it can't hurt you any more.

"Can you open that umbrella and hold it over my shoulder. There's some glare coming off my lens." The photographer placed me where he wanted me. I looked at Geronimo. He nodded his head. At least I thought he nodded his head because he hadn't really moved. He still stared off into the distance, but somehow I knew he had said it was okay. I opened the umbrella and held it over the photographer and camera.

"We have to wait for a few minutes," the photographer said. He stood up and stretched, then he looked at me for the first time.

"Hey, what kind of get up is that? Why are you dressed up in that silly outfit?" He pointed at my buckskin pants with fringe along the seams, leather moccasins, leather vest, paint on my chest and face.

I didn't answer. My arm ached, holding the umbrella. "How much longer?"

"Just stay there." He put his head back under the black cloth. A disembodied voice spoke to me as if the camera itself could talk, "Aren't you a bit white to be dressed in that getup?"

Geronimo looked over at us without actually moving his head. I almost thought he winked at me, but he knew the drill, stay still unless you wanted to do it all over again.

I focused on the umbrella, the bear and the eagle. My father would have said that the animals already lived in the wood, that the carver just set them free. "I was in the games just now."

"I can see that, but you seem to be on the wrong side."

"No, I'm part Indian."

He pulled the cloth back and stared at me. "Which part?" I pretended I didn't hear him.

"Never mind. What's your name?" He stood up straight.

"Joseph Barton."

"Well, Joseph Barton, I think we're just about done here." He tossed me a nickel. "Thanks for your help. This light can be pretty tricky, and I thought I'd be doing this much earlier in the day, but the old man was tied up signing autographs and wouldn't sit still for me, not until you came by." He nodded to the old Indian who turned his head and looked at me.

"Thank you," Geronimo reached for the umbrella. I folded it up and gave it to him. "Come with me," he commanded.

I walked beside him. I could sense the line of people behind us. "Young man," he spoke to me in a quiet voice, barely rising above a whisper. "Sometimes the river changes course. It cuts through a bend and creates another path. For a while there is an island, then the old path dries up and the new path is all that remains." He walked straight into the group of people that had gathered. No one crowded him. No one pushed. It was as if he were a magical creature, like a unicorn. The crowd parted and let him through.

He paused in front of a young boy. Geronimo stared at the boy, looked straight at him. The mother tightened her grip on his hand and pulled the boy a little closer. Geronimo was the bogeyman that parents used to frighten their children. It was his vengeance that would punish them if they weren't good. He may have been old, but he could still make them tremble.

"Would you like an autograph?" he asked. The boy nodded. Geronimo pulled an Official Guide to the Louisiana Purchase Exposition from a pouch that hung around his shoulder. He turned to the page with his name and picture on it. He was one of the main attractions. Then he handed me a bottle of ink so he could make a ceremony of dipping his fountain pen. He signed his name, a scrawl of a signature. He looked up at me and smiled. He didn't have many of his teeth left.

"Would you like one too?"

I nodded.

He pulled out another Exposition guide. "What would you like me to write?"

I heard some laughter. Redfeather and the other guys sat under the only shade tree. They were probably reliving the plunge into the mud. Good times. Good friends.

I looked at the old man. "Just write, 'To Pinky, Thanks for the show.'"

# Chapter Thirty-Seven

# SONNY

## 2004

The boat sat in the water tied up next to the fishing dock.

"How the hell are we supposed to get into that thing?" The cigarette bounced up and down in Roy's mouth when he talked.

Frank leaned over. "What the hell were you thinking, Sonny. This looks more like a cigar than a boat. Seemed a whole lot bigger all wrapped up and on dry ground."

"What was I thinking? I'll tell you what I was thinking." Sonny stood nose to nose with Frank. "I'm thinking that this is a goddamn boat that we are going to row in a goddamn race, and I don't want to hear anymore about it. You hear?"

"Okay, Sonny, I was just asking. Don't have a cow or anything." Frank backed away.

"Sorry, Frank. This whole thing is making me tense."

"It's okay, buddy."

"What are those things?" Grace pointed at the cracked leather boots attached to the boat in front of each seat.

"They're for your feet."

"That's a bit gross, if you ask me."

"Look guys, I've inspected each and every one of those shoes, and they are perfectly fine. You've got to keep your feet in them. It's part of the motion, you know, you use your legs. You know, like the bicyclists that attach their shoes to the bike pedals."

Roy laughed and said, "Not in this town. They don't wear any of those sissy shoes."

Not in this town. Not in this town. It was a chant with them, ain't, can't, won't. A mega-barge pulled next to the grain loader up river.

Sonny squatted on the dock. A bit of frayed line hung from a rusted cleat. Hardly anyone used it for boats anymore. A mile upstream was a boat ramp that let you drive the trailer right into the water. There was no reason to use this dock anymore, except for fishing. It was a good place to maybe catch a catfish, maybe catch a boot.

Grace looked at her watch. "What're we waiting for, Sonny? Why don't we all get in? I gotta get back to work soon."

"Just making sure it's not taking on water.

"You don't know?"

Roy threw his cigarette butt in the river. "Are you saying we're all gonna sink if we get in that thing."

"No. I'm not saying that."

"You know something, Sonny, I think the land of fruit and nuts has gotten to you." Roy lit up another cigarette.

Sonny looked at his watch. Ten minutes and still bone dry. That was a good sign. "I think we can get in now."

"Back to what I said earlier, how the hell are we supposed to get into that thing?"

"Hey, Sonny." Charlie dropped one of the oars on the plastic dock. "These things are a bitch. Why did I have to carry them?"

"Because the rest of us carried the boat."

"Oh, yeah. The boat. By the way, Sonny, I noticed there weren't any cup holders on board."

"There aren't supposed to be any cup holders. It's a racing boat, not a yacht."

"Where am I supposed to put my beer?"

"You need to keep both hands on the oars, Charlie. You won't be able to hold a beer."

"No beer. No boat."

"You know better, Charlie. No boat. No money."

Grace stepped between them. "I'll bring you a holder, Charlie."

"Hell, Grace, he can go thirty minutes without a goddamn beer."

"I'll bring him a holder, Sonny."

Sonny sat on the dock and untied his shoelaces. "Okay, let's get our shoes off, and give it a try."

Grace kicked off her shoes. Her toenails were painted bright blue.

Roy pointed at the dock. "If I sit down, I'll never get myself back up again."

"Here, I'll do it." Grace knelt down helped Frank and Roy and Charlie off with their shoes.

"I could get used to this, Grace."

"Can it, Charlie."

Sonny stood in his stocking feet. "Tell you what. I'll get in first. Then I'll hold on to the dock and keep it steady for the rest of you."

Frank handed Sonny a bright orange life jacket. The price tag hung off the side stuck to the label, On Sale $3.99. "Don't forget to wear this."

He smiled. "I knew I forgot something. Thanks."

Frank adjusted the shoulder straps and clicked the buckle. "Good Luck."

"Yeah." The boat rocked up and down on the waves that lapped against the dock.

"Okay, Frank, you hold her steady while I get in."

"Sure thing." Frank squatted next to the boat.

"Just hold it, Frank. Keep it steady, steady, st— . . ."

"Step on the center of that little cross bar, not on the hull," Charlie shouted, "or else you'll stick a foot through the boat."

Sonny looked at his brother. "How the hell do you know that?"

Charlie shrugged his shoulders. "Just know it. Must have remembered hearing it or something."

He was right. Sonny stepped in, being careful not to let his weight rest on the bottom of the boat. With one foot still on the dock, he felt the boat roll beneath him. He had to balance as if on a surfboard, and he had never really done that, only tried that once. There was something about the ocean waves that scared him. They weren't like the meandering river braids that wove here and there into nooks and crannies, creating islands and hideaways.

"Here, Sonny, take my hand." Grace held out her arm.

"Just hold it steady, Frank."

"I'm trying. Get in already. I can't stay like this forever."

It was like trying to step onto a floating log. The ground moved beneath him. He let go of Grace's arm and balanced.

"You gotta sit down, Sonny."

Sit. He had to sit. No problem. He squatted as slowly as he could, the boat rocking beneath him, his arms out like a tightrope walker grabbing onto the air for balance.

"Oh, shit," he heard someone say, "Grab him."

Sonny wasn't sure who the 'him' was, not until he heard the splash and felt the cold and wet Mississippi wash over him.

"I wish I had a camera. Hey, Roy, go get a camera." Frank was doubled over holding his side.

"I fail to see what's so funny." Sonny stood up. The river was only chest high. No chance of drowning here, but the river mud seeped into the top of his socks.

"Don't just stand there. I need a hand."

"Oh, Lord, I can't, it hurts." Charlie rolled on the dock laughing. "Help me, I'm stuck."

Grace reached over to give him a hand, but her arm wasn't long enough.

Charlie handed one end of the long oar to Sonny. "Here you go. Grab onto this. But I still think we should get a picture."

Sonny took hold of the paddle. Frank, Charlie, Roy, and Grace all held onto the other end and pulled. "Pull harder. I can't get loose from the bottom." It's like a tug of war and the damn river's winning."

It was funny. He knew it was funny, the four of them trying to break him loose, and him standing there dripping with Mississippi River slime and who knew what else. Sonny couldn't quite remember the first time he dipped his feet in the Mississippi Mud. He knew that was Grandpa Joe's idea of a baptism. He always said that no one could really know God until they'd let themselves sink into the ooze. Sometimes Sonny's memories of the river seemed to come from a time before memories, before Grandpa Joe, before people themselves. Amphibious memories of a tadpole before the frog, or maybe even earlier still, a time of fire and water when the continent cracked in two and the Mississippi was still a sea. It had been a long time since he'd felt the ooze between his toes. It was good to be back.

"Okay, guys, pull harder, just pull." The four of them held onto one end and he held onto the paddle end. The harder he pulled the more the river's bottom sucked him in. It was as if he was cemented down. And then suddenly he was loose. The river let him go. But instead of being pulled out of the water onto the dry dock, he fell backward, still holding on to the paddle. And the whole gang tumbled into the river after him.

## Chapter Thirty-Eight

# ANNIE

## 1904

December 4

Dear Diary,

Today is my birthday. I almost forgot, what with the fair and coming home and all. Imagine that, forgetting that I'm a grown woman, eighteen years old today. I'm practically an old maid. But Daddy didn't forget. He never does. I know he looks at me and remembers my mother. It was so long ago, she was barely older than I am now when he lost her, and I've been here longer than he ever knew her. He came into my room, kissed me on the cheek, and sat down on the chair in front of my dressing table. The chair creaked, and I was afraid it might break under the weight of him, but it didn't. Then Daddy said he had something to show me.

I waited with my hands folded in my lap. It never does any good to rush him, and I'd learned long ago that the quieter I am, the sooner he gets where he wants to be. He cleared his throat and took a small box out of his pocket. It wasn't wrapped or tied up with a ribbon or anything, just a plain white box. He handed it to me and told me to open it.

Inside the box was a bed of tissue paper. I unfolded the paper, and there lay a string of perfect pearls, like tiny eggs in a nest. I lifted them out of the box. It was a choker-sized strand, and right in the middle was one large pearl, and on either side of it, they got smaller and smaller until the pearls at the end by the clasp were hardly bigger than a teardrop.

He said it was my mother's idea, even before I was born. She knew I was a girl because I kicked differently than my brother. Of course she'd have known. I could tell from her picture, from looking at her eyes, that she would have known all sorts of things other people didn't know.

He told me that the big pearl in the middle was my mother's—that it had been given to her by my grandmother, daughter to daughter. It was a tradition. On my first birthday, he and my mother picked out the tiniest pair together. He almost couldn't say the word "together"; it died at the end, and he didn't say anything for a few moments. He just sat there looking at me and at the pearls. I wanted to go to him and tell him it was all right, but I didn't.

"I've been collecting these pearls your whole life," he said to me. Imagine that, Diary, my whole life. He took a deep breath, kissed the top of my head, and said, "Happy birthday, Poppy, from your mother and me."

Poppy. I can't even remember the last time he'd called me Poppy. Then I hugged him and told him they were perfect. "Daddy" I called him, and I said it out loud. I haven't called him Daddy out loud in a very long time. I hugged him and he stiffened a bit. He never likes it much when I hug him, but it doesn't matter. I let my head rest against his, my nose nestled into his neck. The edge of his collar was stained dark from the sweat of him. That's enough, Poppy, he said and he pushed me away. But he was smiling.

He wanted to lock the pearls in the safe, but I asked him to leave them with me, just for today. It's amazing when I look at the strand. The large pearl in the middle had been my mother's. It had rested against her skin. Some of her must have soaked into it. When I hold the pearls in my hand I feel the softness of all the women behind me, as if they, too, are holding me. And in the light, there is a soft golden tinge on the middle one. It's a golden egg, and I am looking at layers upon layers of Sunday outings and apple pies and stolen kisses. Layers of my grandmother, my mother, and now me.

## Chapter Thirty-Nine

# NATHAN

*Spring*
*John Greer*
*Dear friend,*
*We are almost home. So I will be handing you this letter, if I decide to.*
*I have all the letters here. No way to mail them, but I am in the habit of*
*writing them, and so I will go ahead and write this. Moon is frightened.*
*Damn, frightened doesn't even begin to cover it. The poor woman is terrified.*
*She is shrinking into the bonnet I've told her she has to wear in order to look*
*civilized and demure. We got her shoes, too. Not that she isn't used to things*
*on her feet. We think of civilized as our way, but if I've learned anything, it is*
*that civilized just means you live together without killing each other. And it's*
*harder than it sounds, believe me. I guess that maybe we aren't as civilized as*
*we pretend to be. We think it's in the shoes. The more your feet get stuffed into*
*some ungodly hard leather, the more civilized you are. Her feet are hurting,*
*and that's a fact. And so are mine, but I expect that's because my shoes have*
*shrunk.*
*Your friend Nathan Barton*

# Chapter Forty

# JOE

# 1904

Aday was waiting for me when I came out of the bunkhouse. He held up a pair of white shoes. "They want me to wear these for the race, my friend, but I don't want to wear them."

"Well then, don't," I replied.

"They tell me I have to. They say they can't have me running around the town without shoes on my feet. That it isn't right. That it's uncivilized," he practically spit out the word uncivilized.

I looked at his feet. I'd gotten used to seeing the natives at the fair running around barefoot, but I had to agree with the committee, it didn't seem civilized. "You know, Aday, you're probably going to be better off wearing the shoes. I don't see how you can run around on these streets without them. This isn't South Africa. We've got roads, not dirt tracks." I looked over his shoulder at the map of the route. "See, here," I pointed, "You're running through the heart of downtown. You definitely need shoes there. The roads are brick and stone and uneven from all the horse carts. Plus you don't want to think about what ends up on the ground. I sure wouldn't want to step in it."

I found myself staring at Aday's feet. They were bleached white from all the dust and dirt and calluses that had built up over the years. It was odd looking at so much whiteness on a black man, as if he'd been rubbed down to where there was no more color. "Just put them on, Aday. You're faster than anyone else here, and you know it. What difference could the shoes make?"

Aday sat down on the ground. "Ayyyyyyy, Joseph Barton. I cannot even squeeze my poor toes into these."

"Stop griping and just put the damn things on."

He pushed his feet into the shoes, muttering the whole time. I recognized the swearing, even if I didn't know the words.

"Well?" I asked, "How do they feel?"

"Like a prison."

"Just walk around a little. I'm sure they'll loosen up."

"Since when do prison bars loosen, my friend?" Aday stood up and grabbed onto my shoulder for balance. "My head cannot feel my feet. My feet cannot feel the earth. I am a baby again. I must learn to walk. I must count my steps. What could they do to me if I refuse to wear these shoes?"

"They might not let you run. Rules are rules after all." After my experience I was sure the committee would find any excuse to be able to kick Aday, a black man, out of the race. Each country had its own guidelines about who could represent it, and the South Africans weren't as particular as the American Olympic committee. When it came to winning, they'd let anyone on their team.

Aday put his arm around my shoulder. "You are a good friend, Joseph. But you know what is the strangest thing about your country? It is not your strange clothes and these silly things you like to put on your feet. It is the noise. There is so much noise."

I stopped for a moment and listened. I had gotten so used to the fair sounds that I hardly heard them anymore. "It's not like this everywhere. If you saw where I come from, you'd understand. Out on the river I swear that if you listen hard enough you can hear the clouds move."

Aday looked up at the sky then back at me. "Don't worry, Joseph. I will wear the shoes, and I will run."

❧

It was one of those thick days that didn't rain, when the wetness sits in the air, but it doesn't go anywhere. It doesn't rain down; it doesn't move at all. It was like sitting in a group steam bath.

I walked with Aday to the stadium. He pulled a cloth out of pocket and wiped his forehead. "Why doesn't it rain, Joseph? I do not understand this weather. The water doesn't know where it belongs. Should it be up in the clouds? Should it be down on the ground? Should it flow to the river?" Aday wagged his finger at me, as if the weather were my fault. "Where I come from the water knows its place. It is not indecisive, not like this."

Aday wore the shoes. They looked odd on his body, as if his long, black legs ended in odd-shaped white boats, white weights.

"Are you ready?" I asked.

He shrugged. "I am always ready."

A few people gathered at the starting line.

"It is odd this." Aday said.

"What?"

"That we do this for sport."

I knew what he meant.

"You know, Aday, you never told me why you came here?"

He seemed startled that I'd asked. "I had no choice, Joseph. I had to come."

"Racers, to the starting line." A voice announced over a megaphone.

Aday stood up. I could tell that the shoes bothered him; his walk was not as fluid as it usually was.

"Are you okay?"

Aday smiled and his face seemed to soften. "I will be fine, my friend."

He walked over to the starting line and let himself bend forward as if he were going to sprint for one hundred meters at full speed, not pace himself for twenty-six miles. Twenty-six miles, I tried to imagine moving nonstop for twenty-six miles. I recognized some of the other athletes. I'd seen them hanging around with Greer and the guys. A few of them were from Chicago and St. Louis, even a group from back East. Aday was the only black man running, and of course, there were no Indians. Aday focused on the ground in front of him. He was going inward. An athlete has to go inward in order to put so much out. That was what I had discovered. That was why I loved being in the boat, pulling and pushing. When I row, my body takes on a rhythm and beat of its own. It's as if I move to a special song, as if I hear with every fiber, and my body dances to the sound. It's not a social dance like the Virginia Reel. There's no fiddle music or piano music or opera or any other kind of music. It's beyond that. Aday knew. I'd say everyone out there knew.

"On your marks."

"Get set."

"Go." The Go was lost in the boom of the starting gun.

The runners were headed out of the stadium to the open road. The road was Aday's river. Aday and I were not that different after all. We both went out and pushed ourselves away from other's eyes and thoughts.

I could see Aday in the front of the pack; the black of his legs against the white of his shorts turned the corner ahead of everyone else.

I knew I had some time before Aday would be back at the finish line. He told me to look for him after two and half hours. The record for a marathon was over three hours.

"You can't run that far in two and half hours," I'd said to him.

"No, my friend. *You* cannot run that far in two hours. For me, it is nothing. I will be there. If you do not want to wait, I understand."

"I'll be there," I promised.

* * *

I realized I hadn't had a day off since I'd arrived at the fair, and I wanted to be alone. In my pocket was a letter from Annie with all the latest news. It seemed like so much had happened in the past couple of months. John was off to the University following in his father's footsteps, studying to be a doctor. Smith was working at the bank, and Tucker was taking care of his farm. I thought about my land. Maybe I'd sell it. Maybe it would come to that. I pulled the letter out of my pocket. It was the last line, "Dear Joe. When are you coming home?" That was the question.

When was I going home? That was the topic on my mind as I wandered around the streets of the fair.

Colonel Mulhall had called me into his office the day before. Up until that moment, I didn't even know he had an office like a lawyer or a banker. It seemed that the Wild West was big business.

"Come in, Pinky. Have a seat."

That was easier said than done. Every surface was covered with promotional posters and newspaper articles and photos.

He waved at a pile. "Put those on the corner of the desk."

I picked up the papers and perched on the edge of the straight-backed chair. His chair squeaked as he leaned back and crooked his thumbs in the sleeves of his vest. For a moment, I thought he might fall over backward, but he didn't.

"You know, Pinky, I been watching you, and I think you'd make a good horseman. You're smart. I watched you on that paint yesterday, and you did good, real good."

I'd ridden horses most of my life, but not one like that horse, not a horse that felt wild from the inside out.

He pulled a cigar out of his breast pocket. "So what I'm saying here, Pinky, is that if you want it, the job is yours."

"Job?"

"With the show." He lit the end of the cigar, and the smoke filled the room. "You can come with us, be a permanent member. It's a good life, boy. It's a real good life."

I hadn't thought about staying with the show. Wasn't even sure why I'd stayed at the fair as long as I had. I should have left months ago, gone back with John and Tucker and Smith. Gone back with Annie.

"Well, Pinky boy. What do you think? You want to come on the road, see the world, and become famous?"

He must have thought me pretty stupid because I didn't say anything, just watched the smoke from his cigar as if I could see my future in the haze.

He leaned forward and pulled a gold pocket watch out of his vest. "I got to go now, but you let me know." He stood up and held out his hand for me to shake. He had a big hand and a strong grip. I was shaking Colonel Mulhall's hand.

So I walked around the fair with the letter from Annie in my pocket. When are you coming home? I didn't know. I could be a rider with the Wild West Show. I'd get to see the world. I'd get to travel and hang out with Redfeather and all the other guys. I'd be one of them. And I'd be famous. Kids would see us coming and follow along hoping for an autograph or even a bit of used leather fringe. I might get to live in my own tepee. I wondered if I could bring Annie, if she'd come, if she'd even like to live in a tepee.

I got back early. A few people were already in the stadium, but no one really expected the runners to be back so early. I realized that there's nothing lonelier than an empty stadium. There was a large bell tower that struck the hours and quarter hours. It chimed ten o'clock.

I looked toward the entrance. It had only been two hours, but I was expecting miracles from Aday. No one appeared except a small boy running away from his nurse.

The clock said quarter past ten, then ten thirty. He should be coming. Ten forty-five. Eleven o'clock. Someone played a song on the campanile. Hickory-Dickory-Dock the mouse ran up the clock. Where were the runners?

Outside the stadium someone shouted, "They're coming. Clear the path. They're coming."

I took the flag out of my pocket. Aday had asked me to carry the flag of his country.

"Wave it for me when I win, my friend. You can be my family."

But it wasn't Aday who crossed the line first, or second, or third. No gold, no silver, no bronze. I waved the flag at the winners.

I left the stadium and walked up the race route. All the other runners were arriving in clumps, but there was no sign of Aday.

Then I saw him. He was limping, and there was some dried blood on his leg. I ran over to him.

"Aday?"

"I'm sorry, sir, please get off the course. Runners only." An official pulled me by the arm. I tried to shake him off, but he dragged me to the side. "Make way for the runners, sir." None of the remaining runners looked good.

"Are you okay?" I shouted at Aday and waved the flag as he ran alongside the course.

"Pino's dinner" is what I though I heard him say.

"Go, Aday!" I shouted, but I don't think he heard me.

---

I found him in the stadium where he sat on the ground with his head between his legs. The white shoes were off and were no longer white. I poured some cold water over the back of his neck.

"Ahhh, thank you. That feels good Joseph."

"What happened?"

"No one told me that you had wild dogs roaming the streets of your cities. Wild, vicious animals."

"We don't have vicious animals around here, Aday."

He waved his finger at me. "I was in front. I was way out in front, and I passed by a house. It was not an ordinary house. I tell you that demons live in that house. You may not have wild animals, but there are demons. I'm warning you. Do not run by the demon house. They came out howling and chased me. I got turned around, ran down an alley, and had to climb over a wall." He pointed at his leg. "Even the walls bite."

Poor Aday was shaken, but at least he wasn't hurt.

I didn't mean to smile, but somehow the thought of Aday jumping over a brick wall struck me as a bit funny.

"Do not laugh at me. I see you trying to laugh, but it wasn't funny. The demon foamed at the mouth. I am only here because it did not have wings. In my country, the demons have wings. You have inferior demons here."

"Aday. I'm not laughing. Really, I'm not."

"Your mouth looks like it's laughing."

"I think maybe you went and got yourself chased by a dog. You probably scared it or something."

"It was not a dog." Aday stood up. "It was a demon. I will tell the Filipino chief where to find their next dinner."

I put out my hand to help him to his feet. "Let's get out of here."

Aday ignored my hand. He reached over for the shoes, tied the laces together, then slung them over his shoulder. Barefoot, he limped out of the stadium.

# Chapter Forty-One

# SONNY

## 2004

Grace perched on the edge of the old, red armchair. "This is why I make sure my life can fit in the trunk of my car. I can't stand the packing tape."

Sonny laughed, "Here's to the damned packing tape."

His parent's life, and Sonny's and Charlie's childhood, was spread around the floor: the plaster handprint Sonny had made when he was in kindergarten, his father's ship-in-a-bottle collection, Charlie's 4-H ribbons, Sonny's report cards from school. Most of it Sonny had hardly noticed when he was young. There were dozens of small figurines. His mother had collected angels, Hummel angels, perfect porcelain children. Sonny wrapped some newspaper around an angel playing a piano. "I'd always wanted to learn to play the piano. Thought I could be a great musician."

"Did you ever learn?"

"No, a piano was too expensive, so they rented me a violin." Sonny put the figurine in a box. "It was embarrassing; nobody played the violin, at least not anyone I knew. I'd hide the case in the bushes behind the school, so I didn't have to carry it around. I was a terrible violin player, worse than terrible. I don't think I ever got one decent note out of that poor instrument."

Sonny put the 4-H ribbons in a separate pile.

"One morning, after I'd spent an hour on 'Twinkle Little Star,' Grandpa Joe took me aside. 'Sonny,' he said, 'let's make a deal. You don't ever try to play that god-awful thing again, and I'll take you out for ice cream.'"

Sonny looked at Grace. "That was the best ice cream I ever had."

Grace fanned herself. Sonny felt the air move between them. "I was wondering, Sonny. Have you thought about staying?"

"I've thought about it."

She looked at him, "And?"

A stray hair fell across her face. He wanted to brush it back off her forehead.

"I appreciate the invitation, Grace, but I can't stay."

"No strings?"

"It's not that. You could always come with me." The thought of Grace in California was appealing. She would fit right in.

She shook her head, "No, I promised myself I was finished with following men."

"Fair enough."

"As far as I can tell, you can be anywhere."

He nodded. "Yes, but here I'm Charlie's big brother. I'm Grandpa Joe's grandson. I'm forever, Sonny. "

"Everyone has relationships."

"Grandpa Joe used to tell us that he was the real Indian Joe."

"And he wasn't?"

"Highly unlikely," He picked up a ticket stub, Burlington, Iowa, to Chicago, Illinois. Sonny had never been to Chicago. He wished he'd gone, wished he'd seen the Cubs play.

"He also told us that he'd fought in dozens of battles."

"And he didn't?"

"Apparently not."

Sonny put the ticket stub in his pocket. "And he told us that he rowed in the Olympics. Guess I shouldn't have believed that one either."

Grace bent over and reached into her handbag. "I have a surprise for you." She took out a leather bound book and handed it to Sonny.

"What is it?"

"I sorted through the books you gave me, and I found this." She paused. "I think it was your grandmother's."

Sonny ran his hand over the surface. Embossed on the cover in gold was the word "Diary." The leather was worn smooth on the top and frayed along the edges. He opened it. At the top of the page was written, "October 31, 1904." The handwriting was loopy and the ink had faded. Sonny could barely make out the words, "Dear Diary, At last I got a letter from Joe."

He turned to another page. "The boat itself is like a layer cake, a frosted cake with frills and candy."

"At first, I didn't know what it was," Grace said. "I thought it was just another old book." Grace sat still, lost in the chair, like a child.

Outside, somewhere in the distance, a car alarm went off and a dog barked. It was getting dark, time to turn on the lights.

Sonny couldn't take his eyes off the perfectly formed letters. He tried to imagine the hand that wrote it, but he'd never even seen a picture of her.

"I can't believe I almost lost this," he said.

When Sonny had been younger no one had alarms, not for their cars, not for their houses. People didn't go where they weren't invited. Everyone knew where they were supposed to be. He stood up. It was hard to breathe in that room. "I just hope we don't screw up that race tomorrow. I need some air." He turned his back and went outside.

It was a clear night. Sonny sat on the porch swing. The hinges needed oil. The fireflies were already out, and heat lightening lit up the sky. It wasn't real lightening, not the lightening that rips the clouds and brings the floods. But it still made a good show. At least he could breathe out here. The door opened. Grace's shadow darkened the porch. It seemed as if there were two Graces, the silhouette in the doorway and the shadow at her feet. The door closed. The real Grace sat on the porch swing next to him. She let her foot drag on the ground as she pushed, rocking them back and forth on the swing.

Now would be the perfect time to light up a cigarette. It would be the perfect moment to strike a match, light the tip, and inhale. The end would smolder. He'd take a few long drags, suck the smoke into his lungs. Then he would casually toss the cigarette into the house. Carelessly, without a second thought, he would toss it in, walk away, and let it burn. That would show him. That would show Grandpa Joe.

"I was in such a goddamn hurry." Sonny felt the wind change.

Grace stood up and walked down the steps. She stopped at the bottom by the bush rose. Sonny never understood why his parents planted flowers that didn't smell.

"Emily wanted an egg this morning. Over easy. That's how she likes them, over easy with the yolk nice and runny in the middle. I'd made them for her dozens of times, but today I couldn't get it right. No matter how careful I was, the yolk ran and got hard before I could flip it. And then I ran out of eggs. Emily was polite enough. 'It doesn't matter, Mommy,' she said, tried to make me feel better. She pushed the egg around her plate, but she never did eat it."

A mosquito buzzed around his ear. He hated mosquitoes.

"We used to sit on his lap in that big red chair that takes up half the damn room, and Grandpa Joe would tell us stories, crazy stories, about Indians, and wild men from the darkest jungles of Africa, and the river. It always came back to the river.

Grace climbed back up the stairs and stood in front of him. "Don't be mad at him, Sonny."

"Damn it, Grace. It's all so complicated."

"It doesn't have to be."

# Chapter Forty-Two

# ANNIE

## 1904

October 15

Dear Diary,

I wish I knew when Joe was coming home. I've written him lots of letters asking when he's coming home, but he never gives me a solid answer. Soon, he says. I know it's soon, because the fair will end, so he'll have to come back, but I want to know when, exactly when.

I spent the day berry picking. I have enough to make five or six pies, and the rest I'll save for preserves.

Daddy seems pretty tired these days. I think the trip to St. Louis wore him out. I wish I'd been able to see Captain Irene on the way back. I think about her a lot. I got the book Mr. Clemens gave me to give Joe all wrapped up for his birthday. It will be his homecoming present. That and a pie.

## Chapter Forty-Three

# JOE

## 1904

My hands and face were numb from the cold as I made my way through the empty streets. The Sioux were leaving, and I wanted to say goodbye to Redfeather's grandfather and little sister. And I wanted to see the tepees one more time. There was still a chance I'd go with them and become a nomad, a wanderer, a real Indian. As if I could become an Indian, as if it was a career track like becoming a doctor or a lawyer or a farmer.

The tourists were gone, and the fair was over. The train wasn't running anymore, so I had to walk. It was further than I remembered. The space seemed so much bigger now that it was empty. We'd already had a light snow, and everyone was anxious to have the place mostly cleaned up before winter hit. The vendors had packed up and left. The palaces and exhibitions were closed. Some of the buildings were being dismantled, brick by brick, the ones that weren't wanted for anything.

It was as if it had all been a dream, a magic place that appeared out of nothing and then disappeared back where it came from, a mirage, a story.

When I got to the place where I thought Jake's family had been camped, there was nobody left except for Jake. He raised his hand to let me know he saw me. I raised mine back. He didn't get up, though, just sat in the middle of a ring of stones and waited.

"Redfeather," I said when I got close enough.

"Joe."

I sat down next to him. My legs didn't cross the way his did, but I managed. The two of us sat there and watched the shadows move around us. The ground was cold and my backside was numb from sitting on the ground, but I didn't get up.

"It's so quiet when the camp is down and everyone is gone." Redfeather drew a circle in the dirt. "Don't think we'll ever be back here. I'll miss it."

"I decided to take Mulhall up on his offer and go with you and the show to Europe."

Redfeather stood up and brushed the circle away with his foot. "You can't come with us, Joe."

"Not your place to say, Jake."

"This ain't real, Joe." He pointed at all the stone rings left behind that marked where the tepees had been. "None of it."

"Seems real to me."

"It's just a show, Joe. A story about what once was, but it's gone. You got something real waiting for you, Joe. A chance for a life in the real world with a real family."

I didn't move. I couldn't.

"Tell you what, Joe. I'll spin you. After I let go, just keep on spinning until you want to stop. Let the spinning set your path." Redfeather put his arm around my shoulders. "Close your eyes. I'm going to spin you now. When you stop spinning all you got to do is open your eyes. Whichever way you're facing is the way you're gonna go."

Redfeather had been the first one to spin me at the Indian school. I might have been one of the oldest kids, but I'd never spun before.

—✦—

The other kids stood around me in a circle while Redfeather spun me around and around until I could barely stand up. Then he let me go, and I stumbled around for a few minutes until someone caught me just before I fell. Everyone laughed including me. It was fun being that dizzy.

"What did you see?" Redfeather asked me later that night after everyone was asleep. "Not much." I hadn't seen anything except wild shadows of light and dark, like a kaleidoscope. "What was I supposed to see?" I asked him.

"Oh, I'm sure you saw it. You just didn't know what it was."

—✦—

My breath hung white on the cold morning air. I closed my eyes tight. If he was going to spin me, I didn't want to let myself cheat. "Okay, I'm ready."

Redfeather took me by both my shoulders. We were a lot bigger now, bigger and heavier. I had further to fall, and not so many people to catch me if I did. He turned me around and around with his big hands like huge bear paws. Seemed like I went around and around more times than the paddle on a riverboat, nearly drowning in my own dizziness.

"I'm gonna let you go now, but don't open your eyes. I won't let you fall."

He took his hands off my shoulders, and I kept spinning. I wasn't sure which way was up or down, it felt like a whiteout in the middle of winter. I staggered around for a few seconds, held my hands out to grab hold of something, but there was nothing around except Jake. I knew he was watching out for me. And then I stopped. I stood still for a moment, not ready to open my eyes.

"You can open them now," Jake said. I was almost afraid to look, but I did. The rising sun was just behind my right shoulder. I was facing Northeast, up toward the Mississippi. I was facing Quinley, Annie, home.

<hr>

I stayed with Redfeather the rest of the day. I didn't know when I'd see him again, if ever. I didn't get back until late, and when I finally got back to the bunkhouse, Aday was waiting for me. He stood outside the door. "How long have you been here?" I asked.

"I am not here," he said.

He said things like that. I used to think it was the language, but as I look back I think he meant it. I think he wasn't there. That's what happens to people like Aday, people who run for long distances by themselves. They seem to end up living in a lot of places at the same time.

"Today I got this." He pushed a piece of paper into my hand.

It was a telegram from the British Ministry.

He looked at me.

"You got some news from back home?"

"Read it." He looked up at sky.

On the horizon I saw the three stars of Orion's belt.

"My father used to say that when Orion wakes up, its time for all God's creatures to sleep."

Aday put his hand on my arm. "Please read it, Joseph."

I opened the telegram. There were only seven words. Village burned. All your family died. Regrets.

Aday squatted and laid both hands flat on the ground. "I couldn't feel them anymore, Joseph, and I thought it was the shoes. I thought that when I put on the shoes I lost them. I thought it was me. . . ."

# Chapter Forty-Four

# SONNY

## 2004

Sonny, Frank, and Roy took the boat down from the lumber rack on Roy's pick-up. Sonny didn't have to tell them where to go. Each of them knew their place. Grace and Frank's wife, Jane, carried the oars while Emily brought up the rear with a cooler on wheels. Charlie walked near them, but not with them. "Look, Sonny," Emily said practically running to keep up. "We made a picnic for after you win the race."

After they win the race? He'd be happy with just crossing the finish line.

They couldn't have asked for better weather. No wind, no clouds, low humidity. Banners were strung across every entrance into the town: *Welcome to Greater Mississippi River Days.* Sonny felt as if he was out of time; this place, this day, this scene was out of a *Happy Families* book. At the far end of the parking lot a small carnival set up shop. The Ferris wheel was already filled with people. Sonny wished he was up at the top, so he could see all the way down the river. Later, maybe, after they were done.

Sonny, Frank, and Roy carried the boat from the car to the launching dock. They held it high above their heads. Sonny's arms hurt, but he liked the way the crowds looked at them as they walked by. Rows of vendors selling homemade crafts and souvenirs were scattered around the grounds. The sound of "Test, Test" came from the stage area. Sonny looked around for the cotton candy. He had to remember to get some for Emily.

"Sweet Jesus, we are totally fucked!" Roy put his end of the boat down on the ground. "Look at what we're up against, Sonny." He pointed at the other teams scattered around the dock area.

Sonny had already seen. There were at least twenty teams, each of them wearing sets of matching warm-up suits and life jackets. "They look good."

"Damn right, they look good." Charlie took a swig from a flask. "Damn it, Sonny, we're making fools of ourselves."

"This isn't a beauty contest." Grace took the flask out of Charlie's hand and put it in her purse.

"Hope not." Roy patted his hair.

They all laughed. Laughing was a good sign.

"Huddle up, everyone," Sonny turned to Grace. "Hand me that bag I gave you." Grace handed him a canvas shopping bag with the picture of an old-fashioned paddle wheeler printed on it. Sonny reached in and pulled out a T-shirt. "Ta da. Here it is, our official uniform." He unfolded the shirt. East Side Badgers was printed in block letters across the top, and under the words was a photo of the badger that lived in the glass case at the club. "What do you think?"

"You got to be kidding." Charlie pulled the shirt out of Sonny's hand and held it up high. "It looks like it's eating a chocolate ice cream cone."

Charlie was right. The outstretched paw had gotten smudged in the printing.

It didn't matter. They were a team. He handed out the shirts.

"I got you an extra-extra large, Roy, so no complaints."

Roy took the shirt and pulled it over his head. "Fits like a glove, Sonny, thanks."

"And I didn't forget you two, our cheerleaders." Sonny turned toward Jane and Emily. Emily jumped up and down. He wasn't used to being around so much energy. "I got a small one just for you, Emily."

Emily ran her hand over the badger and smiled. "He's beautiful, not at all scary."

Jane and Frank held hands. Sonny turned away and looked at the river. The morning sunlight made the muddy brown look almost silver. They were such an oddly matched couple: Jane the sensitive artist, Frank the regular guy. He handed Jane one of the shirts.

"Very thoughtful, Sonny. Thanks."

Grace walked up and down the dock modeling the shirt as if she was on a fashion runway. "I think we should sell these at the club."

"Yeah. For when everyone gets too drunk to see." Charlie pulled the T-shirt over his head.

"Not bad, Charlie." Frank slapped him on the back. "Not bad at all."

Sonny reached into his bag again. He felt like Santa handing out gifts. "One more thing, Grace. I got this for you." He pulled out a bright red megaphone.

"I can't believe that fit in there." She turned it around and around in her hands.

"What's it for?"

"So we can hear you." Sonny smiled.

"Yeah, mom. You'll have to sing on key."

Grace put her mouth against the opening as if she was about to play an instrument, and she sang, "Row, row, row your boat." Her voice came out gravelly, but loud.

"Guess it works." Frank stood next to Jane with his arm around her shoulder.

"Okay, let's put her in." Sonny and Frank each picked up one end of the boat and lowered it into the water."

"She looks good, Sonny," Frank said.

"She does, doesn't she?" Sonny looked at the other boats that floated next to the dock. The sleek fiberglass hulls reminded him of thoroughbred horses. He leaned down and rubbed his hand over the surface of their boat. The wood seemed to soak up the heat of the sun. "You know, Frank, I'm glad she's made of wood. It seems right. Makes her more real."

Roy came up behind them carrying the bright orange life jackets. "Nice new flotation devices." Sonny noticed the price tags were still attached.

"Thanks, Roy. Glad you remembered."

"No problem, Sonny."

Strains of "Alexander's Ragtime Band" came from the shore. The trumpet was out of tune.

"Maybe we should have sprung for the zip-up kind."

"These will work just fine."

❦

"Okay, guys, it's time. Everyone in the boat."

"Wait." Jane pulled a camera out of her bag. "Team picture. We need a team picture."

Sonny, Frank, Charlie, Roy, and Grace stood on the dock in front of the boat. The men each held an oar like a wizard's staff, and Grace held the megaphone like a trophy.

"Smile everyone. Say Mississippi."

Grace whispered to Sonny, "Looks like we're finally getting a new team picture for the wall."

They each got into the boat with no hesitation, no wobbles, no fear, as if they'd been doing this their whole lives. Maybe they had been, maybe it was in their genes.

A teenager walked over to them. He wore red, high-top sneakers and carried a clipboard. "East Side Boat Club? You're up next. Make your way over to the starting line." He untied the line from the cleat on the dock, leaned his toe against the side of the boat, and pushed. "And good luck. I hope I'm still doing this when I'm your age."

Jane and Emily stood together on the dock, "Have a great time, and break a leg, or whatever you do," Jane called out.

"Maybe break a paddle," Charlie quipped.

The protected bay wasn't long enough for the racing lanes, instead the organizers had marked a course on one side of the main channel, not quite in the shipping lanes, but close enough so that buoys were set up clearly marking the course.

The shore was lined with waving, smiling, cheering people. Emily held an orange flag. Sonny watched it bounce up and down as Emily and Jane made their way to a good view spot.

The smell of frying catfish and funnel cakes followed them away from the shore. Sonny was hungry. He should have eaten more than a stale donut and coffee.

The other five boats in their group were already lined up at the starting point. Two men in a motorboat faced them. One of the men stood up and addressed the waiting teams.

"Each lane is clearly marked, so be sure to stay in your lanes. When you cross the finish line, wait there until we give you the signal to row back to the dock."

Frank sat up straight and rigid. "Relax, Frank." Sonny patted his friend on the back.

Sonny noticed Charlie reach forward. The next thing he knew, Charlie was twisted around waving a flask. "I got whiskey? Anyone thirsty?"

"I thought Grace took that away from him."

"She did. He must have had a spare. He's getting smart in his old age." Roy laughed. Sonny wanted to smack them both.

The other teams sat focused in their boats. The official looked over at them. Sonny prayed he hadn't heard what Charlie said.

"Shut up, Charlie." Shut up. Shut up, Charlie. He was tired of saying shut up, Charlie. It was his theme song. It didn't even have any meaning anymore. He might as well have said eat beans, Charlie, or wear blue, Charlie, or fly away, Charlie.

"Can it, Charlie." Sonny felt the boat rock as Roy clipped the back of Charlie's head. "Put the damn flask away. We got a race to row."

Charlie put the flask back in his pocket. "Sure, Roy. I was just fooling."

"On the ready."

Sonny put his hands on the oar.

"Set."

Out of the corner of his eye he saw the men in the next boat lift their oars.

"Oars up." The megaphone made Grace sound like a disembodied spirit.

"Go." A starting gun went off.

The boat next to them pulled away with a smooth glide. "Now," Sonny yelled.

Grace didn't say anything. She seemed frozen.

"Come on, guys, row." Sonny called out.

Frank put his oar in and pulled, and then Roy.

Charlie leaned forward and laughed, "Pretty funny guys, pretty funny."

Sonny knew something wasn't right. At first the people on the shore were on his left, then they were in front of him, then they were on his right.

"Everyone stop. We're going in circles." Sonny pulled his oars out of the water. The other boats were already halfway to the finish line.

"I said stop." They all lifted their oars. "Let's start again. Slow guys. We know what we got to do, slow and steady. Now, Grace, sing. Show us what you got. Sing for us, Grace, sing."

She lifted the megaphone and began to sing "Hickory Dickory Dock."

Hickory meant all pull together; dickory was Sonny and Charlie's cue; dock was Roy and Frank's cue.

"The mouse ran up the clock." Pull, push, pull, push. Grace relaxed. Sonny heard it in her voice.

They were moving, and they were moving in a straight line.

Sonny could feel the pull of his oar as it moved through the water. Each time he lifted it, he felt a spray of water. It felt good, the way it splashed his face. A horn sounded off to their right. It was the Mississippi Queen.

He heard a cheer from the shore. One of the teams had already crossed the finish line.

"Keep going," he said, "just keep going."

"Row, row, row your boat," Grace picked up the beat.

They were pulling harder than they had in practice. It seemed as if he barely had enough time to catch a breath. Roy wheezed. Don't have a heart attack, Sonny prayed. Don't let Roy keel over, don't let Grace get laryngitis, don't let Frank get a cramp, and don't let Charlie . . . Sonny couldn't pray for Charlie.

He gripped the oars. Out of the corner of his eye, he saw the orange buoys. They seemed to zip by. The other boats were already waiting at the finish line. Everyone was cheering them on.

"Hickory dickory dock." The purple streak in Grace's hair seemed to have come loose from her ponytail. It flapped in the wind, their wind.

He saw Charlie lean forward and take one hand off his oar. What was he doing? And then the boat gave a pull, just the slightest catch, and they were out of synch. Charlie's oar hit the water at the exact moment when they were all gliding forward. It hit the water and then pushed back, and Sonny saw Charlie flip out of the boat. It was so fast, he hardly knew if it was real. It looked as if someone reached over, picked Charlie up, and tossed him out. Leave it to him to be the one to catch a crab.

Sonny heard the splash, but they had already pulled past the place where Charlie landed. They'd already crossed the finish line without him. Sonny twisted around and saw Charlie bobbing in the water. The safety boat was already alongside Charlie. They had tossed him a life ring and were pulling him toward the boat when Sonny caught Charlie's eye. Then Sonny saw Charlie unhook his life jacket and begin to swim. Charlie was swimming, his arms moving fast and furious, and his legs kicking behind him. A roar went up from the crowd on the shore. He only had about twenty-five yards to go.

"Hickory dickory dock," Grace sang into the megaphone.

"Go, Charlie. Go!" Frank and Roy shouted from the boat. Sonny shook his head, and then Charlie crossed the finish line.

"Way to go, bro," Sonny called to his brother. Charlie laughed and held up his hand. He hadn't let go of the flask. He made a gesture toward Sonny, a salute, or maybe it was a toast. The rescue boat motored up next to Charlie and extended the hook. Sonny watched them pull him in as if he were a fish or an old boot. But it didn't matter. They'd done it. They'd finished the damn race.

# Chapter Forty-Five

# ANNIE

# 1904

October 31

Dear Diary,

At last I got a letter from Joe, and HE'S COMING HOME! Finally.

But he's bringing the little black man with him because he lost his whole family, and Joe says we're all he's got left. I'm not sure I understand what Joe is thinking. What will we do with him? Where will he sleep?

Joe said he couldn't imagine what it would be like if everyone he knew was dead or dying, if your whole world was split in two by people fighting who didn't have anything to do with you. I wonder what it would be like for me if people came and moved into our house and then fought over it as if we weren't there—like the civil war did to people, or that's what I heard.

Joe never talked like that before, not in riddles and questions. He used to talk about normal things, like when the cow was calving, which field to plant, which fence to mend.

# Chapter Forty-Six

# JOE

# 1905

Yahe na howenohomenuhahe yaheyue. The voice rode on the wind. It was a lullaby, a hymn, and a love song all in one. I could not remember having heard those words before, yet they seemed familiar. I wasn't even sure that they were real words. They felt more as if they came out of the earth and air at the same time. I stopped where I was in the middle of a crowd and closed my eyes. And then the crowd was gone, and there was a flute as well as a voice. I let myself be pulled toward the sound. I found them in a shaded spot near the man-made creek that ran through the grounds. A young woman carried a baby in a cotton sling that draped from her neck. Her body swayed and rocked the baby as she ground a bowl of yellow grain. She sang as she worked. Sitting next to her was Redfeather's grandfather playing a flute. I was surprised because I thought they were all long gone, that I was long gone, but I must have been mistaken.

I stood off to one side and listened. The old man stopped playing

"Please don't stop."

The old man gestured for me to sit down. "You are late."

The woman with the baby continued her motion. She used a large stone bowl and a rounded pestle that fit inside the bowl. I could see the effort, with every circular motion of her arm as the vein on her neck swelled.

"Here, have something to drink." The old man handed me a metal cup. I held it up my nose. It smelled like peppermint.

"What is it?"

"Some tea, just some tea."

I took a sip. It was sweeter than I expected. I drank it down.

The old man nodded while I drank.

He patted the ground next to him, "Come closer."

I scooted over. The old man put his hand on my face and turned it toward the light. I felt like a piece of fruit being inspected at the market. He leant close to me and smelled me, then he ran his fingers over the top of my head.

"Aaaah," he said, then picked up his flute and began to play it again.

I looked over at the woman who fixed her gaze on the bow. She was trying hard not to laugh. "What just happened?" I asked.

She giggled. The baby let out a small cry, more of a squeak. She tucked it inside her shirt, so it could find her breast.

The old man put his flute down.

"You need to visit the island." He lifted the flute again and played. It was as if he hadn't said anything, but he had.

"What island?" I asked. The river is full of islands. Bits of land that don't even last past the next year's flood, while others seem to have been there forever, filled with forests and small ponds.

"The island of your past." He leaned forward to say again, "You need to visit the island."

This should seem strange, I thought, but it didn't. I was sitting cross-legged on the ground, and some crazy old Indian was telling me to go to an island. That could sound crazy, but somehow it just seemed normal.

"One more thing," the old man added. "You'll need to go at night when the moon is full."

He handed me a blanket. It was coarse wool, probably horsehair, woven into a diamond pattern.

"And after I find this island, what then?" I asked.

"Don't worry. You will know."

"Silly old coot." I turned to walk away, and then I woke up. I was alone in my bedroom, and today was the day I was going to ask Annie to marry me.

⚜

I sat across from Dr. Greer in the sitting room. Annie was upstairs. She knew I would come; she knew I had to come. This was the last thing I needed to do. John was with us in the corner by the fireplace. I was with all the Greer men.

"So, Joe," Dr. Greer said. He sat in a leather wingback chair, his legs crossed. "What can I do for you?"

"Sir, I've come to ask if I can have Annie's hand in marriage."

He must have known why I was there. I'd Bartoned myself up as best I could. I had my father's pipe sticking out of my jacket pocket just so Dr. Greer could see it, so he'd remember. I'd put on my newest, blackest shoes, the ones that pinched my toes.

"It's not easy for me, Joe."

"I understand that, sir."

"John, bring me the letters." He didn't look at John as he spoke. John walked over and put a pile of letters on the table.

I recognized the handwriting.

"These were from your father, from before."

He pushed them toward me. "Go ahead. Take them. You might as well have them."

"I don't understand."

Dr. Greer cleared his throat, then he looked straight at me. His blue eyes seemed to have flecks of gold in them.

"You see, Joseph, your father and I were close friends."

"Yes, sir."

"And it would honor me to have his son in my family."

I nodded.

"I would be honored to have his son in my family, but . . ."

Of course there was a "but." If there hadn't been, he would have jumped up and shaken my hand and called Annie down. We'd have set a date, and he and John wouldn't have looked like they'd been told someone had died.

"But I can't have you craving." He pulled out the box of cigars and offered one to me. I shook my head and pulled out the pipe.

"I can't have you wanting." He pointed the cigar at my chest.

Dr. Greer looked at the cigar in his hand and put it back in the box. John hadn't moved from his place in the corner. I tried to catch his eye, but he didn't look at me at all, only at his father.

"I can't have you thinking, talking, or wishing about that other life. It's dead. No. It's not even dead. It never was."

He motioned for John to come over. John stood behind his father, his hands on the back of the chair.

"Do you understand me, Joe? Never a word. You are Nathan Barton's son, and as far as you are concerned your mother died when you were a baby. That's it. Can you do it? It's got to be a solemn promise. I need you to swear, Joe. Swear on your father's letters; swear on that pipe; swear on everything that your father wanted you to be that you will never again mention or think about finding them, those other people." He took a deep breath. "They never existed."

I felt the soft wood of the pipe in my hand. Every piece of wood had a shape, my father used to say.

"What does it look like, Joe?" That's what my father had asked me all those years earlier. "What do you see?"

"I don't see anything," I'd said.

"It's a bird," my father had whispered, "a bird caught in the wood."

## Chapter Forty-Seven

# SONNY

## 2004

Earthquake, Sonny thought from the edge of sleep. The house shook, but it wasn't with the sway of an earthquake, it was more like a pounding jackhammer that came from downstairs. He opened his eyes. Grace slept with her head on his shoulder. Her breath smelled of apple and cinnamon. More pounding. Someone was banging at the front door. He glanced at the clock. It was four in the morning.

He eased Grace off his arm; she barely stirred.

"Coming!" he called out as he ran down the stairs, "I'm coming." He knew they couldn't hear him over the banging and yelling.

"Sonny, open the damn door, Sonny."

He turned the knob. Roy bolted into the room.

"I've been trying to call you for over two hours. Why the hell don't you answer your phone?"

"Sorry. I took it off the hook."

"Who the hell takes a phone off the hook. No one takes the phone off the hook."

"Is everything okay?" Grace stood at the top of the stairs, a sheet wrapped around her like a sarong.

Roy took one look at her and blushed. "Oh hell, Sonny, I'm sorry, but it's Charlie. He took off about two hours ago. He was pissed off. You know how he gets. He was just pissed off." Roy pushed past Sonny and walked into the kitchen. He opened the refrigerator.

"Hell, you don't even have any beer in this place."

Sonny followed him and closed the refrigerator door. "If he does this all the time, what's the big deal?"

"He took the rickety old boat that Parker keeps down at the club, and he's poured so much whiskey down his throat you could probably row down his brain as easily as the goddamn river."

"Here's your clothes, Sonny." Grace stood in the doorway, fully dressed and hair combed. "I'll make some coffee. You get dressed and we'll go."

"Where are we supposed to go?"

"To find him."

"He could be anywhere on this river, at least if he went through the locks we could find out, but other than that . . . damn it." Sonny kicked the dock. There was a steady rhythm from the slosh of the water as it hit the heavy plastic.

Grace held onto his elbow. "This is probably just a lot of worry for nothing. Knowing Charlie, he's over at the IHOP chowing down on blueberry pancakes and hash brown potatoes."

Sonny knew he wasn't at the IHOP. He could see the lights from all the boats on the river. Roy and Frank had rallied the troops. They'd all pulled their share of drunks out of the river.

"Here, Sonny, you can take my boat. You know where he might go, don't you?"

He had no idea where Charlie would go.

"What the hell set him off, Roy? What did you say to him?"

"I've been trying to figure it out, and I just don't know, Sonny. We were sitting around, celebrating. Drinking our share of that beer you promised us. And Charlie, he was playing some pool. We were all just shooting the breeze, you know. What the hell were we talking about, Frank?"

"We were talking about the Evans twins and how much fun it was to watch them pay out on the bet. We were talking about that goddamn finish line and how good it felt to cross to the other side."

"And then?"

"Charlie said his head hurt."

That was his latest excuse. His head seemed to always hurt, especially when Sonny wanted him to do something.

"He must have said something else."

Roy wiped his brow as if the effort of thinking squeezed the moisture out of him. "Well, he stopped dead still and just stared at the souvenir case."

Frank nodded in agreement. "That's right. He was staring at the case, and then he said something about a goddamn badger, and how he'd show Sonny. But he's always saying stuff like that. That he'd show you."

"And then?" Sonny felt the chill of the almost dawn.

"Then he laughed. At least I think he laughed." Frank looked to Roy for confirmation.

"He had that old chart with him. I remember that." Roy blew his nose on a rag.

"That's right. He was carrying that stupid thing around with him all night." Frank kicked at the dock. "I'm really sorry, Sonny. We all thought he'd gone into the pisser. Nobody realized he'd gone to the river 'til old Parker went out and his boat was gone. Then Billy Evans said he saw Charlie take the boat and just assumed Parker said it was okay. Parker was steaming mad."

"He had the chart?" Sonny almost shouted at them. "Do you have another one? I need a river chart."

"Sure, Sonny, we got one right here on the boat, but I don't see how it's going to help you."

"Get in, Grace." Sonny and Grace climbed into the motorboat. He hated motorboats, no rhythm, no soul, but he needed the speed right now.

"There's a CB in the panel, there . . . let us know if you find him; we're on channel 36." Frank untied the boat and patted the hull. "Roy and I will stay here and coordinate the other searchers. Good luck, Sonny."

"Thanks, Frank. You're a good friend."

Sonny started the motor and edged out into the channel.

Grace gripped the side of the boat. Her knuckles were white with the effort. The mist rose on the river like a low fog. He passed the no wake zone and opened the throttle. The sound of the motor echoed off the land. It was deceptive. At first glance, the shoreline looked like a solid line, and then it became obvious that there were islands, dozens of backwaters where the river cut out narrow channels.

"He could be anywhere." Grace offered him a thermos. He didn't remember her getting coffee.

"I don't think so," said Sonny.

"Maybe he's just motoring around."

"I think he knew exactly where he was going."

"You're not worried?" Grace asked.

"I stopped worrying about him long ago."

Grace leaned over the side, her hand in the water. "I bet there's all kinds of things at the bottom of this river. All kinds of stories."

"There's one hell of a lot of mud, that's for sure, and it sucks things up a lot more easily than it spits them out."

Sonny slowed the motor and eased the boat into a narrow channel. "We've got to be careful here. I don't want to get us stuck on a sandbar. Here, Grace, take the tiller for a second. Hold us steady." He opened the map. It looked different than the map he'd found among Grandpa Joe's things. The river had changed a lot since the date of that one.

"What are you looking for, Sonny."

"I've got to get oriented. The braids of this river move and shift with every season, but there's something familiar. Here." He pointed at one of the small Islands. "What does this look like to you?"

Grace leaned forward. The boat rocked with her motion. "Looks a bit like a horseshoe."

"Right."

"Remember the treasure map, and the horseshoe shape? It wasn't a picture of a horseshoe for luck." He ran his finger over the map, tracing the shapes of the islands. "It was an island, this island."

"So you know where we're going?" asked Grace.

"We're going to find X." Sonny revved the motor and took off. It had been a long time since he'd explored the islands. They seemed to have gotten fat and middle-aged, too. What used to be distinct was now overgrown and muddy.

"I need to hug this shoreline, Grace. I'm pretty sure that if I follow it around on this side, we'll come to a break with another island to the North. I need to turn in between the two of them. That should be Horseshoe Island. You take the pole and keep testing the bottom. Make sure we've got enough water under us. I don't fancy getting stuck in this mud.

The few lights visible from the town shone brightly. So many people still asleep in their beds, most of them didn't even know these nooks and crannies existed on the river. They saw the big open channel where the paddle wheelers and the barges and the yachts made their way to gambling and adventure. But now, as they headed into this backwater, Sonny realized that they were in a completely different world, yet barely a quarter mile from the highway.

"It's getting shallow, Sonny."

He turned the motor down so he could hear the sound of the water on the island. He used to be able to know a lot by that sound. Now he wasn't sure. It seemed that as he got older he'd stopped listening. It was dark between the islands. They were in the shadow of the trees. The city lights didn't reach here. He stopped the boat and pulled out the flashlight. The water was still. He heard a splash, and then quiet. He shined the flashlight up along the shore.

"Sonny, over there, behind that tree. I thought I saw something." She was right. Up ahead, Sonny saw a faint hint of a reflection on the water that didn't look anything like a tree.

He eased the boat down the narrow channel toward the shadow. "This is it, Grace. We found it. I'll be damned. We found it."

Sonny pulled his boat as close as he could to the bank. There was no easy entry here. They'd have to wade in the Mississippi muck and climb the embankment.

"You stay in the boat, and then toss me the line. I'll pull you as close as I can."

He jumped out as high up the bank as he could manage and grabbed onto a tree root, then pulled himself up. He was amazed at how strong he had become over the past few weeks. He pulled the boat in and reached out for Grace's hand. "You can do it. I won't let you fall." He knew he couldn't promise that, but he said it anyway. Grace held onto his hand and then seemed to fly out of the boat and land on the shore next to him.

They stood for a moment and listened to the island settle back down to sleep. Sonny shined the flashlight over the woods. The brush was thick, but he could make out the spot where Charlie had hacked a path.

"Over here," Sonny whispered. It wasn't wide enough for two people, but Grace held on to the back of his shirt. She hadn't spoken a word since they'd landed.

Sonny saw the opening in front of them, a place where the trees didn't grow. It was just a small meadow, but Sonny knew exactly where they were. This was the badger spot. Grandpa Joe had brought him and Charlie here before.

⁂

It had been an early autumn evening. He remembered that they'd been eating pomegranates. His father had come home from the store, and in the bag were the deep red globes. Sonny had never seen anything like them before. They were better than caramel apples, better than carving pumpkins, this fruit was a mystery fruit, a fairytale fruit. His father cut it open and handed him and his brother each a quarter. He had made them wear old kitchen aprons like bibs, but Sonny didn't mind.

"Take them out on the porch, boys."

He and Charlie sat on the top step. Grandpa Joe came outside and sat next to them. "This is going to be a real treat, boys. Best time you ever had with a fruit. Here, like this." Then he peeled the red skin back and showed them the seeds all clumped together. "Now take a bite." Sonny bit down. The seed juice exploded in his mouth and squirted down the front of the apron.

Grandpa Joe laughed. "Not bad," he'd said. Then he spit the seeds out on the ground. The spitting out was the best part.

Charlie put his piece down on the porch and made a face. "It's messy. I don't like it." Sonny picked it up.

"His loss, Sonny, now there's more for you." The red juice dribbled down Grandpa Joe's chin.

Inside the house the phone rang. His father shouted into it, "Hello!" He always shouted at the phone when he talked. Then he came out on the porch. "Joe, I've got to go out for a little bit. The Leahy's cow is calving, and they need my help. Can you watch the boys?"

Grandpa Joe winked at Sonny. "What do you think Sonny? Can I watch you?"

"I mean it, Joe." Sonny heard the car start and saw his father back it out of the garage. He honked the horn.

"Don't you worry. Me and the boys will do just fine, won't we?" Grandpa Joe winked again.

Sonny watched his father drive away. Grandpa Joe clapped his hand against his forehead. "I almost forgot. Do you know what day this is?"

Sonny shook his head.

"It's the badger day. Hard to believe it's been over fifty years. Okay, boys, we're going to go and have an adventure. We'll be explorers, like Louis and Clark."

Sonny didn't know who Lewis and Clark were. All he knew was that they were going on an adventure with Grandpa Joe, and that was always a good thing. Grandpa Joe jumped up and went into the house, leaving the pomegranate peels on the ground. It must be a real big adventure if he didn't make them pick up. Sonny followed and Grandpa Joe told him to go get a blanket and some rope and meet him at the tuck. By the time Sonny found everything, Charlie was already in the front seat and Grandpa Joe was loading a canvas bag and a shovel into the truck bed.

The next thing Sonny knew, he and Charlie and Grandpa Joe were crowded into the front seat of the old pickup truck and on their way to the adventure.

Grandpa Joe took them down to the river. Sonny had never been on the river at night before. He never went anywhere at night. The moon was full, and the river was brighter than he could have imagined. Even the trees along the side cast dark shadows. Sonny could see his reflection.

Grandpa Joe put some cushions on the floor of the rowboat, then he made them each put on a life jacket. He wrapped them together in a blanket. The wool scratched against Sonny's cheek. He didn't want to be wrapped in a blanket like a baby; he wanted to feel the moon light on his skin. "Where are we going, Grandpa Joe?" Sonny asked.

"I told you, to the badger place. Where I got that badger a long, long time ago." Sonny wondered how long ago that might be. He knew that Grandpa Joe was old. But somehow Sonny couldn't really fathom how old. Older than time, he seemed. As old as the river, maybe even older than the river. Grandpa Joe seemed that old; seemed like he was forever.

※

Sonny didn't know how long it took to get where they were going, just that he and Charlie must have both dozed off, because he didn't remember the trip very much. All he remembered was the bright moon and being huddled in the wool blanket so tight that his own breath heated him. He remembered the creak of the oar locks, and Grandpa telling him to be quiet, and then Grandpa leaning close to his ear and whispering, "Charlie, Sonny, time to get up, boys. We're here. Sonny, you take this." He handed Sonny the shovel.

"I'm going to tie a rope around my waist and then wrap it around each of yours." Grandpa Joe tied one of those sailor knots, so we couldn't wiggle loose.

"Now none of us can get lost. Me included." He picked up the canvas bag and tossed it over his shoulder.

Grandpa Joe led them through the brush into an opening in the middle of the trees. It was a meadow.

Charlie held his crotch. "I need to pee."

"Well don't pee in your pants, okay. I think we're there," Sonny told him.

Grandpa Joe stopped. He looked at them. "You boys doing okay?"

"Charlie's gotta pee," Sonny said.

"Okay, Charlie. You let loose."

He didn't untie them, and Sonny could hear the stream of urine, feel the heat of it rise off the cold ground.

"I'm gonna untie us now, and I don't want either of you wandering around. Just stay right near by. Sonny, you're gonna start digging over here by this tree. And you too, Charlie. Can you do that for me?"

They nodded. Grandpa Joe sat down. "Thanks, boys. I just need to rest a minute." He watched them for a few minutes. "Come here, boys. I got to tell you something. I never told you this before. Never even told your dad, but it's something you got to know." Sonny put down the shovel and took Charlie by the hand. They sat on the gound by Grandpa Joe. The meadow grass was damp. "Boys, what I got to tell you is that deep down inside, we're not really Bartons." His voice got quiet, almost a whisper, and Sonny had to lean in close to be sure he heard every word. "No, boys. We're not Bartons, we're badgers. That's what we are. Seems like some people forget how to pronounce who they really are."

Charlie tried not to cry, but he couldn't hold it in.

Grandpa Joe stood up. He picked the shovel up from where Sonny had left it and dug the hole deep enough so Sonny could stand in it up to his knees.

"Ready." He pointed to the canvas bag that lay on the ground. "Hand that over, please." Sonny picked up the bag. It felt lumpy.

"We're going to put this in here. Okay. There ain't nothing to be afraid of boys, not when you got the moon watching over you. When the moon is full and just before the snows come, that's when you got to make sure you got yourself clear, that's when you got to just check in and come home, that's when you got to make your peace with who you really are."

Sonny looked up. He wanted to know the place. He wanted to know where he belonged, where they belonged. The leaves were mostly off the tree and the branches crisscrossed in front of the moon.

⚜

Sonny never imagined the place would still exist after all these years of the river rising and falling. The moonlight made its way into the meadow. Under an old cottonwood tree was his brother. Charlie had fallen asleep with his hand still grasping the neck of an empty whiskey bottle, and on his lap was a pile of old shoes.

Sonny looked down at his brother. All the drink, all the disappointment, all the life had drained out of Charlie's face, and Sonny saw him as he used to be—the little kid in the flannel pajamas.

Grace knelt next to Charlie. The moon was full. To the right of the tree was a pile of dirt.

"He dug something up."

"The treasure," said Sonny. "He wanted to beat me to it. He wanted to make sure I never found it."

"But why?"

"Because he thinks that Grandpa Joe loved me more." Sonny watched Grace. The moonlight changed the shadows on her face. A sweater covered her arm, but he was able to see just the faintest hint of the blue feather on the back of her hand.

Above them an owl cried. They'd probably scared away his dinner.

Sonny picked up the shoes that were on his brother's lap. "This must have been the big treasure."

He held up a pair of old, white shoes and a pair of black, lace-up boots. The laces were covered in green mold, and something grew in the soft bends and creases of the leather.

"They're so small." Grace took one of the black shoes. Who do you think they belonged to? Your grandmother? Why would he bury your grandmother's shoes?"

"I don't know," said Sonny. "I really don't know."

"Where am I?" Charlie moaned.

"Well, look who's finally awake?" said Sonny. "I better go call off the search parties, let them know he's okay."

"I'll go," said Grace. "You stay with your brother."

He didn't really want to stay with Charlie. He was sick of all the drama, sick of all the neediness. He wanted to walk away and just leave him here, let him swim back.

"Channel 36 on the CB," Sonny called after Grace.

"Got it." She disappeared into the darkness.

Charlie opened his eyes. "Where the hell am I?"

"Badger Island."

"Oh, yeah." He sat up. "I've really fucked up, haven't I? I'm just one big fuck up. I fall out of a goddamn boat, and I can't even find a decent buried treasure. All I find are some old shoes. Someone else must have dug it up the real treasure years ago."

Sonny sat on the ground next to him. It was wet and cold. He could feel the moisture soak into his pants. He wished he had something to sit on. He shifted his weight. There wasn't anything he could say. He wasn't going to tell Charlie that it was all okay. It wasn't okay.

"What's going to happen to me?"

"I don't know, Charlie. I really don't know."

Sonny was sick of the mud and the mosquitoes and the rusted out boats and the buildings in need of paint. He didn't expect to be so damn cold. He didn't expect his fingers or the tips of his ears to hurt. He didn't expect to wish that he could make it all go away.

He saw the light from Grace's flashlight through the trees. "It's okay," she called out, "I was able to contact Frank. I told him we found Charlie, and that he's okay." She was out of breath when she reached them.

Sonny looked at her, and then back at his brother.

"We need to get you home, Charlie. I'm soaking wet from sitting here for five minutes. I can't imagine what you feel like."

"I don't feel anything."

"Maybe not now, but as soon as you sober up, you're gonna feel plenty."

"You were always the good one, always the goody two shoes. You know, Sonny, dad cried when you took off and left. You'd of thought you'd died the way he hardly talked and locked the door to his room. It was like living in a fucking funeral home."

Sonny didn't know. He'd never asked.

"Well, it was just me and dad, and you know what, Sonny? You know what? We did okay. The two of us, we did okay without you, and without Grandpa Joe. We were okay. We really were."

Grace stood off to the side. The light from her flashlight made a circle on the ground.

"We were okay, the two of us."

Sonny pulled Charlie to his feet.

"I know you were, Charlie. You did good."

# Chapter Forty-Eight

# ANNIE

## 1905

January 31

Dear Diary,

I thought about the modern nursery today. The one they'd had at the fair. They put little babies in machines that kept them warm. "Incubators" they called them. Several women were standing around looking at the tiny babies. They were smaller than I imagined a real person could be. One of the ladies wiggled her finger at the tiny thing. A garnish of joy she called it. I laughed. Who ever thought of a baby as a garnish.

A sprig of parsley is a garnish. Sweet cranberry sauce is a garnish. A baby isn't a garnish. A garnish is something that adds to the main dish, an accent, something that is nice to have but doesn't really mean anything.

I never thought about a baby before. Me and Joe. Not even sure I know how to have a baby. Not everyone has a machine to keep them in. Mrs. Macavey said my monthly bleeding has to do with having babies. Not sure I want one, the little things floating on a river of blood. Doesn't seem right. The machines look clean enough, so I suppose it will be okay. Me and Joe, we don't need a garnish. We're good, just the two of us. Well, maybe three. Me and Joe and his crazy river.

# Chapter Forty-Nine

# NATHAN

My Dear Son Joseph,

I've asked my good friend Dr. Greer to give you this letter on your 18th birthday. Maybe I should have done it sooner, but I am first and foremost a coward. That is clear to me. But I had to go. I had to find out. I couldn't live without her.

Now that you're 18 the farm is yours. Maybe I'll make it back there someday. I would love to go out on the river with you and catch a catfish and swap stories. It would be fun to hear your stories. I am sure that when it is time, my spirit will find its way to you. Funny to hear me write about spirits. Look for me. I'm sure you'll know me, and I, I will always know you.

I think I will come back to the island when it is time. You know the one I mean. That is where I will go. I will miss the river. It is dry and cold where I'm going, but I am dry and cold without her. I know that sounds foreign and odd, but please don't judge me too harshly.

I want you to have children and grandchildren and not worry about what happened to your old dad.

Don't miss me. Know that I am fine.

Your Father Nathan Barton

# Chapter Fifty

# JOE

# 1911

Aday came back to Quinley with me after the fair. "For a while, Joseph Barton," was what he'd said, but the while just kept on growing until he stopped talking about going home. He was always very careful about not intruding, almost too careful. He never came in the house, even though Annie and I both invited him in. Instead he made himself a room out in the barn and stayed there until he could get himself a place of his own.

"I want to live down by your river," he said. "Just in case."

He never told me what the just in case was, and I never could figure out exactly what he meant. But I'd gotten used to his odd way of thinking.

"What's he going to do?" Annie asked me when we first came home. She worried about him and how he'd fit in. But it turned out Aday was good with the animals. The cows practically dripped milk when they saw him coming, and the chickens laid more eggs when he was around. He never complained about the work.

We just had a long, hot summer, and poor Annie needed a break. She'd had her third miscarriage, and I could see how tired she looked. I thought if I took Aday away for a night on the river, the time alone would do Annie good.

Annie tried to make us take a big picnic, but I told her we were planning on catching our dinner, so she gave us some corn muffins and apples just in case. That was Annie. It was hard to argue with corn muffins. I wrapped my overnight gear in the horsehair blanket I'd brought back from the fair. Aday brought his spear and the white running shoes that he carried around his neck like a charm. "To throw at the dog devils."

"And what the hell are you going to do with a spear?"

"Catch a fish," he said.

"Not in this river. It's way too deep."

"No matter." He threw the spear up in the air. I watched it fly straight up, no wobble. It seemed to get caught in the sun, and I had to close my eyes, but Aday didn't. He never took his eyes off the spear, and then he grabbed it out of the air, as if he'd trained it to come when he called.

"Just be careful where you aim that thing," I said.

I was looking forward to the trip. It would be good to hang out on the river, let my feet hang off the side of the boat, jump in and get good and wet if I felt like it. I stowed my bundle under the seat, and we set off across the water.

Aday, all stiff knuckled, held on to the sides of the boat. I didn't know he could get that white.

"Addy, it's okay. You can relax."

"I am relaxed, Joseph Barton."

I headed us a bit upstream, so that I could tuck behind the bay on the east side of the river channel and get us out of the main current. From there we paddled north a little over a mile and then northwest up the static channel another three-quarters of a mile before turning west and rowing through the narrow passage that leads to what I always called Horseshoe Island. It was my secret spot. No one ever came back here. The river was still; the current seemed to have lost its way. I loved the rhythm of the oars, the feel of the paddle as it sliced through the water. It was a game I played with myself, seeing how clean and silent I could make my stroke. I always felt a bit like Moses parting the Red Sea.

I ran the bow as close to the bank as I could manage. I took off my shoes.

"Here, Aday, you take the oars while I jump out." The water was cold and the river bottom was soft. It sucked at my leg like a calf sucking on a cow's teat. I scrambled up the muddy bank. "Okay, toss me the rope." I turned toward the center of the island and pulled the boat behind me, then I tied the rope off to a tree.

"So what do you think?"

Aday hadn't moved from the boat. "What do I think about what?"

"About our island? We have our own private island here. Just you and me."

"Just you and me and who knows what else. You, yourself, have read me the stories of that Jim and the Huck person." He crossed his arms. "I know better than to get out here. There could be murderers and thieves on this island."

"That was just a story."

"Where I come from our stories are real."

"Suit yourself, but I'm going to set up camp a bit further inland. I took off without looking behind me. The next thing I knew, Aday was next to me. He was as quiet as he was fast.

I broke off a branch and used it to hack at the underbrush. I knew exactly where I was going. After about ten minutes, we came upon an open space in the middle of the island. It was covered with soft river grasses.

"Look at this meadow, Addy. It's a great place to camp, but first, let's get our lines wet and catch ourselves some dinner."

The day had been hot and the early evening was cooling off just enough to be comfortable. I got my pole and the bait and cast my line out into the deep water. Aday walked up and down the embankment looking for a place to spear his fish. "I told you, Aday, that won't work in this here river. Here let me show you how to use a line."

Aday rested his spear against a tree. I handed him a fishing pole. I'd already stuck a worm on the end of the hook. "What's that for?" he asked.

"So the fish tries to eat the worm and gets stuck on the hook."

"So you trick him?" he asked.

"I suppose I do."

He hesitated. "Come on, Aday. You know, sometimes the fish gets the bait and the hook doesn't get him. If he's smart, he tricks us."

A fish jumped up out of the water and made a splash right in front of us. Aday laughed. "I will play your game, Joseph Barton. Hand me that pole."

Once Aday got the hang of it, he was an incredible fisherman. He had a sense of how to move the line around in just the right way so that no fish could resist it. We were going to eat very well.

I didn't notice that Aday had wandered off until he came back. It was spooky the way he appeared and disappeared. "Look what I found, to cook with the fish." He dumped a pile of mushrooms in front of me. "Shouldn't eat those," I said. "They could make you sick."

He laughed. "Just cook them, Joseph."

I put them in a pan on the fire, but I made sure not to mix them up with my fish. There's nothing better than fresh fish seared on a campfire after being out on the river all day.

I got my gear out and spread it on the ground not to far from the fire. Aday wanted to sleep in the boat. "I do not trust this island at night."

"Suit yourself," I said, but he didn't budge. I don't think he fancied finding his way back to the boat in the dark.

I lay on my back and looked at the stars. I liked to find my own patterns, make up my own constellation names. I thought I heard a sound in the woods. Almost like a man walking. Maybe there were murderers and thieves here. If someone killed us, they could take the boat and no one would ever know. We'd become ghosts on the river. Aday's family would be able to find his spirit. But then again, maybe Aday was right, maybe he was lost to them forever. I held my breath. Aday snored. I wanted to reach over and push him so he'd stop, but he was too far away, and I didn't want to get out of the sleeping bag. The sound stopped.

I felt myself drifting between sleeping and waking. Then I heard the sound again. A shadow came out of the woods. The creature was low to the ground and walked with an odd lumbering gait, and then it stopped, frozen, as if it had just sensed that it was not alone. I didn't move. I wanted it to think that I was part of the meadow, just a mound of earth that it had never seen before.

Whatever it was, it came right up to the edge of the smoldering fire. It didn't seem to mind that it was still hot. We hadn't washed the plates, and I'd just left the cleaned-out guts lying on the ground next to the fire. I'd thrown some of Aday's cooked mushrooms on top of the garbage pile. I was going to dig a hole and bury it in the morning.

The creature came up close to me. It looked like a small squat bear. A badger, I thought. I lay very still because I'd heard they could be nasty. I'd never seen one up close before. It smelled me, then it opened its mouth and let out a chittering that sounded like na na na nan. I thought maybe I was dreaming. I tried to open my eyes, but realized they weren't closed. Aday snored. The badger was talking to me, but I couldn't understand what it said. He wanted to me to listen, and he continued to chatter at me. I felt as if I should know what he wanted, but I didn't. Then he turned and left, and I fell asleep.

While I slept, I dreamed. I dreamed that the badger was a constellation in the sky, and that I was part of it. And that the star creature sprouted fur and claws, and it spoke to me. It said, "na na na nan." Only this time I understood. It said, "I got you. You're it."

When I awakened, the stars were already faded, all except for Venus, which was still bright in the sky.

Aday's spear was in my hand, and at my feet lay the badger, very real and very dead. I stared at the critter and the spear, then back at the critter and the spear. Then I looked at Aday, who had hardly moved. I went over and shook him.

"Aday, wake up."

He stretched like a cat. "I am not ready to wake up yet, Joseph Barton. My dreams have not yet left me."

"Well, my dream hasn't left me either. Look."

He opened one eye and looked at the dead badger.

"What is this?"

"My dream."

He pushed himself to sitting.

"You didn't get up in the middle of the night and do some hunting did you?" I asked.

"I am not a night hunter, my friend." He almost seemed offended, as if I had insulted him. "I stand in the sunlight, so that whatever I hunt can see me."

"It's your spear."

"It is by your bed."

I couldn't deny that.

"I think you must have done this, Joseph Barton."

I thought I would have remembered grabbing a spear. I most definitely would have remembered the feel of it as it pierced through living flesh. "I didn't do this. I swear. At least I don't remember it. But in my dreams there was a mountain lion and this badger, and I swear the badger was trying to protect me. I wouldn't have killed it.

Aday picked up his spear and looked at the tip. "I do not think he was killed by my spear. There is no blood on the tip." He walked over to a bush to relieve himself.

"That doesn't make any sense." I leaned closer. It was true. There was no wound at all. The badger had just up and died at my feet.

Aday pulled a leaf off one of the trees and polished his teeth. "I do not know how your animal spirits work on this side of the world. It could be that this creature has broken free from the dream world into this. Perhaps that is what has happened."

He made it sound like an everyday event. "That sounds like hogwash to me. There's no such thing as animal spirits."

He tilted his head and looked at me. "I am hungry now."

I touched the dead badger. It was real enough. Not a dream spirit kind of animal. It was the kind that bled real honest-to-goodness blood. "It is odd, though," I said. "You don't see badgers around here much. They live further west out on the prairies, where they dig tunnels and hunt prairie dogs."

Aday took one of Annie's corn muffins and broke it in half. He handed me a piece before he took a bite. "It must have got confused coming out of the dream world. Or maybe it was sent by someone. It happens like that sometimes."

The badger's teeth were bared and his forepaw extended, his body already in the death freeze. I knelt down and put my hand on its fur. "I'm sorry if I did this to you. I didn't mean to."

Then I turned to Aday. "I guess we should bury him."

"No." He stood up and frowned at me. "He came to you from a great distance. You must take him home with you."

"But he'll rot."

Aday lifted the badger and placed it on his sleeping mat. Then he folded the sides over so that it was protected. "Joseph Barton, I do not understand you. We are taking this spirit made flesh, and we will bring it to one of the people in the town that makes the dead bodies immortal. You will take him home and honor him. You will always remember the sacrifice he made for you."

I didn't understand a word Aday said, but I did it anyway.

# Chapter Fifty-One

# SONNY

## 2004

Sonny walked past the for sale sign and headed out across the field behind the house. He used to walk out that way with his dog, Justine. Grandpa Joe had given him the dog when he turned eight. "The boys don't need a dog," his father had said. They already got plenty to take care of around here."

"She isn't for the boys," Grandpa Joe said. "She's for Sonny. He's old enough now to have a dog of his own." It was an honor, having Grandpa Joe think Sonny was old enough to have his own dog. She'd was a funny looking mutt, an in-between dog, not a German Shepherd, not a Golden Retriever, not a Collie. She was just a dog.

"I found her by the old oak tree, and I think she'll fit right in. What do you think we should call her?" Grandpa Joe whispered in the dog's ear as he combed out the matted fur with a small, forked gardening tool. "She needs to have a name."

"I don't know. She's just a dog."

Grandpa slapped him on the back. "Justine. Good name for dog."

Justine.

Justine had been his first real love. Sonny realized he could pack up the old china and the toys. He could sort through the bits and pieces of the past one hundred years. He could call the Salvation Army to cart the junk away, or he could box it up and keep it in the garage. But he didn't know what he could do about the buried bones, or the snow forts that had melted, or the fish that were never caught. He couldn't take those things with him, and he couldn't leave without one last goodbye. Sonny headed to find the spot in the woods where he'd buried her. Back by where Justine had been found, near the old tree house under the oak tree.

They'd buried a lot of things in the woods. He and his brother had carved their names into trees and climbed just about every branch that would hold their weight, and several that wouldn't. But the woods were smaller than they used to be. His father had sold off the land in bits and pieces until they weren't really woods anymore, just a bunch of trees.

Sonny walked to the top of the hill behind the house. It was the highest point on the farm, and it wasn't even that high, more of a mound than a hill. The boys knew it was officially summer when their dad brought out the big piece of plastic and set it on the hill. He'd string dozens of hoses together until they stretched from the house to the top of the hill, and then he'd run back to the house and turn on the water. Sonny and his brother would wait by the end of the hose, watching for the sign of life, for the trickle of water to cover the distance. Sonny would wave and his father would come back, and they'd all watch the water run down the plastic. They had their own private waterfall. He and Charlie had spent hours sliding down that mound on the wet plastic.

The oak tree was at the back of the property, toward where the Leahys used to live, by the River Meadows subdivision. Out in the middle of nowhere was where they used to live, but nowhere didn't exist anymore. It was all filled in.

At least he was taller now. From the top of the hill, he spotted the tree and headed toward it through the tall grass. No one had bothered to mow it down. Sonny sneezed. He'd forgotten about hay fever, and he had forgotten about ticks. There were always ticks in the tall grass. Sonny hesitated, then continued. After Justine died, Sonny never got another dog. The last couple years of her life were spent curled up at Grandpa Joe's feet in front of the red chair. The two of them had been very old together. Sonny wondered if there were dogs in Grandpa Joe's spirit world.

The tree house was still there. It was in good shape, better shape than the tree itself. His father had built it strong, had poured his heart into it, seemed to pour all his dreams into it, too. It was a luxurious tree house, with two stories, a trap door, and a wrap-around porch, so he and Charlie could sit outside and see for miles all the way down to the river. Sonny tried to remember what his father was like the summer that they built the tree house. His father always seemed to fade away, seemed to live in Grandpa Joe's shadow, as if he were a shadow himself.

But that was because Grandpa Joe was always around. Sonny knew that now. Grandpa Joe was the one who raised them while his dad worked. Sonny didn't know it back then, didn't know that his father was tired to the bone and didn't have anything left to give them. The summer after their mother died, his father hadn't rolled out the hoses or put plastic out on the hill. He hadn't been around very much at all, and when he was he didn't say much. Then one night Grandpa Joe and Sonny and Charlie sat at the kitchen table building houses of cards when Sonny's dad burst into the house. "What's wrong, Junior?" Grandpa Joe always called him Junior.

"Nothing's wrong, Dad. Boys, I've got something to show you. Something I been thinking about for a while." He carried a rolled up piece of paper the size of a chart and spread it on the table. Sonny had never seen anything like it before. A ghostly blue paper covered with white lines.

"What's that?" Sonny asked.

"It's a blueprint. It's what they use to build houses with." Sonny had never seen his father so excited. "We're gonna build ourselves a house, a tree house, out in that oak tree."

"Can we have a swing on it?" Charlie asked.

"Sure we can have a swing."

Grandpa Joe clapped his hands together. "Great idea. I've always wanted a tree house."

The four of them spent the whole summer building the tree house. They'd rush to get their chores done, so they could work on the tree house. Sometimes it would get so dark that Sonny could barely see the top of the tree, but they all kept working. Sonny wished he'd thought to thank his father.

❧

Sonny put a foot on the first rung of the ladder. It felt solid. He climbed up to the landing. It was even higher than he remembered. It had been a long time since he'd been in a tree. The door hung by one hinge, but it still covered the opening. He pushed it open holding his breath in case the whole structure collapsed from his touch.

A rumpled sleeping bag lay on a cot. Empty beer cans were thrown around, so many they were almost like a carpet. A copy of *Playboy* peeked out from under a pillow. Charlie must be hanging out here; no one else would bother.

A shelf was filled with rocks and pinecones. Sonny picked up one of the rocks. He couldn't remember why he'd kept this one, or for that matter, why he'd kept any of them. An old jean jacket hung from a nail. Something had made a nest out of an old sock, but it was long gone, the babies grown. Sonny was amazed that the roof was still good and that it was dry inside. All these years, his father must have kept it patched. Or maybe it was Charlie.

Sonny sat on the cot. The hinges creaked from his weight. He pulled the small leather diary out of his pocket and opened it to the last page, the page with the important dates jotted down for quick reference.

> *October 15*
> *I'm a married woman now. . . .*

That was what it said. He could almost feel her blush, Annie, his grandmother. It was so long ago, 1906. She and Grandpa Joe were married. She wrote no more words for what came next. She wrote no more down. She had a husband, and there was a family to start. No more time for dear diaries. Diaries were frivolous girlish activities. Grown women didn't have the luxury. There wouldn't be time for confiding to the blank pages of a book.

Sonny wanted the rest of Annie's life. He wanted the happily ever after, because that's how it was supposed to end, that faraway life connected to him through his DNA. He wished he'd known her. He wished he'd known her happily ever after.

He stared at the five words that began the final page. And then he realized there was one more page. The last page was stuck to the back cover. Some water must had glued it shut, fused it. Water did that. Sonny reached into his pocket and took out a small Swiss army knife. He pulled out the nail file and stuck it in the small gap and pried the pages apart.

There was something written. It was in a different handwriting than the rest of the diary, not the round flowing script that he had come to know as his grandmother's, but spidery, almost shaky as if the letters wouldn't come easily.

The ink had run, bled into the page, dying the yellow parchment a pale blue. But he could just make out the lines, fainter than a watermark.

> *Joseph Barton, Jr., born July 4, 1919*
> *My Beloved Annie died July 5, 1919. She will not write again.*

Annie had been gone since 1919. So much had passed since 1919: Prohibition, the Depression, World War II, and Viet Nam.

Sonny climbed down from the tree house and walked toward the apple tree. No one knew who planted the tree so far from the house, but Sonny didn't mind. He always thought of it as his Johnny Appleseed tree. Out by the tree house on the edge of their world seemed like a perfect place to plant an apple tree. He would climb up its branches and get bushels of apples. He could spend all day in the tree house and never get hungry. Autumn came with three arrivals: colored leaves, pomegranates, and caramel apples. They'd pick the good tart apples right from their own tree, and Sonny and Charlie and Grandpa Joe would make a mess in the kitchen, dipping the apples in caramel, rolling them in chopped peanuts.

Most of the branches were dead, and the tree now had a scraggly witch's silhouette. But good witches are never ugly. A few dried-up apples still hung on. They were so dry that they were more like hardened rock fossils. Like him. He stubbed his toe and nearly tripped over it, but the grave marker was still there. Sonny squatted beside the stone. He ran his fingers over the lettering. Sonny had spent hours scratching in the word, "Justine." Just a dog. Should he take the marker with him he wondered, or leave it here for whoever bought this place? Would they build more of those little houses, or was the boom over? Had the people stopped coming? Were they all going away like him now? Would someone plow over this field and cut down the tree and let Justine's dust blow away in the wind?

A breeze came up. The dinner bell sounded. He turned. He couldn't imagine who might be ringing it. It was the bell that used to summon the family to dinner, and it meant that he had ten minutes, not a second more, to get his butt back home and in his seat at the dinner table. There were no questions asked and no extensions. You were there, or you went to bed hungry. That was Grandpa Joe's rule. "We all sit together. No matter where you've been, no matter what you're doing. This is when we look each other in the eye and remember what matters."

Sonny left the marker where it lay, then turned and ran. He was out of breath by the time he got back to the house. He hadn't run that hard in a long time. "Hello? Charlie?" No one answered. Charlie wasn't around. At least his truck wasn't there.

Sonny went into the house and opened the refrigerator. No beers missing. It definitely hadn't been Charlie. The wind changed. It came out of the north. He stood at the front door and watched the clouds. "If you don't like the weather, wait five minutes" was the local wisdom.

Sonny stepped outside and walked over to the for sale sign. He unhooked the chain and removed the swinging piece of wood. "Guess I'll hang a lamp there." He carried the sign back to the house and laid it face down on the ground. He looked at his watch. Ten minutes since he'd heard the bell. He went into the kitchen and sat down. "Looks like I made it, Grandpa Joe."

# Chapter Fifty-Two

# ANNIE

## 1906

October 15

Dear Diary,

I'm a married woman now. Me and Joe. Till death do us part. I wore my mother's pearl necklace. It was the something old, and the gift from Redfeather was the something new. I had a blue ribbon in my hair, and I've come to realize that my Joe himself is borrowed. He's from a place I'll never know, and I've got him on loan.

I never told Joe about going to see Redfeather that day at the fair, or even about the present he gave me. I know Daddy would be angry if he saw the necklace, because Joe promised to put all that Indian stuff behind him. But I didn't make any promises. And this is about me, not Joe. So I put Redfeather's special necklace on a belt and wore it around my waist, where no one else could see it. When I took it off, I noticed that the feathers left a mark on my belly that looked like my very own wings.

# Chapter Fifty-Three

# JOE

## 1917

Greer, Smith, Johnson, and me were the last to leave the cemetery, because we wanted to be the ones to fill in the hole. None of us talked very much. The funeral had been a major event for the whole town. Tucker had the distinction of being the first one to come back in a box. We got used to it after that. So many died during the Great War. If the Germans didn't get them, then the influenza did. It came to me that I hadn't known real grief up until then, not the kind that makes you so sick you can hardly move with the pain of it. I thought about Aday and how he'd managed to live with his grief. He'd uprooted himself and created a new life. That's what people did. They carried on. But the day when Tucker came back, we were still in the newness of it and weren't sure what we were supposed to do.

It took a long time to fill in the hole because the shovel seemed heavier than usual. Here I was a farmer's son, used to digging and pitching and pushing, and I could barely lift it. That shovel was heavier and the hole was bigger than anything I'd ever seen. It took all we could do to get every last bit of dirt back in and Tucker covered up.

We finished our job, but we still hadn't talked much. Everyone else had gone back to the Tucker's to be with the family, but we just drifted to the club. Someone had written a sign, "Closed for Funeral," and tacked it to the door.

It was cold inside. The stove wasn't lit, but then it wasn't supposed to be cold enough outside for heating yet. I got some wood and started the fire, and John went behind the bar for a bottle of Jim Beam. "I could use some of this.

How bout you?"

"Sure." I rubbed my hands together to warm them up." That's what we all need right now. A nice hot fire."

He took out the glasses and poured each of us a shot. Back in those days I could throw it down my throat without choking on it, just let it burn all the way down.

It was Smith who got the team picture off the wall, the one of the guys before the big Olympic race.

"Hey. Look at Tucker. He was so damn happy that day."

"Yep. Happy he hadn't landed in the water," Greer took the picture away from Smith.

I looked at the picture over their shoulder. They were smiling, all of them. This was the picture of possibility. Anything could have happened at that point, no one was thinking about catching crabs or even losing. They were a row of winning faces in starched whites. Under the faces was printed in gold lettering, *1904 St. Louis World's Fair Olympic Games.* It was the official team picture.

I'd just gotten the letter that they wouldn't let me row with the team, but I showed up for the picture anyway, just in case. I stood behind the photographer. I wasn't in that picture. I wasn't a part of the team anymore. It was their Olympics, not mine.

"Just look at us. We were so damn young." Greer seemed to be talking more to himself than anybody else. "And Tucker." We all knew what he meant. Tucker young and alive then. Tucker six feet under now.

Greer had some white in his hair that was mixed in with the blond. I hadn't noticed the white before or the lines in his forehead or the sag in his shoulders. "It was a good time wasn't it? Hell, they even had some Krauts at the fair. They used to be good guys, those Germans, weren't they?"

"Used to be," Johnson echoed and Smith nodded.

I'd always kept my word. Never talked about what had happened back then. Never talked about what I was or what I might have been. Even after old Dr. Greer had died. Besides, it was Tucker we were remembering.

Greer must have noticed I wasn't saying much. "You know, Joe. I always thought there was something wrong with this picture." He poured himself another shot of whiskey. "Me and Tucker always thought it wasn't right. We always meant to do something about it."

I wasn't sure what they could have done.

He gulped the whiskey down in one swallow then slammed the glass down on the bar. He stormed off. I looked at Smith, but neither of us said anything. Then Greer came out of the club office carrying a box filled with pictures, a jar of rubber cement, and a large pair of scissors.

"Look at all these pictures. Where'd they come from?" I pulled out a handful of photos.

"Careful." Smith reached in and laid them out on the bar. Smith was always the orderly one.

Greer nodded. "These were the rejects, the ones that never made it on the wall. I've been collecting them over the years. Never knew why."

There were so many: Greer and I standing in front of the dock pointing at something no one else could see, Smith and Tucker modeling their team sweaters, Greer hanging the new sign for the club. There were pictures of people whose names I couldn't quite recollect, people just passing through taking turns on the river. There were so many challenges and victories and good times that I'd lost count.

John rummaged through the box until he found the one he was looking for. It was the picture we'd taken so many years ago, before we left for St. Louis. The day we tried on our new whites, the ones we'd gotten special for the fair. We had lined up a row of chairs, and Dr. Greer had stood with his back to the big picture window and snapped the shot. I'd forgotten about that picture. I was grinning though. We all looked happy enough.

Greer took out a pair of scissors and began to cut. I watched him. He was always good with scissors. He could cut a row of dancing children out of a newspaper. With a pair of scissors that size, I'd probably have cut off my finger, but somehow he managed to cut that tiny picture without cutting off my head or anything else.

Then he took the little picture of me and pasted it onto the official picture of the team, as if I'd always been there. He pasted me right where I belonged.

# Epilogue

# MOON

## 1887

The cow sounded sick, as though it had asthma. It moaned from way deep in its belly. Or a growl, maybe it was growling like a dog, growling at her.

"Moooooo," Moon growled back at it, although that wasn't a cow's real sound. Moooooo was what they sang to the small children in this town of people who lived in their tight shoes. Her people had a sound for the cry that came from deep within. It was in their songs. She missed the songs. Missed the sounds. More than anything, she missed the sounds. She couldn't laugh in these words. She couldn't live in these words.

She hated these things on her feet. She couldn't breathe. She was used to breathing from the bottom to the top. She was used to feeling the sounds, feeling the rocks and the pebbles and the wormholes. She looked at the walls of her kitchen. It was a wonderful room. It was a wonderful house. He was a loving man. Nathan spared no expense in giving her the best of everything. But she missed her grandmother's bones. She missed crawling under her grandmother's skirt into the tepee.

Her husband, Nathan, and their son, little Joseph, sat at the kitchen table. The boy was so much like his father. She looked hard to see anything of her in his face. He had a light red sheen to his hair, not like hers. Her hair had a red inside the black, a hidden red.

She looked at her husband. He was good to her, gave her a nice home and treated her well. He always asked what he could do for her. How could she tell him there was nothing he could do? He was focused on a pile of papers spread out in front of him.

The boy ate solid food now, at least what didn't end up on the floor. They will be fine, she thought.

"Can I get you anything else?" she asked as she brushed the crumbs of corn bread off the table.

The boy held up his spoon. She smiled at him. Her breasts ached, but the milk had stopped long ago. They weren't aching from being full, they were aching from being empty.

She bent over and kissed the top of his head.

"I am going now," she said to her husband. "Take care of the little one."

Nathan nodded. He didn't understand.

She took one last look around. The dishes were washed, the floor was clean, the chickens fed. She opened the door and went outside. The air was thick with the smell of honeysuckle and manure. She untied her shoes and pulled them off. She placed them by the side of the door on the mat that said Welcome. Then she turned to face the setting sun. She turned to go home.